MW00444464

Robin's Lake Road

C. L. Avery

Toulon Publishing
Dallas, Texas MMXVIII

Also by C. L. Avery

Mary Full of Grace

On the Edge of Darkness

Copyright © 2018 C. L. Avery

All rights reserved.

ISBN: 978-0-9600335-2-2

Printed in the United States of America

*For Soms, a secret agent from heaven
sent to spread happiness everywhere she goes.*

ACKNOWLEDGMENTS

All a writer ever does is try to entertain at least one person. When it happens, the satisfaction of it becomes the narcotic that justifies writing the next book, so that at least one *more* person can be entertained. There's no end. With that in mind, I consider myself truly blessed by all of you who have thanked me for entertaining you. From the bottom of *my* heart, thank you for letting me! I hope you are inspired to be the pebble that starts the avalanche that one day sweeps away hate and leaves us a tolerant and loving society.

The writing of this story would not have been possible without the help of a special group of my friends who invited me into their private lives in a very personal way. Without their loving insight and enthusiastic support, this book would not exist. To be honest, I feel adopted. And I couldn't be more proud.

As always, I am in deep gratitude to my editor and dear friend, Shannon McHale. Because of her professionalism and keen eye for perfection, I can concentrate on telling a story. Nothing I write will ever be complete without her.

Lastly, but most importantly, I once again give tribute to my muse, who is and always has been a bottomless well of inspiration—and who still has that uncanny ability to make me believe I can actually fly. You know who you are.

Robin's Lake Road

"To love is to burn, to be on fire."

— Jane Austen

1

Welp, here we go again.

"Jermy, *stop* it!"

He cruises right past me without missing a beat, just like always. Now I'm *really* pissed—and I scream back into my phone at the top of my voice.

"*Jermy!!*"

It doesn't help.

I clench my teeth as the onslaught continues with no end in sight. The sound of his voice makes me cringe, like hearing fingernails scraping across a chalkboard. To my left, Orm minds his driving, but the wide-eyed glance he just gave me tells me he's never seen *this* side of me. To be honest, neither have I.

Jermy's nonstop tirade continues to boil out of my phone like soda from a shaken bottle. If we were in person, there's no doubt he'd have his finger in my face while throwing around a lot of admonishments like "you need to" and "I told you."

I put my phone in a choke hold and keep it at arm's length until finally, he gasses out. "Now, what is it you was saying?" he wheezes with his last gasp of breath.

"I'm warning you, Jermy," I say, starting over for the third time, "stop calling me! Whatever you think we had—and I'm *not* going to argue with you about what it was—is *over!*" Without waiting for him to start spiraling again, I disconnect the call and toss the phone into my purse.

When I look toward Orm, he has a surprised expression on his face. "Hold on," he says, "you mean you *broke up* with Jermy??"

"Orm, don't even!" I exhale and lean back in my seat. I can't remember being on edge like this.

"So, he's the one—"

"Who's been blowing up my phone all afternoon? Yes!"

He pauses to take it all in. I knew this would surprise him. After all,

Jeremy McIvers, whom everyone calls "Jermy," is his cousin, and he kind of got us together. He turns his head to stare at me.

"You're just kidding. You didn't really break up with him . . . did you?"

"I'm *not* kidding," I snap back at him. "And keep your eyes on the road!"

He takes a quick glance at the road ahead, then turns back towards me. Confusion is written all over his face.

"Seriously . . . why? I thought you were pretty desperate for a boyfriend."

He has a point.

"Well, maybe I *did* make you think I was a bit desperate. But it just wasn't working." I can see that sailed right over his head. "Okay, I don't *feel* anything for him. I know you meant well setting us up, but I knew three weeks ago it wasn't going to work for me. I mean, *he* thought there was something there because he made a move on me last night. And I shut him down, hard. And believe me, he wasn't too happy about it."

"And—"

"And he's been calling me nonstop."

"But . . . you were *dating* him!"

"See, right there, that makes me crazy! You think because I went on a date with him I'm somehow obligated to do anything *he* wants to do??"

"Um . . ."

"I *hate* it when you guys think like that!" I break eye contact and slump back with my arms crossed.

"I didn't mean it that way! Sorry!"

"Ah, forget it," I sigh. I wonder whether another girl would have even had a problem with it. Jermy's not bad looking. Is it just me?

After another minute or two of silence, he says, "Well, sorry about you and Jermy."

"Don't be." I pause for a second, then add, "And sorry for snapping at you. I'm just . . . hell, I don't know. I'm not myself lately."

"Yeah, I've noticed that, Ash."

Orm is the only person who calls me Ash, the shortened version of Asher, my given name. Could be worse, though, if I went by my middle name of Kendall. On the other hand, everyone knows Ormand by his shortened name.

We go a long way back, the two of us. It's not romantic or anything, and never has been, but we've been best friends since fifth grade. I was the tall one back then, but now he's taller, probably right around six foot one, thin, with blue eyes and dark hair that's just this side of curly. He's not athletically inclined and is bookish, so yeah, he's a geek. But he's well-liked by everyone.

I don't know what I'd do without Orm. And one of the reasons we're best friends is that he's *always* on my side. I wouldn't hesitate to share any secret I have with him. In fact, I *have* shared my secrets with him. *All* of them. Even my closest ones.

Me? I'm the senior student photographer at Sagebrush High School. There're two others—Roy Nellums, a sophomore, and Evie Patterson, a junior—but as the senior, I'm in charge of the yearbook photo assignments. My real passion, though, is photo art. My dream for college is to gain a fine arts scholarship to the nationally prestigious Winston Institute for the Arts in Chicago.

I pull down my visor, take a last look at my face in the mirror, then close it and sit up straight. For a while, I wonder whether I really know myself. I mean, I think I do. But do I? And do I know what love is? Would I even recognize it? I steal a sideways glance to my left. I can tell Orm's mind is a million miles away. It's time. I've carried this burning question around way too long. I take a deep breath and turn towards him.

"Hey!"

"Yeah?" he replies, negotiating a turn in the road.

"I've got a question for you."

"Sure." He adjusts his rearview mirror and leans back.

"Have you ever been in love?"

That gets his attention. He straightens up and makes eye contact with me for a split second. After a moment of thought, he turns back to me and gives me a quizzical expression—like I'm supposed to know better.

And maybe I do.

But this is serious, especially after what happened last night. My need to know a certain *something* is greater than it's ever been. I'm desperate. If anyone else knew I was this clueless, I'd be the laughing stock of the entire school. It's bad enough having to go to a guy about it, even if it *is* Orm. Worse, this isn't even the *real* question. But to get to it, I need him to answer this one first.

He clears his throat and squirms slightly. "Well, yeah," he finally replies. "Did you forget about Charlene?"

I expected that.

"No."

"Then why'd you ask?" he says, throwing up his hand.

Here goes nothing.

"Because . . . I wanna know how you *knew* you were in love."

"How did I *know?*" he parrots back to me.

"Yeah, exactly! How did you *know?* Was it something your brain told you? Was it a feeling? Were you horny? I mean, what *was* it?"

It's not like I want to know if I'm in love right now. I already *know* I'm not in love right now. In fact, I've got an excellent idea of what "in love" *isn't.* My problem is that I don't know what "in love" *is*—and I feel that at 18, I should know this.

So as of now, I'm done with fantasizing—I want to *know.* Orm and Charlene were a hot item, so I figure he at least has a clue. I watch him as he fidgets a bit, as if he knows this topic is heavier than our usual conversation. And he would be right about that—it is.

"Why are you asking all this?" he finally replies.

I expected that, too. "Okay," I admit, deciding short and quick is best for confessions. "Don't you think it's kinda pathetic that I've never been in love even a single time in my whole life?" There, I said it.

"You mean not even *once?*" He gives me a look of sympathy, which of course confirms my fear that the problem really is serious.

"I don't think so," I say, shaking my head. "I feel kinda left out. Does that make sense? Here I am about to graduate from high school, and I've never been in love. I guess the whole 'Jermy' thing has me worrying about myself, so that's why I wanna know how you know when you're in love."

He holds his gaze on me for another few seconds, then returns his focus to the road ahead. "Well, I guess I'd have to say I knew I was in love because . . ." He nervously taps his fingers on the steering wheel as he stares out into space. "Because I felt *alive,*" he finally says. He pauses as if contemplating whether he used the right word. Then he nods. "Yeah, that's definitely it. I felt alive. *Really* alive."

"Alive?" He watches me as I try to make sense of his reply. "What does *that* mean?"

"It means I hungered for her presence," he smiles. "She was in every thought. She was my purpose for waking up each day, and I wanted to make her the happiest girl ever. Even the touch of her hand was exciting. It was like every part of me was *alive* with anticipation of being with her."

Well, fuck my life. I don't know what to say. His description is entirely foreign to me. And it definitely confirms what I already knew about whether I've ever been in love. I breathe out a sigh of disappointment and file Orm's definition away in hopes it will be useful someday. I feel banished—like I'm on the outside of life, looking in.

"So . . . does that answer your question?" he says.

"Yeah . . . I suppose."

"Okaaay." He goes silent. I know he's searching for some sappy sentiment he can give me to make me forget about Jermy.

But who am I kidding? It's not Jermy—it's *much* bigger, if I'm going to be perfectly honest with myself. It seems all the girls in my school are happily dating their boyfriends. Me? I don't think I've ever felt a need to *have* a boyfriend. Maybe that's the problem. Sure, a few boys at my school are cute. But I've never had romantic feelings for any of them.

And it's not like I haven't gone out on dates—like last night with Jermy. Yet, for all four years of high school, all I have are five platonic kisses from three different boys to show for it. And, I guess I'd have to throw in that awkward moment with Jermy last night that went sour in less than thirty seconds.

Orm reaches over to rest his hand on my shoulder and gives it a reassuring squeeze. "Look at yourself. You're smart, and you're talented. And . . . you're beautiful. Ash, you can get *any* guy you want!"

"That's just *it,*" I sigh. "After this *thing* with Jermy, I'm not sure I *want* any guy I can get."

"Why?"

"Because it's the same thing, every time—as in no stars, no fireworks, no *nothing*. And definitely no *alive*, like you described. Everyone else seems to be in love . . . everyone else seems to know the secret!" I look over at him and shake my head. "Orm, I seriously think there's something wrong with me."

He pulls into a parking space in the nearly empty lot in front of the auditorium at school, turns off the car, then turns to face me.

"There's nothing wrong with you," he tells me, raising his brow. "You're perfect just the way you are."

"Think so?" I stuff my purse under the seat. "Well, maybe I'm not as perfect as you think I am."

"Are you kidding me? No one is smarter or more level-headed than you, Ash. And did I mention you're beautiful?"

That's Orm, all right, defending my honor at the least provocation.

Sometimes I wonder why I don't just say, "Orm, praise me," instead of hinting around that I need a boost.

At five feet seven, I'm 130 pounds soaking wet. I have long, board-straight hair that stretches to mid-back in a V-cut, with short bangs in front. Even though I dyed it blonde one summer right after ninth grade, I've since kept it at its natural medium brown. So, yeah. Maybe I *am* pretty.

"Okay, Orm, whatever." He gives my hand a squeeze, and then we pile out to unload my stuff. It's the night of the spring art and talent show, which starts in forty-five minutes, and I have three photo art entries to set up.

It's a clear March evening with a chill in the air, so I pull my sweater in tight before I retrieve the wooden easels from the trunk and start toward the auditorium. With only the three easels to carry, I easily outpace Orm, who has three heavy maplewood frames to manage. Once inside, the aroma of "school" and stale popcorn assaults my senses. God, I hate popcorn. Why does there always have to be popcorn? Already, I can't wait for the show to be over.

I turn to study the display map posted beside the door that shows my designated display area. I hear the door open again, and I motion for Orm to follow. Handling those three frames, I know he's struggling, but he smiles anyway. My spot is on the left side of the auditorium about halfway down. As soon as we arrive there, we get to work, Orm setting a frame in each easel as I finish assembling it.

"Ash," he says, no doubt seeking to lift my spirits, "you're just gonna be famous!"

"You always say that!" I smile.

I get my prints positioned just as I want them. He stands back and pretends to know something about staging artwork, then gives me an approving nod. "Are we gonna be carrying these right back out later tonight?"

"Nah, the artwork stays for the next three days, so everyone has time to see them and vote."

"You're gonna win! Just like last year!" He give me a grin. I wave him off with a smile as we retreat toward the back to find seats and relax as the audience slowly begins to fill the auditorium.

Sagebrush, Oklahoma is a small town with a population of about five thousand. It's set smack in the middle of the flat land that makes up the Oklahoma Panhandle, between Kansas to the north and Texas to the south, with New Mexico and Colorado just a stone's throw to the west. From the looks of it, the entire town is present, and the air is abuzz. When the house lights finally dim, we sit up straight, just in time for Principal Lowrey to come out and make her annual "aren't our students talented!" speech.

Then the show begins with what always seems to be the first act in any school gathering: the pep squad. We're forced to endure a full five minutes of cheerleading. Orm knows how I feel about it, and when I look over at him, he's snickering at me.

Once the cheerleaders are gone, we get two songs from the marching band, then two more from the orchestra. Then, we see a juggling act, a dog acrobatics act, a couple of rap acts, a magician, a clown on a unicycle, a solo comic act, and then two guys performing the classic "Who's on First" comedy routine. It's one act too many for me, and what with people on both sides of us eating popcorn, I'm anxious to leave. Orm knows it, too.

"Hey," he leans over to say in my ear, "just one more act and we'll be out of here!"

Ugh. "I'm sure I can live without it," I mumble in reply. Orm doesn't budge, so it looks like I'm sitting through it to the bitter end.

The last act of the evening is the theater department's one-act play. To set the mood, the orchestra plays a short intro, and then the curtain rises to three actors—a guy and two girls—who launch into a well-performed skit centered on a comedic debate over whether girls today expect the same genteel courtesies as their grandmothers did. At the comic expense of the guy, some of the lines are hilarious, and I actually find myself laughing. After another few minutes, a last clever punch line delivered from one of the girls draws riotous laughing and deafening applause as the curtain comes down and the lights go up.

"That was good," I say to Orm as we rise in applause.

I'm glad we stayed for that one, but now I'm ready to leave. I gesture to him to get a head start on the crowd, but suddenly the curtain rises again, and the house lights go dark. After everyone has taken their seat, an upbeat music track comes pounding out of the sound system, and slowly at first, but then gathering steam, the audience joins in, clapping to the beat. Then, with an electronic laser sound, a lone, white-hot spotlight explodes onto a small circle in the center of the stage.

It illuminates a girl in a sequined white gown trimmed in red who begins belting out "Born this Way" by Lady Gaga. She's graceful and slender, with short, red hair that curls ever so slightly at the bottom of her ears. Although she looks vaguely familiar, I can't recall her name. But boy, does she ever have my attention.

Her voice is pure and pitch-perfect as she ranges from lows to highs and everything in between. She gyrates her body to the beat as the audience cheers, and I'm mesmerized beyond description. This is a rather racy song for a small, rural school, but they're eating it up. My eyes are glued to her as she masterfully scoops up her audience and takes them on a wild ride, delivering the perfect facial gestures at the perfect times while showing a body rhythm that, for some reason, makes me squirm. As she finishes the song, the audience practically leaps to its collective feet in deafening applause.

I stand up in a daze. Did I really just see that? I'm not sure why, but I have butterflies in my stomach and can barely breathe. She takes her bows while long-stem roses rain in from the audience. I lean into Orm while keeping my eyes on her.

"Who *is* that?"

He turns to me, still applauding, and smiles. "*That* girl," he announces with a flourish, "is Robin O'Leary."

2

My head is still spinning as we walk toward the exits.

We're slowed by a sizable crowd in the hallway. The air is a bit stuffy, and I can tell Orm wants to be outside as soon as possible. Over to the side in the main hallway, I see the problem. There, holding court, is Robin O'Leary.

I feel like I'm in the presence of celebrity. She's holding a small bouquet of flowers and standing next to Dillard Drummond, more popularly known as "Dill," who's the quarterback of our football team. Amid accolades for her performance, she maintains a smile while a man and woman, apparently her parents, seem to be in charge—almost as if she is a professional and they are her managers. While her mother is all smiles, her father has a scowl on his face that looks creepy.

"She'll be famous someday," Orm says. "At least, that's what a lot of people say."

"I've never noticed her before." At least I don't think I have, because I can't get my eyes off her now. I silently curse myself for giving away the theater department photo assignment to Evie Patterson.

I size her up and decide she's slightly taller than me by about two or three inches. Her lithe figure is highlighted by nicely proportioned hips and a medium bustline. It's the most feminine figure I've ever seen. She easily outpoints me, that much I know for sure. Her facial features are elfin, and utterly captivating in a way that's hard to define. She has bright eyes that are set above a small, ever-so-slightly upturned nose, and her lips frame a perfectly-shaped mouth.

Her best feature is definitely her eyes—they're a deep emerald green, and she has a way of looking at people by training her eyes on them without her face being entirely squared up. It gives her a coy expression that I wonder if I can copy. I watch—or rather *stare*—as she shakes hands and exchanges hugs with her well-wishers.

"She transferred in last fall, right before Thanksgiving," Orm leans in and says. "I think she's from Texas."

We pass slowly, partly because the crowd around her is taking up most of the width of the hallway, but also because I'm purposely dragging my feet. Orm puts his hand on my shoulder to try to steer me through the tight spots in the crowd, but I stiffen up and resist. He gets it and holds back next to me without saying a word.

My eyes continue to examine her every feature, from her slender fingers that I could stare at forever, to her perfectly formed nose and baby-smooth skin. I can't remember the last time I was in the presence of such beauty. With the insistence of the crowd pushing up from behind us, we're eventually forced back into motion toward the exits. On the way through the parking lot to Orm's car, he gives me an intense stare.

"What?" I say.

"You're acting strange."

I shake my head and pretend I don't know what he's talking about. "Really?"

Orm always seems to "know," which can be annoying when I *don't* want him to know, but very handy when I need personal advice from him. Right now, I'm in no mood for advice or inquisition, so I say nothing.

With the slow traffic on the highway, the drive to my house takes longer than the usual ten minutes. As I get out of the car, I turn back to him.

"Sorry, Orm."

He gives me a forced smile. "Forget it! See ya in the morning!"

I'm not sure why I was short with him to begin with. I wave as he backs out. Then, chased by a chilly gust of wind, I hurry inside and go up to my room, where, once in bed for the evening, I use my phone to dig through Instagram and Facebook for photos of Robin O'Leary.

The next morning, a car horn takes me by surprise. It's Orm, which means the time must be right around 8:30 a.m. I thought I had another fifteen minutes. Orm likes to be in his first-period class at least five minutes ahead of the bell, which is okay most of the time, but sometimes his attention to punctuality drives me nuts. This might be one of those times. I didn't get that much sleep last night.

It takes me a minute to gather my books into my backpack, during which Orm gives another series of horn blasts. Grams calls out to me as if I can't hear his horn. She seems to be on a mission of making sure I'm never late to school. Truth be told, I probably would be tardy every day if it weren't for her and Orm.

Grams is the only family I have. I never knew my dad. Mom told me that he left town the day after I was born, headed for Albuquerque to find work as a trucker, and never returned. Until I was ten, it was just me and Mom living with Grams. Then one day, Mom started bringing this guy named Harley around.

I never liked him. Sometimes at night, I could hear them arguing. Grams would have to bang on their bedroom door to stop it. I'll never forget the day that Mom took me aside and tearfully told me she was moving to Tucson to find a better job. Well, at least she told the truth. She did go to Tucson. She's been there with Harley for the last eight years. I hear from her about two or three times a year when she calls me—always from a different phone number that I can never return a call to. So it's just me and Grams.

I take one more look at another Instagram photo of Robin O'Leary on my phone before clicking it off and stuffing it into my purse. By the time I make it to Orm's car, I can see he's on the verge of honking yet again.

"Chill, will ya?" I admonish him as I close the passenger door.

I have the visor mirror down before the car even gets rolling, inspecting my face and hair. The hair is okay. It's my eyeshadow. Right eye is okay, but thanks to Orm's timeliness, the left one needs a bit more work.

"You know, I could probably fill up a vacuum cleaner with all the powder and shit that's fallen into that seat," he says, giving me a wry grin as I take out my eyeshadow. It's a good icebreaker from the awkwardness of last night's ride home, and I feel my face stretching into a smile.

"Yeah, well, a girl's gotta do what a girl's gotta do." With my eyeshadow brush, I pick up a shade called "Blossomy" and apply it as best I can, considering Orm's not exactly a steady driver. "Sorry I was stuck-up last night on the way home." I sneak a sideways glance to see how Orm receives my apology. He's still staring at the road straight ahead, but I see him smile, so I return to fixing up my eyes.

"Ah, forget it," he chirps. "What I want to know is whether you've made note cards for that history test next week."

"Huh? You're asking *me*? You know I don't take studying to *your* level!"

"Thought so! Then you can study with me because I *did!*"

I shake my head. "You dork, I *always* study with you." I stuff my makeup kit back into my purse just as we find a parking spot—and I see my phone. I'm tempted to take it out, but I fight the urge and instead close my purse to check out what the girls walking across the parking lot are wearing. It's early March, and the temperature is in the thirties this time of day, so I'm in a long-sleeved gray sweater and tight black jeans. I throw my heavy jacket into the back seat. I'm in no mood to have to babysit it all day.

Once we're in the hallway, we head in different directions, but not before he calls out, "See ya, Ash!"

Then, with no one to distract me, I look around for any sight of Robin O'Leary. Nothing. I get to my English classroom a good two minutes before the bell. It doesn't take but a minute to notice—someone is wearing way too much cologne, and I spot him immediately.

It's Danny Tucker, and he's sitting across the aisle from me. He's smiling at me and moving his mouth ever so slightly, almost like he's muttering something to himself. He asked me out right before Christmas, but I turned him down. He may not have gotten the message. I pull out my textbook and open it to a random page, making like I'm prepping for class. Out of the corner of my eye, I see him starting to lean in, but then I'm saved by the bell and the chipper voice of Mrs. Ledbetter, who smiles and calls out with "Good morning, students!"

English just might be my favorite class—next to photography, of course. Literature appeals to my artistic need for expression. In fact, many of my photos are inspired by imagined scenery from a book or story I'm reading. I'm especially attracted to a good romance. It really sucks that I'm so lacking in that department.

Fifth grade saw my first and only crush. My fixation on Jacob Hearn lasted all of two weeks. As I moved through middle school, I was inundated with the graphic details of romance and sex from other girls I knew. Frankly, I didn't get it. Even now, I see boys as crude, opportunistic, and braggarts. Yet I've always had boy *friends*—just not in the romantic sense.

Math is my most challenging class, and today, it's boring. Mr. Harrison is droning on and on about something to do with factorials. I zone out to the mental image of Robin O'Leary being showered with roses last night. I'm a bit jealous. It would be kind of nice if *I* were the star of a show for my photographic art. But people don't stand in line to look at art. They want entertainment, and Robin serves it up by the boatload. People *will* stand in line to hear *her* sing.

The mental image of Dill Drummond standing in Robin's shadow also pops into my mind. He seemed rather nice, allowing her to receive her applause and accolades. But that's nothing new to Dill. He's used to earning his own accolades, that's for sure, because as the star quarterback for the high school football team, he regularly has crowds standing and going batshit for his on-field heroics. So I guess they make a good couple—both stars with spotlights following them.

The thought of them having sex is a different matter. The idea of it is awkward, and honestly, a bit repugnant. It's hard for me to imagine Dill having his way with Robin's body like that. Or that she could possibly enjoy it. Maybe they haven't. It would show, somehow, and it doesn't. At least that's what I tell myself.

By the time sixth period is over and I'm seating myself into Orm's car, the temperature is almost warm enough for short sleeves. As we leave the parking lot, I catch a glimpse of Dill, and sure enough, there's my first sighting of Robin. They're walking hand-in-hand, and when they arrive at Dill's car, he opens the door for her. That's a nice gesture, but it annoys me for some reason.

I turn to Orm. "Let's go for ice cream."

He smiles and gives a short chuckle. "Just what I was thinking!" He guns the car as we take a turn onto the main highway that runs through Sagebrush, slinging me against the door and causing me to squeal. It makes me laugh every time he does that.

Orm is always a lot of fun. I've even imagined being Orm's girlfriend. But, the notion of it crashes and burns when I try to imagine kissing him— or even holding hands in a romantic way. No, Orm is definitely "best friend" material, nothing more. Orm understands, and every girl he's expressed interest in has had to come to the acceptance of the fact that *I'm* his best friend. Well, all of them except for Charlene Madsen. But the others got it. I guess that makes me feel special, but Orm's definitely *not* the guy I'm waiting for.

Big Sam's Cones and Shakes is still on the empty side as we take our seats in our favorite booth. It won't be long before the place starts to fill up, as it's a favorite after-school hangout. Big Sam looks at me from the counter and gives me a raised brow. I nod, indicating "the usual," and he sets to work on a double-dip chocolate cone for me, and a banana split with whipped cream for Orm.

I need to know more about Robin, but I don't want Orm to think I *need* to know. So, I clear my throat and start with my best nonchalant attitude.

"Did you see Dill in the parking lot?" I ask, my eyes cast out the window to the highway.

"When we were leaving? What about it?"

I strategically pause before replying, hoping he'll add something—preferably some comment about their relationship. But he doesn't.

"Nothing, really. Just wondering."

"Whatever."

"Well, did you see who he was with?" This time I make brief eye contact. My phone vibrates, but I ignore it.

"Yeah."

That's all. Just "yeah."

"Okay, who was it, then?" I'm irritated that I now have to be more direct.

"Robin!" he replies, aiming a forefinger at me as if having passed a pop quiz.

I let out a sigh and turn my head back to the window.

"What?" he says. I'm trying to think of a response that won't seem so obvious, but just then, he gets a clue. "Oh, you want to talk about Robin, don't you?" he triumphantly announces.

I finally have him headed in the right direction. "I guess I do," I confess.

"Can you believe it? I mean, Dill always gets the most popular girls! And Robin . . . well, she's the latest. *And* the most popular."

"Who's *she* been dating? Before Dill, I mean."

He takes a deep breath and holds it in, as if searching his memory, then lets it all out. "I dunno. She's only been here since November." He pauses for only a second, then adds, "Hold on, are you hot for *Dill?*"

"No!"

He studies my face. "You really want to know who *Robin* has been dating, don't you?"

Now, it's my turn to pause. I don't want him to start making assumptions. But hell, I've been telling him my secrets for years now.

"I was curious. I mean, I barely knew she existed before last night. Well, maybe I knew of her *existence*, but now that I know how talented and popular she is, well . . ."

"Well, what?"

"Well, I guess she's had her pick of the boys?"

"I suppose," he nods, smiling.

"A lot of them?"

This seems to stump him. "I guess. Well, maybe not a *lot*. Just several. Kinda." He lets out with a sigh of exasperation. "Hell, I don't keep up with that stuff, Ash! And she hasn't been here that long."

"Serious boyfriends?" I persist.

"Ash, how could I know that? And *why* do you want to know that?"

"Well, we were talking about her . . . so?"

"I just don't know." Right then, Big Sam shows up with our order.

"Nice to see you kids!" he smiles, carefully setting down our orders and then laying out a pair of napkins and a spoon for each of us before walking away. I adjust one of the napkins around the cone before finally taking the first bite. I gesture to Orm. I have to keep him on track, or we'll be starting all over again.

"So, are they together all the time?"

He slowly finishes his first bite of banana split, his eyes fixed on the food before him. He's spooning up his next mouthful when I reach out to stop his hand. "Well?"

"As far as I can tell, yeah. Pretty much all the time. I have two classes with both of them, so I—"

"Do they hold hands?"

"Um, I think so, but I'm not—"

"Do they sit together? Have you seen them hug? Or even kiss?"

He lets out another sigh. "Ash, I just don't know, or I'd tell you! And what's with your fixation on Robin O'Leary?"

It's at that point I realize I might have revealed too much. I open my mouth to speak, but he beats me to it.

"I think I get it, Ash," he says in a low voice.

"You do? What do you get?"

He smiles and gives me a wink. "You want to get to know her because she's a fellow artist, right?"

"Umm—"

"I'll see what I can find out!"

I have no idea how he arrived at that interpretation of my interest in Robin. Most of the time Orm is pretty observant, but then sometimes he's out on a tangent like that, expecting me to understand his meaning or how he got there. I'm going to let him keep this one. And yes, I do ask a lot of questions. And he knows I'm nosy as hell.

"Thanks, Orm," I smile. He chuckles, pulls his dark brown hair back from his face, and dives back into his banana split.

Orm doesn't let me down. A couple of days later, he takes me aside in the hallway at school.

"Okay, just found this out! Jennifer Dixon is having a party on Saturday night. Her parents are at a wedding down in Lubbock, so pretty much anyone can come, and guess who's gonna be there!"

"Is it Robin and Dill?"

"Yes!" Okay, now he's got my attention. "Ash, you can crash this party!"

It's entirely out of Orm's character to suggest a risky activity such as party crashing. It's out of *my* character to be intrigued by it, and definitely out of my social stratum to actually do it.

A whirlwind of possibilities races through my mind. I don't see myself as a party girl, but then again I've been to a couple over the past year. I'm scheming now. I hear a faint "Later, Ash!" in the background as I resume my course through the hallway.

There's a part of me that wants to go just so I can see more of Robin. But there's also a part of me that wants to creep on the two of them to see just how serious they are. I ask myself why it matters and can't come up with anything logical. Yet I can't get them out of my head.

Saturday finally comes around. Orm has been over studying for history with me and now asks if I want him to go with me to the party. I think about it but tell him this is a lone-wolf mission. Now, all that's left is for me to figure out what to wear.

I finally decide on a pair of tight jeans with sequins arranged in a soft curve down the left side that, in my opinion, makes my butt look good. For the top, I choose a turquoise button-up long sleeve with frills. I've got a new pair of low pumps I've never worn, and I almost decide to wear them, but then decide on a pair of almost-new white Reeboks.

Around seven, I scrub my face clean and do my makeup fresh. It's light, but just the right degree of noticeable. I choose a sample size perfume vial and put it in my purse for after I make it out of the house. I'm pretty sure Grams is going to notice I'm dressed up for something, and I don't want her asking questions that I'm not sure I can answer. I decide to use the trusty old "kitchen dash."

"Hey Grams," I call out, breezing through the kitchen where she is busy scrutinizing a recipe that looks like it was cut from the newspaper. "I'm headed over to Jennifer's if that's okay with you!"

"Okay, sweetie!" she calls out. "Just be safe out there!"

I know she's watching me from the window, so even though I can't see her, I wave goodbye and get in my car, a used and somewhat beat up Honda Civic. It's nowhere as showy as Orm's, but it's mine, and it gets me where I need to be in a small town. It has a slightly musty smell inside, but it's been over a week since I've driven it. A few squirts of perfume clears it up.

The parking situation at Jennifer's is absolute mayhem. There are more cars than I care to count. Some are parked in an orderly fashion next to the curb, but a lot of them are askew and stretched out on both sides of the street as if jammed in by an impatient valet. I want no part of having a hard time getting out, so I choose to park a long way from the driveway and walk in.

Nobody notices my entrance. Nearly everyone has an alcoholic beverage in their hands, and the odor of beer permeates the room. I take a deep breath and wade in. A few notice my arrival and call me by name. I nod and smile . . . and keep moving. Near the bar next to the kitchen, I find a cooler full of beers. I take one and open it, hoping I'll blend in.

Now, to find Robin.

A half hour later, I'm on my ninth or tenth circuit through every room in which people are gathered, I've sipped half my beer away, and I haven't seen *her*. Seeing as I haven't stopped to visit with anyone, I'm pretty sure my behavior is starting to look strange. I decide to do a better job of mixing, so I finish off the beer I'm carrying, grab another one, and slow down. Not having had anything to eat since lunch, I'm starting to feel lightheaded. When spoken to, I stop and chat, but my eyes don't stop scanning.

After another fifteen minutes, I'm getting bored and a bit tipsy—and wondering why I thought it was so important to be at a party that Robin O'Leary might be attending. The whole "Robin" thing now seems ridiculous. I start planning my exit.

Just then, I see Jennifer Dixon. Someone puts a bottle of Corona in her hand, and she suddenly makes a beeline for me. Her eyes make contact with mine. Panic sets in. I have no desire to be outed as a party crasher. I move back into the kitchen, hoping not to be seen, but in an instant, she catches up to me. I open my mouth to explain my presence, but she breezes past me to the refrigerator, where she spends nearly a minute rummaging about and talking to herself. Finally, she closes the door in a huff. She looks up and sees me staring at her.

"God, I just need a fresh lime!" she says as she pushes past me, to which I mumble, "I know what you mean."

All of a sudden, Danny Tucker appears out of nowhere. His hair is mussed, his jeans are riding too low, and he's got a cell phone in one hand and a beer in the other. "Asher!" he calls out in a loud voice, turning more than just a few heads. "Boy am I glad you're here!" He stumbles toward me, parting the crowd, and before I can get out of the way, he clasps me in a bear hug. The smell of beer and weed on his breath makes me cringe. "What are you drinking?" he asks, after releasing me.

"Uh, this beer," I reply, backing away.

I slowly drink from my beer to ensure he doesn't try to kiss me. The can is almost empty before Danny gets distracted and looks away. About that time, Andrea Mitchell forces her way into the kitchen, still dancing to the tune blaring over the speaker system. "Oh, hiya, Asher!" she croons as she performs a whirl, which knocks Danny's phone out of his hand. Some guy I don't even know takes her into his arms and leads her into the living room area. I follow them out, leaving Danny on all fours trying to retrieve his phone.

There's a crowd in front of the television, and they're conversing loudly. Perfect. I mix in with them, hoping Danny Tucker won't be able to find me. When I turn toward the kitchen to keep watch, I see three couples lounging on the couch, and Gary Holmes is busy taunting them into tossing shots of vodka. I'm not surprised. It's exactly how I envision Gary and his future: a lifetime of drinking and getting others drunk. All three guys and one of the girls accept the challenge. With no warning, he calls me by name.

"Hey, Asher!" Spittle flies from his mouth, and I hear some girl cry out, "Eww!" I don't really know him, but he's feverishly waving me over. A gathering crowd cheers me on, and I feel someone behind me nudge me out into the couch area. "Hey, guys, this is Asher!" Gary bellows out, to which there is a loud response of cheers and whistles. He turns to me. "Three shots! Are you ready?"

It's a dare. What the hell. I take another swig of beer, crumple the can, and respond, "Sure!" There's another outburst of cheering, almost like they're waiting for a show to begin. At least Danny Tucker won't be able to mess with me.

My inhibitions have clearly left me. I've never done more than a single shot. Yet here I am taking on a three-shot challenge. Someone has already filled "my" shot glasses and set them out on the coffee table in front of the couch. I kneel down in front.

Gary, now in full emcee mode, calls for more applause. It seems one more guy has taken up the dare, so there are now six contestants. I belly up to the shot glasses. To my horror, Danny Tucker appears once again, announcing that he will kiss the winner if the winner is female. I'm pretty sure there's no "winner" to this challenge, but since I'm one of the only two female participants, I cringe. He points to me as if saying I should get ready.

I turn away from Danny just in time to hear Gary shout, "Now!" The crowd starts clapping in unison. I pick up the first shot glass and slug it down. My throat is instantly aflame, but I hear a loud cheer. I pick up the second. "Go, go, go!" the crowd urges. Taking a deep breath, I down it in one gulp. Once again, my throat feels as if it has been doused in molten lava. I feel something touch my shoulder and turn to find that Danny Tucker is on his knees by my side, with an arm around me as if claiming me for something.

"Go, baby, go!" he says, to which the crowd starts chanting, "Three! Three! Three!"

I hold off as long as I can to let the fire in my mouth and throat cool down. The other contestants have their shot glasses up and ready, so I wriggle free from Danny and raise mine. Gary is grinning and pointing to me, and people are cheering.

I take a deep breath and slam it. My throat belches smoke and fire, and I hear raucous applause. Danny zeroes in for a kiss, but I manage to dodge him and rise to my feet while calling out, "Dude, get *off* me!" He interprets that as playfulness, gets up and sweeps me up into his arms. Now I feel my head *really* spin. The music is a dull throb in the background. Somehow, I end up on the couch, with Danny on top of me.

"Asher!" he moans, as he tries to land a kiss. I'm pushing against him and trying to talk, all the while keeping my mouth away from him, but my head is spinning so fast I'm on the verge of vertigo. There's another guy next to Danny who seems intent on "taking over," but Danny pushes him away and comes in again for a kiss. It's only a miracle that I'm able to evade his open mouth, but his lips and tongue land on the side of my neck. My arms are limp and useless. I let my head fall back and close my eyes, knowing full well I'm completely exposed and vulnerable. The room is spinning like a merry-go-round on overdrive.

Suddenly, out of nowhere, there's Robin, and she's looking into my eyes as if I'm a crash victim on a stretcher. Am I dreaming? She turns back to the crowd. "Back off!" she orders in a loud voice, and Danny and the other guy retreat under protest.

I feel her arms under mine, lifting me from the couch. "Are you okay?" she asks, her face only inches from mine. I can smell a faint vanilla fragrance. With my left arm slung over her shoulder, we head somewhere away from the living area. I try to give an intelligent response to her question, but the only sound I hear coming from my mouth is thick-tongued gibberish.

I don't know how we manage to get there, but we're on the top landing of the staircase, headed for the hallway bathroom. The sound of Danny and the other guys are far away in the background, and it's just the two of us. I feel her hand take mine and give it a reassuring squeeze as we enter the bathroom. I try to give her hand a return squeeze, but I barely have any control over my body. She eases me down in front of the toilet, and I immediately feel how sensual the cold tile in the bathroom feels on my skin.

"Aren't you Asher?" she asks. I turn to look up at her, and she smiles into my eyes.

"Yeah," I grunt. There's a volcano brewing in the pit of my stomach.

"Well, don't worry, I'm going to take care of you," she says. "Just let it out, hon."

I wish I could express my gratitude, but all I can do is nod my thanks. With no one else around, at least my embarrassment factor is way down. And, can you believe it, I'm in a room alone with Robin. I'm wretchedly sick to my stomach, but she somehow makes everything okay.

From a sitting position, I pull myself over and hold my head above the toilet. It's coming, just a matter of when. Behind me, I hear Robin's voice commanding someone to "find another one," and then the sound of the bathroom door being closed. I feel her hand on my back.

The event itself is violent. I find myself heaving and retching for the longest time—and in a stranger's house, no less. But Robin's arms are holding me up, and she's comforting me with her words. When I'm finally done, I manage to operate the flush lever before leaning back. She allows my body to settle into her arms and applies a cold, damp rag across my forehead. I'm in survival mode, too drunk to be embarrassed by the fact of having made my acquaintance to her by vomiting in her presence.

"It's okay," I hear her say. "Just relax, you're safe." After a minute or two, she cranes her neck around to smile into my face and asks me, "Do you think you're done?" I manage to give her a nod. She eases me into a sitting position against the wall next to the door with her arm around me, and then gently positions my head on her shoulder. "Let's just sit here and catch your breath before we go anywhere else, okay?"

This moment of relief simply cannot ever be equaled. It is simultaneously comforting and sensual. I surrender all control of my body to her. With the room still spinning, I desperately need to close my eyes. And in her arms, I'm safe to let the room spin and go dark.

When I come to, I see Orm hovering over my face. "Ash, it's me."

After a second or two, I realize I'm lying on a bed. My tongue feels thick and dry, and there's a foul, acidic taste in my mouth. The music and loud voices are gone. I look around the room. It's dark, but not completely black. I hear a familiar voice.

"Are you okay, Asher?"

It takes some effort, but I turn my head and focus on the source of the voice. It's Robin. She's still with me, sitting on the other side of the bed from Orm.

"What time is it?" I manage to force out. My own voice sounds foreign to me.

"Oh, about four in the morning," I hear Orm reply, stifling a yawn.

"You've been in and out for about six hours," Robin adds, giving me a smile.

"C'mon, Ash, let's get you out of here," Orm says. I can feel his strong arms lifting me. As I go up, I realize Robin's hand is clasped to mine, and I instinctively squeeze it. Both he and Robin help me walk outside. "You're not gonna throw up in my car, are you?"

I shake my head in response as he lowers me into his car. My mouth is thick, and I try to wet my tongue. At least there's no nausea, but my head spins, and I feel like something on the inside of my skull is trying to jack-hammer its way out.

Suddenly, Robin's face is in front of mine. She checks me out like a mother hen, then smiles at me. It's a comforting smile that conveys safety.

"Get plenty of rest, okay?" she says.

I don't want her to leave me. I peer into those captivating green eyes as if I'm hoping time will stand still. She sees what I'm doing and smiles again.

I can tell from the conversation she's turning me over to Orm.

"Well, I'll see you Monday," she says to me, before withdrawing from the car and standing up.

I can hear Orm thanking Robin in the background before coming around and getting into the car. He drives deliberately slowly, to keep from resurrecting my nausea. My head spins again, so I close my eyes. Presently, I find myself being tucked into a soft, warm resting place with familiar odors, and a blanket being pulled over me and up to my neck. And that's the last thing I remember before waking up this morning in Orm's house.

He spends the morning and early afternoon patiently nursing me back from a wicked hangover while we watch television. Later, we retrieve my car, and when I get home early in the evening, Grams hardly notices—probably because I'm in Orm's company. When I get in bed for the evening, I drift off to sleep while replaying in my mind what little I can remember of Robin's attention to me.

3

It's the first day of the new school week, and I'm fully recovered.

The usual Monday morning smell of pine oil permeates C wing as I enter the school from the parking lot. Yes, I'm sure a lot of people are aware that I got stupid drunk at Jennifer's party on Saturday, but in a way that only makes sense on a high school campus—it's a badge of honor. And as I make my way to my locker, a few people give me smiles, and one guy I've seen but whose name I don't know gives me a fist bump and a "Hey!" It feels good. The only person I *don't* want to see is Danny Tucker, and fortunately, he's nowhere in sight.

I'm pulling books out of my locker when I'm startled by a cheery "Hi!" from over my left shoulder. I turn around to find myself face-to-face with Robin O'Leary. Dill is standing off to the side as if having been deposited there by Robin with instructions to "stay." For some stupid reason, I'm suddenly a bit short of breath.

"Hey!" I respond, pulling my books in toward my body and clasping both arms around them.

She smiles at me, studies me for a second, and then starts in as if we were already engaged in conversation. "You look great! Me, I was a bit hungover yesterday, but it could have been worse. Not like you, though!" she laughs. "Dill wanted me to go to church with him the next morning, so I had to moderate." There's a pause, and then she keeps going. "My first three classes are my hardest, but my favorite is theater. That's fourth period, right after government. That's my hump class of the day. It's all downhill after that. Speaking of period, I've got bitching cramps today. But, hey, enough about me, what about you?"

"Uh, yeah. I'm okay. I, uh, slept on Orm's couch." Oh, geez, how stupid can I possibly sound? I'm always flustered when put on the spot, a character trait I despise. I find myself trying to take a deep breath when Robin starts in again.

"That's cool. Is Ormand your boyfriend? I've seen the two of you hanging out with each other during the school day, and you know, I even told Dill last week when I saw y'all leaving together after school, 'They make a good couple!' Don't get the wrong idea, I don't creep on people, and I don't gossip. At least, I try not to. So, it was just an observation that—"

"He's not."

"Oh, sorry, what?"

I release the hold on my books long enough to pull a strand of hair out of my face. "Orm. He's not my boyfriend."

"Really?" Her eyes lock onto mine. "Like, I see y'all together all the time."

"A lot of people assume the same thing," I tell her, "but the truth is that he's just a friend. I don't mean *just*, 'cause he's like my *best* friend." I pause for a moment to see if she gets it, but her expression doesn't move. "We've known each other since fifth grade, and I guess we just found each other on . . . on a friend level." I pause again. "I know that sounds weird and—"

"No, not at all! It sounds *great!*" she trills, adjusting her stance so that she's just a bit closer. "So, is there a *real* boyfriend?" she asks, in a lower voice.

For some reason, I hesitate. Is this a social acceptance test of some kind? If I tell her the truth, that I don't, and never have had a real one, and that I've only dated three boys, will I fail and be rejected? And if I pass, will I be admitted to her social group? No time to think, so I go ahead and jump right in the deep end. "Um, no."

"No?"

"Yeah."

"Well, that's okay, Asher!" she smiles. "I spent just about the first two months after I moved here last year before hardly even speaking to a boy! Not until after the Christmas show, actually. That's when I dated Terry Thurston for a whole two weeks. And then, when school started up again in January, me and Leland Hall kinda dated—until he got a little too aggressive, that is. Dill and I have been together for the past two months."

"Oh," I manage to reply. She pauses, like it's *my* turn to confess my dating history. "I guess I haven't found the right boy yet," I finally manage, followed by a halfhearted shrug.

She doesn't say anything right away, but slowly, she gets a smile on her lips. Maybe I managed to pass after all. Then, she cocks her head to one side and gives me a sideways stare that almost takes my breath away. "What lunch period do you have?" she asks, her voice practically a whisper.

"B."

"So do I!" she replies in an exuberant but constrained voice. "Tell you what. Why don't we sit together at lunch, so we can talk some more? Where do you sit?"

I can't believe what I just heard. Robin O'Leary wants to sit with *me?* For a second, all I can see is the fevered mob that descended upon her after the Spring Show. And now she's inviting me into that inner circle? I just hope to God I didn't misunderstand her question.

"Okay," I whisper, to which she leans in close to my ear and says, "So . . . where do you sit?"

I tell her. She nods and, after another smile, walks away with Dill. But before turning the corner into the classroom corridor, she faces back to me and mouths, "See ya!"

I don't dare tell anybody, out of fear that she won't show up after all and I'll look like a delusional wannabe. But it's almost too good to contain. My mood is ecstatic for the first three periods, and in history, I can hardly follow the class discussion. Orm sits behind me, and even from there he senses I'm not myself. He nudges me and leans forward.

"What's going on?"

"Nothing!" I emphatically whisper over my right shoulder. He gets the hint and doesn't pursue it. When the bell rings, I rise, but suddenly find myself slightly wobbly. This is it. The moment of truth. I try to steel myself for the ultimate rejection.

I breeze through the lunch line, grabbing only a slice of pizza and a glass of water. I'm so nervous I almost spill the water as I walk to my usual table. As I take my seat, I glance up and see Robin and Dill in the lunch line. They'll be out in less than a minute. I settle in and try not to stare.

Orm is sitting across from me, but he's engaged in a lively discussion with two other girls about St. Patrick's Day. I pray I'm not sore-thumb obvious with my nervousness. I pick up my pizza to take a small bite, but just then, someone plops their lunch tray down beside me. It's Robin. Dill grabs the seat on her other side.

"Asher!" she sings out, followed by a laugh. Her smile is stretching from ear to ear. And, it's not fake. I can't help but smile in return.

"Hey, Robin!" I reply, after which I immediately notice that nearly everyone at my table has stopped their conversations and is now staring at the unexpected display of familiarity as if a Pulitzer Prize winner had just been announced.

"Oh. My. God!" she says, her eyes wide and beseeching everyone in earshot. "Can you believe that Dill has decided on Texas Tech?" She smiles at Dill, who nods slightly and continues chewing his food. "It's true!" she says, to everyone except Dill. "Are y'all gonna be here for signing day?"

"I will," a voice calls out, which results in a few others responding in the affirmative.

"You gonna follow Dill?" another voice asks.

Robin pounces on the question, almost as if she has a prepared response.

"Nope!" she responds with a shrug. "I'm hoping to get accepted to the Winston Institute for the Arts. I've heard they only take one for every thousand that apply, so I'm sweating it out big time. But, if I get in, I'll be in Chicago this time next year!"

A chill runs up my spine.

"Wow, the Winston!" Laura Harkens replies. She's sitting next to Orm. "But, hey, if *you* can't get in, nobody can!"

Orm immediately opens his mouth to speak, but I manage to shush him with "the look." He shrugs with a look of confusion seen by a few, including Robin, then turns away and rejoins his discussion about St. Patrick's Day.

I had absolutely no idea that anyone else at tiny Sagebrush High School aspired to attend the Winston Institute. This means that Robin and I are alike in more ways than I thought. I can actually feel tiny shivers of excitement coursing through my body.

As she's the social queen bee, the topic of discussion is left to Robin. At first, she engages in a group discussion about something to do with the lunch menus, but after a few minutes when that conversation has its own momentum, she leaves it and turns away from the group to speaks only to me. Her voice is much lower, and she turns her chair slightly sideways to face towards me.

It's not so hard to speak with her since she broke the ice this morning. We talk first about history, probably because it's her hard subject. That topic of discussion melds into a critique of the high school yearbook staff—in particular, the person who interviewed her—after which she puts a hand to her mouth as if to shush herself.

"Asher, are *you* on the yearbook staff?" she asks.

"Yeah, but that wasn't me." I give her a shrug. "Cameras," I add, "just cameras."

"Really! That's nice!" she responds.

"Yeah, you should see her photos, too," Laura pipes up. "She is so good! In fact, she's so good that she—"

"You should see the portrait she did of me!" Orm interjects. I had no idea our conversation was being followed.

"Portrait?" Robin asks, looking first at Orm, then turning to me. "You do portraits?"

"Yeah, I do."

"Do me!" she blurts out. "Will you do me?"

"Um, sure."

"She's gonna do my portrait!" she says to Orm, who smiles.

"You won't regret it," he assures her.

Robin gleefully claps her hands without making a sound, clenches them into fists, and turns to Dill. "She's gonna do my portrait!"

We continue with small talk until finally, I can hear the clatter of trays and silverware at the bussing station, so I know the lunch period is at an end. Robin hurriedly finishes her last bite of green beans, dabs at her mouth with a napkin, then crumples it and pushes back from the table. Out of the corner of my eye, I see her rise and tilt her face up to Dill, who gives her a quick kiss. And then, without warning, she turns back to me for an instant.

"See ya!" she says, and she lightly touches the back of my hand before turning back to Dill and walking away with him.

For a few seconds, all I can do is stare at the back of my hand where she touched me. I'm not sure what that was all about, but I get an immediate head rush. Dazed, I rise from the table and begin wandering away in the general direction of the cafeteria exit. Behind me, I hear Orm calling out, as I've walked away without him. I pause and let him catch up.

"See ya after school!" he says, before heading off to his fifth-period class.

I spend the last two periods of the day trying to figure out how I feel about my newly-found social status, finally deciding it's most likely just temporary. On the way home after school, Orm is talkative and goes on and on about how some people are already posting on social media about me.

"Why do you think she came over to sit beside you? Was she checking up on you?"

"Yeah, probably." I start to add that she checked up on me that morning but decide to keep my mouth shut.

"You think so?" he asks, keeping the topic alive.

"Yeah, I do think so. What's the big deal, anyway?" I don't want Orm making more out of this than it is.

"The big deal is that Robin O'Leary—you know, that girl you didn't even know a week ago?"

"So?"

"Well, now she's like your bosom buddy!"

"Geez, Orm, drop it, okay? Tomorrow I'll go back to just being Asher, the camera girl."

I'm opening the car door to get out at my house when Orm asks me a question.

"Do you like Robin?"

"What kind of question *is* that?" I demand, turning to face him.

He's unfazed. "Well, *do* you?" He has a weird expression on his face—something between a smile and a smirk.

"Get that stupid look off your face!"

"Well?" he says, this time a bit louder.

"No!" I shoot back, surprising even myself. Orm's question unsettles me in a way that feels kind of like anger, but it isn't. I get out and slam the car door behind me.

"Ash!" he calls after me. I keep walking to the house, completely ignoring him. I get a text message just as soon as I get inside.

WTF??

I delete it without answering and head upstairs to my bedroom. After four hours, my homework is done, and I'm finally getting over my attitude from what I've now decided was nothing more than an innocent question. Now I'm wondering why I even had attitude.

Grams and I eat dinner in uncharacteristic silence. I help her clean up, after which I retreat to my room and try to watch television. But I can't. It's like I'm caught in some kind of limbo between tense and relaxed. I head to bed and am almost asleep when my phone rings. Yawning, I raise my phone to my face, press the answer button and offer a timid, "Hello?"

"Hi Asher!" a girl's voice replies. "Did I wake you up?"

It's Robin. She's using the same chipper tone of voice I heard at lunch earlier today. But why would *she* be calling me?

"No!" I answer immediately, even though it was half-true. I scrunch my pillow up and plop my head onto it. "I was just, um, watching TV."

It's a full two or three seconds before she says something, and when she does, her voice is softer, almost a whisper.

"Good. I was hoping you were awake."

"You were?"

"Yes." I hear her take a deep breath. "I just finished my homework and now I'm getting ready for bed."

There's something about the fact that she called me with no specific purpose in mind that stirs me. I fumble around for something to say.

"Sorry about your period." There's a moment of silence. Did I really just say that?

"Thanks," she answers, softly. "I've been cramping all day, so I took some pain pills an hour ago." I can hear her yawning, but then she whispers again. "I'm glad I met you."

"Me, too," I add, hoping I don't sound mushy or anything.

"Well, maybe I'll sit with you again at lunch. If that's okay?"

"Sure!" I reply. "You can sit with me anytime you want to. I mean, with *us*. Like today." For the life of me, I can't figure out why I'm so klutzy when talking to her.

"You really don't mind?" she asks, after another yawn.

"Well, no. I mean, you can sit anywhere you want. In the cafeteria." There I go again.

"I know that, but do *you* want me to sit with you?"

I take a breath. "Yes, I do," I tell her, my own voice now a whisper.

"Good! I was afraid you might say no."

"Really?"

"Yeah."

"Well, I didn't, did I?" I reply, with a giggle.

She returns the giggle. "No. Thank goodness!" She lets out another yawn, and this one provokes a yawn from me. We both burst out laughing. "Well, I'll let you get some sleep, Asher!" We laugh again.

"Okay, Robin. Bye!"

"Bye!"

I'm about to click off, but I hear her voice again.

"Asher?"

"Yeah?" I say, returning the phone to my cheek.

"I'd like to meet up with you at your locker *every* morning."

4

The next morning, as the aroma of bacon and eggs summons me from the fog of slumber, I suddenly remember Robin's request to meet me at my locker.

Now I'm in a panic about what to wear to school. I spring from bed and start digging in my closet. What I wear today is important. It's *way* important.

I think maybe the light blue distressed jeans I picked up over in Boise City a couple of weeks ago. But I do have that pair of black skinnies that would go well with my light blue oxford. Or my black jeans with a dark gray long-sleeve flowy top. If it weren't still chilly in the mornings, I'd consider wearing a tank top with a loose button-up sweater on top.

"Asher!" I hear Grams call out. "Breakfast!"

"Be down in a minute!" I yell.

With no time to waste, I throw on the black jeans and the flowy top. There's static in the air, so my hair is acting possessed. I'm in the process of lacing up my tennis shoes when I impulsively take them off and slide my feet into a pair of low heels I've only worn once. As I make my appearance in the kitchen, Grams' eyes go straight to my heels, but she says nothing.

Without even taking a seat at the table, I wolf down a couple of slices of toast and swig a glass of orange juice. Before Grams can protest, I rise, give her a kiss, and hurry back upstairs to exchange the flowy top for my mauve balloon sweater, and then give my hair a quick brushing. Only thing left to do is brush my teeth.

Orm drives up just as I'm rinsing my mouth. Good, back on schedule. He's smiling at me like the Cheshire cat as I climb into the front passenger seat, his eyes on my low heels.

"What?"

"Oh, nothing." As he pulls away and drives straight ahead, he holds his nose in the air. "But you never wore heels to school for Jermy!"

"Whatever."

I hear a beep, and retrieve my phone from my purse. It's a text message from Robin.

Hey u at school?

I hesitate, trying to compose a message with just the right words, but out of fear she'll think I'm ignoring her, I give up and quickly tap out a response.

Not yet, but almost

OK see ya!

"Who's that?" Orm asks as I put my phone down on my lap. It's not that he thinks getting a text message is out of the ordinary—it's that he can see my reaction to it. I shrug in response, but he guesses who it is. "It's Robin, isn't it?"

"Yeah," I smile, turning to face him. "She wants to meet me when I get to school."

Orm nods his head and gives me a thumbs up. "Don't forget the little people like me on your way to stardom!"

We share a laugh as we pull in, but I'm already scanning the parking lot for any sign of Robin or Dill. Nothing. I head right in without Orm, who usually walks in with me. I'm anxious about meeting Robin, and I don't want to do it with Orm following me.

People are thick in C wing, but as I make my turn into the locker area, I spot her right away. As our eyes meet, I feel a smile spread over my face.

Her outfit is impeccably stylish: distressed jeans and a white, frilly top under a tan vest trimmed in burnt orange that perfectly shows off her figure. She waves and smiles at me, and as she approaches, I feel a tingle sweep through my body.

"Hey, Asher!" she squeals, and then she breezes right into a conversation. "Terrible Tuesday!" she blurts out. "Not as bad as Monday, but at least to-morrow is hump day!"

I force my eyes off her glistening lips and up to her eyes, smile, and offer a timid, "Yeah, Tuesdays." It's only then that I realize Dill isn't with her.

"Where's Dill?" Her smile drops a bit. It's barely perceptible, but there's no doubt.

"He's, um, with Steve Nichols." She pauses for a second, and I get the feeling she doesn't want to have to explain why he's not here. I take the cue.

"Orm's off somewhere, too. I think he has physics first period." She gives me a puzzled look. "Well, not that Orm is my boyfriend," I hurriedly add, "which he's *not*, but sometimes we come in . . . together." I give her a shrug.

"Yeah, I remember." I worry I've said the wrong thing, but then she's bright again. "Well, can I sit with you at lunch today?"

"Sure!" She impulsively takes my left hand between both of hers and pumps it up and down, causing me to smile.

"Yay!" she squeals. Off to the side, I can see some people taking note of the conversation. "Well, see ya!" She gives my hand one more squeeze. Almost in a flash, she's gone, leaving me with all kinds of distracting thoughts.

I'm sort of back to normal by the time I'm in math class, but then I hear the phone in my purse, sitting at my feet, start buzzing. I lean over enough to see the screen of my phone. It's Robin. I wait for the right moment, and when the teacher turns her back to write on the whiteboard, I quickly retrieve the phone from my purse and, leaning over to conceal it, read the message.

Only two more classes til lunch!

I quickly look up to see whether I've been noticed. A grinning Lisa Stowell, sitting across from me, is following my every move. I quickly tap out a smiley and slip the phone back into my purse. Once again, I'm filled with distracting thoughts of Robin.

By the time fourth period is over, and it's time for lunch, I feel like a weekend has arrived. When I get to the lunch line, I see that Robin's already there ahead of me, but she's with Dill. She notices me right away and peels away from Dill to run over to me.

"You don't mind if Dill sits with us, do you?" she asks.

Once again, my newfound social status has me floored. That someone with Robin's social stature would think it necessary to ask permission—the whole idea of it catches me off guard. I start to reply but find myself stuttering.

"Y-yeah, sure!" I give her a smile. She giggles in return, and I can't help but stare into her green eyes. She returns to Dill and they head away from the checkout register.

It's not in the right direction. But then I see Robin tap him on the shoulder from behind and gesture toward my table. He pauses, and then, with her leading, he follows, and they both take a seat. In a move that makes me catch my breath, I see her claim the empty chair next to the one she chooses for herself. And as I finally approach with my tray, she pulls out the chair for me and pats the seat. I look at Orm, who's already in his usual place across the table, and he gives me a smile and an eye roll.

By her very nature, Robin commands everyone's attention. Within a few minutes, she's got everyone charged up and raucous. But after every two or three sentences, she turns to address only me, each time ending her sentence by touching or patting my hand. I like that, and when I don't think anyone is looking, I find myself studying her fingers and how they are immaculately manicured.

Today, she's wearing a soft orange nail polish that perfectly complements her vest, but clashes a bit with my own light peach nail polish. What I'm really staring at are her long, slender fingers. I steal a look at my hand. My fingers are long as well, but I have large knuckles that disrupt a smooth taper from palm to fingertip. Hers are perfect.

Lunch isn't nearly as long as I'd like, and all too soon, Dill is taking Robin away. "See ya!" she calls out over her shoulder as she leaves the lunchroom. Orm politely waits for me to gather my tray, and he walks me to the bussing station where we both plop our plates down.

"I guess I'll see you after school," he says, giving me a wave, "unless you're maybe riding with Robin!"

I quickly look around to see if anyone noticed his comment and get a couple of return smiles from a bevy of girls standing near the exit door. But Orm's words almost turn out to be prophetic after school is out when Robin intercepts me in the parking lot as we're walking to his car.

"Hey!" she greets me.

"Oh, hey!"

I stop, but Orm continues on to his car.

"So, how was your day?" It's obvious she meant for this meeting to occur. I can see she has fresh lipstick, and the wind is playing with the tiny wisps of hair around her ears.

"Good!" I reply, breaking into a smile.

"Really?" She tilts her head ever so slightly and takes a deliberate step into my personal space. I feel my heart racing.

"Yeah. Good!" After a second, I add, "How about you?"

"Same here! Except for history, of course."

"Oh, yeah, my weakness, too. But Orm's pretty good at . . . I mean, he studies me up pretty good."

My mouth is suddenly so dry I can barely swallow. She's really close—so close I can smell her breath. It's sweet and minty, and I breathe it in, hoping she doesn't notice. She shifts her weight from one leg to the other, then back again.

"Good guy to have around!" she observes, looking over my shoulder and giving Orm a small wave of her hand, to which he responds by lifting his chin. Dill calls out, and she turns to him, but says nothing. "Well, I gotta go. See you in the morning?"

"Sure!" I reply, to which she touches my shoulder and then turns to scamper away. I watch her climb into the front seat of Dill's truck. I'm still staring at them as they drive away.

I finish my homework earlier than usual after dinner, and then get ahead of the game and pick out my outfit for the next morning. I'm a little surer about my choice this time.

The next morning, as I come into the kitchen, Grams eyes me, then smiles and gives me a compliment on my appearance. The expression on her face lets me know she suspects something out of the ordinary, and for a minute it looks like she's going to ask about it. Just then, I'm saved by the sound of Orm's car horn. I grab my book bag, give Grams a kiss on the cheek, and head out the door before she can say anything.

Orm warms me with a smile and we spend the drive in trivial conversation. He keeps giving me a curious sideways glance, and I'm almost sure he knows I've got something on my mind. Thankfully, and probably because he knows me so well, he doesn't bring it up.

As I hurry down the corridor of C wing, I'm hoping Robin's already there. Sure enough, she's the first sight I gather in as I turn the corner into the locker area.

"Hey!" she says, as she scans me from toes to nose. I notice that despite the chilly weather, she's wearing a cute little light-yellow sundress trimmed in green underneath an unbuttoned beige sweater. Dill is nowhere in sight.

"Hey!"

We chat for a minute while I gather my books, but then, at her suggestion, we walk together around the corner and sit on one of the large window sills lining the south wall of C wing.

"God, I'm so glad I have you to talk to in the mornings," she says in a low voice, as if confessing a secret. "Dill's not the best conversationalist." She pauses, apparently expecting a reply, and I'm caught off guard. She rescues me with a quick "If you get what I'm saying." She holds an expressionless face for a second, and then we both dissolve into laughter.

"Like, which guy is?" I say. "Unless you wanna talk about football!" More laughter. We're still laughing when we part ways and head to our first-period classes. Later that day, between third and fourth period, I turn the corner into B wing and there she is, a broad smile lighting up her face.

"Wow!" she exclaims. "I didn't expect you *here!*"

I know she perfectly well expected me here, and that's why *she's* here.

"Hey!"

I can't help but giggle at this unexpected delight as I walk up to her. This really makes my day. I pull my hair out of my face and give her a smile. The sun coming through the window reveals her perfect complexion. I guess I'm staring, because she suddenly says, "Don't be fooled, I get pimples!"

"You do?"

"Sure!" She playfully puts her arm in mine and walks me across the hall to a vending machine, where she pulls her arm back and digs in her purse for coins. "I drink a lot of water. Everyone tells me that." She feeds the vending machine and retrieves a bottle of water. "Want a drink?"

"Uh . . . sure." Too late, I see it's a squirt bottle. She pulls up the top and motions for me to tilt my head back and open my mouth. I feel awkward doing it, but I comply anyway, allowing her to fill my mouth with water. The look on her face as she observes me with my mouth full is just too funny, and I can't control myself. The water spews out all over the floor as Robin jumps back out of the way. "Oh my God!" I exclaim, wiping my chin and face.

We're both heaving with laughter. She inadvertently squeezes the bottle, and a long stream of water jumps out onto the floor. We stare at it with wide eyes for a second, look to each other, and exclaim, "Eww!" in perfect unison, and there is another loud chorus of laughter as we step back.

At this, Vice-Principal Morrison steps out from nowhere and lets out with a loud, "Ahem!" We turn around to find him standing with his arms crossed, inspecting the wet floor. After a second, he looks up. "You ladies have a class to go to?"

"Um, yes, sir," I answer, as Robin sobers up.

He gestures toward the hallway. "Well?"

Robin and I exchange a furtive glance and begin walking away in different directions, after which I hear him calling someone for a mop. At lunch, we tell the water bottle story to long peals of laughter from everyone, except Dill. And as Orm and I are riding home from school, he makes a remark about how happy I seem lately. He's right. I *am* happy. In fact, I've never been happier.

As I'm settling into bed for the evening, I get a text message from Robin.

You asleep?

Nah.

A minute or two passes, and I get:

Sometimes I have trouble going to sleep.

Not me.

Wish I knew your secret! You gotta teach me!

I manage a swallow.

Sure! I tap out.

OK, nite!

Nite!

I'm not exactly sure how I'm supposed to teach Robin how to fall asleep, but the idea of doing it races through my mind with reckless abandon. And now it's *me* who's having a hard time falling asleep. I'm curled up with my pillow and staring at the wall when my phone rings, and in anticipation of hearing her voice, I answer in a flash.

"Hey!" I whisper.

"Asher?" It's Jermy's voice. I pull the phone back to look at the caller ID, and sure enough, it's plain as day. This is about the worst possible time for him to call me, and I have to bite my tongue to keep from saying something snarky.

"What do you want?"

He hesitates before replying. "I was just, um, wondering if you wanna go see a movie with me or something." He clears his throat.

"No."

He's ruining the ambiance of my text exchange with Robin, and I'm consumed with the impulse to hang up. A minute or so passes, during which I silently curse myself for not looking at the caller ID before answering. I'm on the verge of disconnecting the call when he speaks up.

"Why not?"

"I don't want to."

"Why not?"

"We broke up, remember?"

"*You* broke up with me."

"Whatever! The fact is, we're broken up!"

"Yeah, but that was then. You're not still mad, are you?"

"I didn't break up with you because I was *mad* at you!"

"You didn't?" he replies, in a tone that reeks of new hope and makes me want to get off the call before he gets the wrong idea. "Wow. I thought I had messed up real bad! So, why *did* you break up with me?"

I don't have the time or desire to explain myself. He wouldn't get it anyway, and I don't want to get another verbal tirade. I take a breath and try to be nice, but firm.

"It just wasn't working, you know? At least it wasn't for me."

There's another long silence. "Look, Asher, I can do better if you give me a chance."

"That's just it, Jermy. I'm not looking for 'better' from you."

"Well, whatcha looking for then?"

"I don't know." I grit my teeth. That's not what I meant to say. He's getting me flustered, and my patience is about at an end.

"Well, if you don't know whatcher looking for, how do you know I can't give it to you?"

"Jermy, c'mon. Please. We're done."

"You owe it to me to give me a second chance."

"I do *not!*" I shoot back.

"Yeah, you *do!* I paid for your meals and stuff for three weeks."

"Dammit, Jermy, you didn't *buy* me! So you sure as hell don't *own* me!"

"Well, I know I *can* give you what you want."

I shudder at the thought of what he thinks I want. "No, you can't. Good night."

"Wait!" He sounds desperate. "How do you know? Just give me a chance!"

"Jermy, you don't *have* what I want." It's blunt, but the situation is about to push me over the edge.

"How do you know I don't have what you want, Asher?" he pleads.

"Because someone else *does!*" I shout in frustration.

Oh God, now I've done it.

"Who?" he demands.

"Goodbye, Jermy! Please don't call me again!"

"Who *is* it?" I hear him demanding as I remove the phone from my ear and end the call.

The Jermy encounter leaves me tense and irritated as I roll onto my back and try to get to sleep. After tossing and turning for what seems forever, a tone alerts me. I'm afraid it's Jermy, but when I look at the screen, I see it's from Robin.

I was just thinking about you! :)

I feel a warm flush spread over me. Funny how a simple text message from her can give me an emotional makeover, but she seems to know just how to do it. I tap out a reply.

I was thinking about you too :)

She replies with a heart emoji, and suddenly I have trouble swallowing. I tap the same heart emoji, and my finger hovers over the send button. But, I can't make myself do it. I'm afraid that if my response is somehow inappropriate, I'll destroy the magic in the air.

I'm withdrawing my finger when I suddenly get pissed at myself. I have three months of school left—and then what? It's now or never. I grit my teeth, close my eyes, and press send.

5

As usual, Robin's waiting for me the next morning when I get to my locker, and thankfully, she has a big smile on her face.

She steps into my personal space and whispers, "I liked your text!"

I feel a warmth shoot through me. "Really?" My eyes follow the neckline of a cute, light blue V-neck tee she's wearing. I can smell the sweet vanilla fragrance of her perfume.

"A lot!" she adds. Dill calls to her, and she says, "see you at lunch!" before walking away with him. My eyes lock onto her figure as she walks away from the locker area.

Up to now, I've never considered school lunch to be anything more than unusual odors, a bit of food, and a lot of solo conversation with Orm. Boy has that ever changed! After a week, lunch has morphed into a daily social event. In fact, it's made me a celebrity. Robin sits beside me, everyone at the table hangs onto every word she utters, which is usually to me, and I get a lot of the spotlight that's coming down on her. People I barely know now greet me as I pass through the hallways. Even my teachers seem to have a new attitude towards me.

One of the things I really like about Robin is that she's very touchy-feely. When she makes a humorous point, or even if it's just a personal sentiment, she'll almost always touch me on the shoulder or hand. Same for compliments, gossip, and, well, most everything. I don't care why she does it. I just like it.

And then there's Dill. I'm amazed that he still accompanies Robin to lunch. It's rare that she speaks to him except in response to something he says. When others laugh, he stares blankly. I've noticed that when she does respond to something he says, it's with impatience in her voice. That sometimes makes me feel a bit awkward, like maybe I'm a relationship intrusion.

The end of the school day still belongs to him, and he makes sure there's no doubt about it. Every day, even when Robin and I visit in the parking lot, I have to endure the sight of the two of them walking hand in hand and driving away together.

"Seems like you can't get your eyes off them," Orm says as I once again follow Dill's car with my eyes from the parking lot after school.

His observation gets my attention. I've been thinking my feelings were my secret, but now I'm sure Orm can see me for what I'm doing. I close my eyes and let out a sigh.

"What are you saying?"

"Nothing, really," he smiles. "What's up?"

"I don't know!"

There's a long silence, and then he says, "I didn't mean anything, Ash."

Then it hits me. What the hell am I thinking? It's *Orm,* for crying out loud. It's time to come clean. I *need* to come clean.

"You're right. I *was* watching them drive away."

He nods, but says nothing. I decide to put a toe in the water.

"I was watching them drive away because . . . I think I'm kind of jealous." There, I said it. I watch his face very closely as a smile appears.

"I thought so."

"Do you think that's . . . weird?"

He frowns and looks into my eyes. "Of course not!"

His blanket acceptance makes me think he knows more than I think he does. But do *I* know? With that, I lean back into the passenger seat and silently try to figure out just what's going on with me lately.

"You okay?" he says, after a long silence.

I turn toward him. "You ever met anyone you just—I don't know—like maybe they made you kind of confused?"

He nods—like he was expecting that question. "You mean like you don't know whether you even like them or not?"

"No, it's not like that, but it's close."

"Go on," he prompts.

"Orm, she's like an itch I can't scratch!"

"Ahh," he smiles, "I think I get it now. You're crushing on her! That's your itch!"

He's right, of course. I am crushing on her. And it feels good to finally admit it to myself. In fact, I can't help but smile, and he sees.

"I don't think I even know *how* to scratch *this* itch!"

"Well, you better figure it out quick, that's all I've gotta say!"

"Why?"

He gets a broad grin across his face. "Because I heard a rumor today!"

"Rumor? What is it?"

He lets out a sarcastic chuckle, as if he wants me to beg for it. That's a familiar game we play.

"Out with it!" I command, giving him a playful slug to the shoulder. He laughs out loud and holds up his hands in surrender.

"Okay, I'll tell you, but you didn't hear it from me."

"Fine!"

"I heard a rumor that they might break up."

I didn't expect *that*. "Seriously?" I face him, almost letting my books slide to the floorboard.

We lock eyes for a few seconds, a comical ritual we use on each other to ferret out "gotchas." If he can hold a straight face, he's telling the truth. He manages a straight face for a few seconds, but then loses it and grins. Yet he defends his claim.

"Seriously, Ash, I *did* hear that today. Some of the guys were saying that Dill wants to end it."

My mind immediately goes to Robin. Will this crush her? Does she have any idea? And why am I all of a sudden feeling kind of guilty?

"Why would he do that?" I force down a hard swallow.

He rolls his eyes. "Aw, c'mon, Ash, I think you know that!" he laughs.

I feel my face flush. "No, I don't," I reply, feigning ignorance. "She hasn't said anything to me about any such thing!"

Orm takes a deep breath and sighs like you do before launching into an explanation of the obvious with a small child. "Ash, you've taken her away from him!"

"I have *not!*" It feels like Orm knows *way* more than he should. He gives me the *you know I'm right* look and says nothing.

The idea that I've somehow taken Robin away from Dill tears through my brain for the rest of the afternoon and long into the evening. Even though I had no intention of mentioning it to her, I blurt it out during our end-of-day phone call.

"Am I taking you away from Dill?" I ask before I can think twice about it.

Robin laughs, but it's short, and in a tone I've never heard from her. "Why do you think *that?*"

"I don't. At least I don't think I do." I hesitate for a second, but then finish. "Okay, Orm told me today." I can't believe I said that. He's gonna kill me now.

"Well, don't pay any attention to it," she responds, after a long pause. "What's going on between me and Dill has been building for a long time."

Before I can catch myself, I respond. "So, y'all *are* gonna break up."

"No!" she shoots back. She pauses before continuing. "Or, at least . . . well, I don't know. He's just kinda . . . I don't know. Lately, I don't know *anything.*"

"Well, if I'm the reason—"

"No, you're not."

"I'm just saying—"

"You don't have anything to apologize for. Trust me."

I don't know how to respond, and it's several awkward minutes before anyone speaks.

"Asher?" she calls out in a timid voice, almost too weak to hear.

"Yeah?"

"Did you ever see a blouse or a sweater, or, I don't know, it could be anything? Like, in a store? And you thought you needed to have it because of what others might think about you if you had it? Like trying to impress them?"

"You mean like trying to fit in?"

"Yeah," she answers, her voice a bit stronger. "That's good. Like trying to fit in."

"Well, yeah. I guess." I think I know where she's going with this, but the thought of Robin being unsure of herself, or thinking she needed to do something to "fit in" is crazy.

"That's sorta how me and Dill ended up together."

"Really?"

"Yeah. He was the football star, and I was the new kid on the block."

I force myself to breathe. "You mean, you're not in—"

"Love?" she interjects. "No. Between you and me . . . I'm *not* in love with Dill. I never was."

"But, you hold hands, and you—"

"Asher, Asher, Asher," she whispers, her voice trailing off.

"You're just keeping up an act?"

"Please don't say anything. Promise?"

"No, I won't say anything. But, does Dill—"

"C'mon, Asher, do you really think he knows?"

"He doesn't have a clue, does he?"

"You got that right."

"But Orm says he might break up with you."

"Geez!" she responds with a sigh.

"So that's not true?"

"Asher, it's *me* that might break up with *him!*"

That revelation makes me catch my breath, and I force down a swallow. I can hear her breathing deeply while nervously tapping on something, probably the phone.

"Are you?" I ask.

"Maybe." I hear another sigh, and then, speaking softly, she adds, "Yes."

Her response makes me once again get butterflies in my stomach. "Well," I manage, "you can call me . . . or whatever. If you need to talk." I pull my covers up to my chin.

"Thanks," she says in a soft voice. "I might need to do that."

"Good." I notice that my hands are trembling. There's a long silence during which we listen to each other breathing.

"Asher?"

"Yeah," I whisper.

"*Are* you trying to take me away from Dill?"

The question makes me squirm. "No," I finally reply.

"I wouldn't be mad if you were," she responds, again in a whisper.

Oh, God, there goes my head, spinning again. "Umm . . . what?"

"Did you understand what I said?"

I swallow and struggle with something to say. "Yeah," I whisper.

There's an overtone of intimacy in our conversation that I really don't know how to handle. Robin finally gets me off the hook.

"Well, I'm getting sleepy. See you at your locker tomorrow morning?"

"Okay."

"Well, then, bye," she says, to which I say the same.

For a long time, I don't press the button to end the call, and neither does she. I can hear the sounds of her handling her phone, as well as her breathing, but only faintly, like maybe she's holding the phone's microphone away from her mouth—but not so far I can't hear her. I don't say a thing, and instead listen to the sounds she's making. I close my eyes, and after a few seconds inadvertently allow the phone to touch my lips. Without even thinking, I reflexively plant a long, soft kiss on the mouthpiece, and to my horror, it makes an audible sound. And she hears it.

"Asher?"

I don't say a thing. I don't even breathe. I can't believe I did something so stupid. After another few seconds of panic, I disconnect the call, but my heart is pounding. I try to think up an excuse, just in case she asks me about it in the morning, but get nowhere. Avoiding her is out of the question. I ball my fists and find myself biting my lip for a long time before surrendering to sleep, but the agony of my predicament greets me within the first microsecond of being awake the next morning.

I see that Robin's waiting for me as I walk up to my locker, and her face has the expression of a child's on Christmas morning.

"Guess what?" she asks, taking care that Dill doesn't hear her, not that he's trying to eavesdrop.

"What?"

"It might be crazy, but I have an idea!" she replies, leaning in closer and speaking almost in a whisper. "Let's sneak off at lunch today, just us! You and me! You wanna?"

"What?" I demand. "Are you crazy? This is a closed campus, you know that!" At least she didn't ask about the strange noise on the phone from last night.

"I didn't say anything about leaving campus," she says through a smile. "We'll just sneak off to the football field and eat lunch in the bleachers! That way, we can have some privacy."

Hearing her say the word "privacy" makes my head spin. "You don't think someone will notice we're gone?"

"Who cares?" she giggles.

"But I didn't bring lunch today!"

"Well, *I* did!" she smiles. "Enough for you *and* me!"

"You planned this!"

"Meet me outside C wing, okay?"

I can barely contain my excitement. At the end of fourth period, I sneak back through C wing, and just as I step outside, a finger taps me on the shoulder. I turn around to find Robin right behind me, and she looks like she's about to explode in mischievous laughter—which, of course, makes me have to put my hands over my own mouth to keep from causing a scene.

"Let's go!" she says. I notice she's carrying a large brown paper bag, rolled at the top.

"What about Dill?"

"I guess he's in line in the lunchroom?" she says, to which we both laugh out loud.

It's a bright, sunshiny day and the temperature is on the warm side. Within a couple of minutes, we're in the bleachers, and she's setting out a two-person lunch: a sandwich, a bag of chips, napkins, and soda for each of us.

"Eat!" she commands, laughing and touching my hand.

"You are so devious!"

"Yep!" she smiles. God how I love her smile. It gets me every time.

She watches as I take my first bite. It's delicious. My mouth is full, so I give her a thumbs up, after which she smiles and starts eating, too.

"Me and Dill had a talk last night," she says, wiping the corner of her mouth.

"What? You mean, after *we* did?"

"Yep, after." She cocks her head and gives me a coy smile.

I can't help but smile back. "What about?"

She acts like it's no secret. "You know!"

"You mean—"

"Yes! We just talked about *it.*"

I wait for her to say more, but she hesitates, apparently wanting me to draw it out of her.

"Just tell me!" I say through a mouthful of chips.

"We talked about our relationship."

I feel the same stirrings of conversational intimacy that I felt last night. "Um . . . and what did he say?"

"A lot of stuff," she replies, fixing her eyes on mine. She takes a sip of her drink. "Do you think we're happy?" she asks.

"Well . . . seeing as how you're not in love . . . I don't know."

"Even after what I told you last night?"

I try to make a sensible reply, but seeing my difficulty, she waves me off. "I told him I'm *not* happy," she says. "Does that surprise you?"

I'm afraid to reply, but more afraid of not replying.

"Maybe not." To my own surprise, I'm now aware of a new feeling building within that I can't quite figure out. She peers into my face, and I wonder if she can see it.

"We've never had sex," she says, finally. "Me and Dill." I'm speechless. "Does *that* surprise you?"

"Geez, Robin, will you stop asking me that?" I take a long draw on my soda, trying to figure out what to say. I'm almost afraid of where's she's going with the conversation—or where my own emotions are taking *me*.

"Well?" she persists.

"Well, what?"

She rolls her eyes. "Are you surprised that—"

"No, Robin, I'm not!" I blurt out.

"Really?" Her brows are raised in surprise. She stares right into my eyes until I look down at what's left of my sandwich. After a few awkward seconds, she laughs and gives me a goofy expression that breaks the tension and makes me burst into laughter. I open my mouth to ask a question, but then shake my head and resume laughing.

"What?" Robin says.

"Nothing!" I reply.

"Bullshit! What?"

What the hell. "I guess I'm wondering if you've . . . done it with some other guy?" Wow. I can't believe I just asked Robin O'Leary if she's a virgin.

The expression on her face looks like relief. "Sorta!" she says, through a smile.

"What do you mean *sorta?*" It dawns on me that I have a creepy need to know what she's done.

"It was a guy I dated in tenth grade," she says. "His name was Marcus. I think he was Italian, or Spanish, or something. This was when I was living in Texas." She smiles again. It's clear she wants me to prod her.

"And what?" I say.

"Well, we went on a movie date, but after, he drove us somewhere secluded and parked the car. That was when he started kissing me. And then . . ." She stops and raises her brows.

"What? He did it?"

She chuckles to herself and looks down. "We were so dorky!"

"Dorky?"

She looks up, grinning. "Yeah, dorky! We didn't have sex, but he tried.

No way was I gonna let him do *that!"*

"What do you mean, *that?"* I reply.

She giggles and leans in. "*Fuck* me," she whispers.

Her daring use of those two words gives me a head rush. A really big one.

"Really?"

"Yeah, really."

"So that was it?" I realize that I'm glad she hasn't gone all the way with a boy.

"Well, I gave him a blow job," she adds, somewhat off-handedly.

"Eww!"

"I know!" she laughs.

"Did he—"

"Yes!"

"Ewwww!"

The two of us are laughing so hard that I'm sure people in the school building a hundred yards away can hear us. I can barely breathe as my chest convulses, and it's all I can do to keep from literally rolling out into the gap between the bleacher seats. Robin sees me leaning and reaches across to steady me.

As our laughter dies down, I feel a closeness we didn't have before we snuck away for lunch, as if we've crossed some kind of emotional milepost. I wish I had something personal on the same level to tell her, but she's clearly way ahead of me. We sit with our eyes focused on each other.

"Well," she says finally. "Are you glad you asked?"

"I don't know."

I'm trying my best to be coy, but she sees right through it. Almost as if in slow motion, she picks up a chip, contemplates it, and then teases my mouth with it, finally allowing me to take it. As I chew it, I can see her scrutinizing every movement and every muscle in my face, especially my mouth—and I allow her to do it. Watching her watch me stirs something inside. When I swallow, she takes a deep breath and exhales slowly.

"Well, we better head back in before someone comes looking for us," she says under her breath. "If someone sees us, just act like you're supposed to be in the hallway."

Just before we reach C wing, and as we're walking side by side, she moves a bit closer, and I notice she's practically staring a hole in the side of my head.

"What?" I say, turning toward her. Our shoulders are touching now.

She tilts her head just a little, smiles, and with her palm extended just far enough to reach me, gives me a soft touch to my lower back—more like a caress than a pat. It doesn't last even for a full second, but her touch makes my body flush with heat. I feel instantly powerless, but in an exotic and forbidden way. I want to say something, but I can't. She continues to hold eye contact with me, almost as if savoring the effect she's having on me.

"C'mon, let's go in," she finally says in a sultry tone, gesturing to the doors.

We walk through the doors into C wing, but then get busted. Vice Principal Morrison chooses that exact moment to round the corner up ahead, and his eyes land squarely on the both of us. He calls us over.

"You girls wanna tell me why you're coming *in* that door?" he says.

At first, there's silence. "We had to get something out of her car," I finally say, to which he shakes his head and hurries us off to class, both of us doing our best to keep from laughing out loud.

"Can you come over to my house today after school?" Robin asks before we part ways. The question catches me completely by surprise. She's clasping her books tightly to her chest while leaning in. My eyes study her face—her wide, green eyes, and especially the way her upper teeth have captured her lower lip.

"Yeah," I hear myself say.

She breaks into a wide smile. "Then you're riding home with me today!" And with that, she's gone. I get the definite feeling the two of us are on a runaway train. After sixth period, I walk out into the parking lot to find her waiting for me.

"Wait . . ." I say as she gestures for me to follow. "Aren't you with Dill?" That didn't come out quite right. "What I mean is, don't you ride with Dill?" I don't want to say it, but I'm not gonna ride third wheel in the back seat behind the two of *them*. I don't care how short the drive is.

"I brought *my* car today," she grins, giving me a wink. Dill is off to the side and obviously hears her, but stares straight ahead. She steps closer. "That way, I can bring you to my house . . ." She mouths *alone*. I look at Dill, then back to Robin, all the while trying to swallow without being noticed.

"You planned this, too!" I whisper, to which she gives me *that* smile again.

I give Grams a quick call to let her know my plans as Robin walks me through the parking lot to a sleek, black Mercedes-Benz sedan. She makes a point of opening the passenger-side door for me. The plush decor of the car takes me by surprise.

"Holy shit, Robin!" I stoop to run my hand over the leather seat cover. "This is *your* car?"

"Yep!" she nods. "Dad bought it for me at the beginning of the school year, when we were still in Texas. Get in!"

I'm immediately overwhelmed by the luxurious interior. She punches a button on the wheel and a song I like titled "Since We Met on Monday" plays from a sound system that comes at me from every direction.

"Oh my God," I exclaim, through a smile. "That's my favorite song!"

She gets an immediate gleeful expression. "Mine too!"

"Then this is *our* song, deal?"

"Deal!"

That we have a song that's "ours" fills me with excitement and anticipation. She must be noticing, because she touches the seat beside me and pretends to sample the softness of the leather. In so doing, her hand brushes my thigh ever so slightly. I look up at her face, and she's smiling into my eyes.

"I've always loved the nicer things in life," she says softly, "and this"— she motions with her eyes to the seat on which her hand is resting—"is nice."

Wow. I swallow and force out a timid, "Yeah."

She takes Halcot Road just north of the high school, which doesn't surprise me. It leads to the only high-end development around, where all the rich people live.

"You're the first person I've brought home with me!" she says, once we enter the subdivision.

I nod. I can't believe Robin O'Leary really is taking me to her home.

"I called my mom already, and she's waiting to meet you!" She touches the back of my hand, which is folded in my lap over my book bag. "You like it when I do that, don't you?" she smiles, to which I can't help but squirm while trying to keep from blushing.

"It tickles," I say, then clear my throat and quickly add, "I'm trying to imagine what the inside of your house looks like!"

She faces the road again. "It's okay, I guess. Most people are afraid to walk around because they think they might break something expensive."

"I won't—"

"No! Don't you even dare be afraid to touch something!" She smiles and gives me a flirtatious look. "Promise?"

"Um, okay." She touches my hand again and gives me a coy smile.

It isn't long before she whips the car into a long driveway that splits off between two separate garages. She takes the smaller of the two.

"Dad gave me this single-car garage," she says, activating a control on her steering wheel that opens the garage door. She gestures to the right. "They use that one." She brings the car to a stop, turns off the ignition, then faces me. I'm fixated on how perfectly her medium-length red hair frames her face. She reaches out and lightly caresses my cheek with her fingers. I'm pretty sure my heart just skipped a beat. Then she moves her face very close to mine and looks straight into my eyes.

"Are you ready?" she whispers.

6

A giggling Robin takes my hand and pulls me through the garage and into the house, letting go right after we're in.

My first sight is Robin's mom. She's slim and petite, and her hair is the same hue of red as her daughter's. She beams at me and gives me a big hug. Her perfectly formed smile stretches across a face adorned with laughing green eyes that make me smile just looking at them.

"So, you're *Asher!*" she exclaims. She holds me out at arm's length to examine me, then pulls me in for another quick hug. "I'm *so* glad to finally meet you, because Robin's told me so much about you!"

"Um, well, I hope it was good," I manage to choke out through a smile. "Thanks for having me over."

"Oh, you're so welcome here!" she responds. "I hear you're a photographer?"

"Yes, ma'am." I glance sideways to a smiling Robin, who gives me a little nod of encouragement.

"She says you won the photo art competition at the spring show?"

"Um, well, yes, ma'am." Being complimented like this up close and personal by someone I don't know pushes me out of my comfort zone, but she immediately sees it and grabs my hand.

"Come and sit. I simply have to know *all* about your photography," she says. She leads me through to their great room which includes an incredibly ornate dining room and a plush living room with a diagonally-set fireplace in the near corner with a hearth of pure marble. The ceiling is high and reveals a second-floor landing, obviously the bedroom area. A gold and glass chandelier hangs down in the center, but most of the lighting comes from recessed fixtures around the room.

I'm led to a cushy gray sofa, and as I sit, Robin's mom settles on the love seat next to me—and I'm not sure I've ever seen anyone take a seat that gracefully. She comes to rest with one leg precisely positioned over the other, facing me.

"Have you been practicing your photography for a very long time?" she asks. I feel Robin sitting down beside me.

"Yes, ma'am, since I was eleven years old and got my first smartphone. And three years ago, my grandma gave me a digital SLR." Robin's mom continues her smile and nods, but I realize I've just geeked her. "Um, that's a digital camera," I explain. "The kind where you look through the lens."

"Is that the kind that the professionals use? Like on *CSI?*"

"Yes, ma'am, they do use those on *CSI,*" I respond with a smile.

"Maybe you can show it to me sometime!"

"Mom," Robin jumps in. "Asher is going to do my portrait!"

I let out a nervous laugh. "Well, I'm one of the photographers on the yearbook staff, so—"

"I can't wait!" Robin adds.

"How wonderful!" her mother chimes in, scooting forward and bringing her palms together. "I am such a fan of the arts, as is my daughter! I so admire the two of you for your passions!"

"Um, thank you." I'm trying my best not to squirm.

"So do you develop your own pictures?"

Robin sighs. "Mom, nobody *develops* pictures anymore!"

"Of course not. How silly of me!" She places her hands on her knees and shakes her head, all the while holding her smile. "Well, there you see how little I know about cameras!" she says through a chuckle.

"Well, we still develop pictures, but it's done on a computer," I say, trying to give her some credit.

"They use picture shop," Robin adds. "That's how they develop pictures on a computer. Right, Asher?"

I almost correct her, but catch myself. "Exactly."

"You kids today—you know so much more than I do!"

At that exact moment, I hear a door open and close, and a man I recognize from the talent show as Robin's father strides into the living room. He stops the second he sees me, and for a long, awkward moment, he stares without smiling.

"Darling!" Robin's mother stands up and positions herself at his side. "This is Robin's friend, Asher. We were just talking about her photography.

Did you know she won the art—"

"What's your name?" he demands, holding up a hand to shush his wife.

"Asher. Sir." I glance to Robin and notice the expression on her face is very different from just a few seconds ago.

He narrows his eyes in my direction. "And *how* do you know Robin?"

"Um, we're in the same school. Sir." How can he not figure that out for himself? There's only one high school in Sagebrush.

"So, you're in theater together?" He cocks his head slightly. I can't help but notice he has a frown on his face that's unnerving. To my side, Robin shifts her position.

"No, Dad!" Robin chimes in. "We're not in any classes together. We just *know* each other."

"How *did* you meet her, then?" he asks, directing the question to Robin.

"How did we *meet?*" she asks, giving him a look.

He makes eye contact with his wife, then me, then back to Robin. "Yes. How did you meet?"

The silence that follows is awkward, even oppressive. Why is he hung up on how Robin and I met? I begin to think maybe I've violated some social grace.

"Dad, we just *met*. Okay?"

The two of them have their eyes fiercely locked onto each other in a silent undercurrent of communication. The stare down finally ends and he walks out of the now-silent room. Robin's mom seems to be trying to say something to us, but no words come from her mouth. The entire performance of the last two minutes leaves my head spinning.

Once he's out of sight, Robin motions for me to get up, which I do. "Mom, we're just gonna be in my room." She leads me up the staircase to a bedroom just off the second-floor landing. I feel like we're sneaking.

"What was *that* all about?" I ask once we're in her bedroom. "Did I do something wrong?"

"No!" she replies, shaking her head as she closes the door. "That's just . . . well, my dad has a hard job and when he comes home . . ." She stops mid-sentence, and I stand there waiting for her to finish it. Her face changes to a look of consternation. "I—I guess he wasn't expecting you. Or something." Her explanation makes no sense, but it's obvious she wants to change the subject.

"Yeah, probably," I reply, letting her off the hook. She breathes a sigh of relief, then gives me a smile.

"What do you think?" she asks, turning on her bedroom lights.

The room is easily three or four times the size of mine. One complete wall is adorned with playbills, presumably from her many theatrical performances. Another wall features a large bay window that bathes the entire room with a warm glow, the sill decorated with small knick-knacks and succulents, along with a couple of greeting cards stood up and slightly open. The view looks out over the large front yard toward the driveway.

"Look at this!" she calls out as she opens her closet door. As I step toward her, she gestures to a spot on the third level of a massive shoe rack toward a pair of small glossy white slippers that look as though they've never been worn. I want to touch them, but I dare not. Robin notices my desire, quickly snatches them up, and puts them in my hands. "I wore these when I was five years old!" she laughs. "Can you believe it?"

"They're so cute!" I gush, turning them over in my hands.

"I knew I wanted to be a dancer, even way back then."

"I wish I could see you dance! Why didn't you dance in the spring show?"

"They already had that one-act play selected. But I did ask for the song I sang."

"It was amazing. Your voice is *so* beautiful."

"Thank you!" she says, gently taking the shoes from my hands and replacing them on the rack. "C'mon, let's listen to some music." She walks to her desk and operates a remote. Soft music fills the air. It's a country song, and one of my favorites. She plops down on her bed, motioning for me to follow, giving me a smile while patting the spot she wants me to occupy. I take a seat and look around the room, taking in the decor.

"This is really nice," I say, finally allowing my head to turn in her direction.

"Yes," she responds in a voice I can barely hear. "This *is* really nice."

Her eyes are transfixed on mine. She has a strange but captivating smile on her face. We remain frozen like this for a long time, and although awkward at first, I relax as I search out the features of her face. Her deep, green eyes seem to go on forever, but what's really bothering me is the perfect shape of her mouth and lips.

She leans in a bit. "You know what, Ash?" she asks, using a nickname I've only heard from Orm.

"What, Rob?"

She giggles, giving me a soft shove on the shoulder. "It's Robin!"

"Well, you called me by a nickname," I grin. "Don't I get to call you by one?"

She laughs and adjusts her position on the bed to face me with both legs crossed. Then she leans over and touches me lightly right on the tip of my nose, almost as if experimenting to see if she can get away with it.

"I guess," she says, "as long as it's a good one."

"Robbie?" I venture.

Her face contorts, and she shakes her head. "No! That's horrible!"

"Well, I guess I'll have to settle with just Robin. So, what's your full name?"

"Robin Cierra O'Leary," she replies with a smile, pronouncing her middle name with a hard "C."

"Cierra?" I say, making sure I'm pronouncing it correctly. "That's an unusual name."

With gleaming eyes, she nods and tilts her head ever so slightly to the side. "That's because it's Irish. My grandfather came to this country right after World War Two. My dad has an Irish name, too. My mom is American."

"Cierra," I whisper, trying out the name again. "It's beautiful!"

I see her eyes light up. She readjusts her position slightly, then leans in again. "So, what's *your* full name?"

"Asher Kendall Sullivan."

"I think that's a *beautiful* name!" She laughs and reaches out to touch my nose again, but this time I dodge her. "Okay," she smiles, "you can do it to me!" A sudden intimacy emerges from this silliness. Smiling, I take the challenge and softly touch the end of her nose. We both dissolve in laughter.

As the laughter dies down, she fixes her eyes on mine. "I just thought of something!"

"What?" There goes that swimming feeling in my head.

"I told you everything I ever did with a guy, but *you* never told me what *you've* done! So let's hear it!"

My stomach knots up. It's not that I'm hesitant to discuss personal details of my life with Robin. It's that I don't have anything to report that in any way comes close to what she's done. I almost make something up, but then decide I'm just gonna be honest. And now that I think about it, I *want* to see her reaction to my sparse boy-girl history.

"I already told you that I've only dated three guys," I begin, trying to set the stage in a way that doesn't create great expectations.

"I remember," she says, smiling with an *it's okay* expression.

I take a deep breath.

"Jermy was the last one, but I've—"

"Why did y'all break up?"

"Well, to be honest, I never even considered myself to be his girlfriend."

"But y'all dated?"

"Unfortunately!"

She giggles and lightly brushes her hand over my calf. I'm sure she sees my reaction. "Keep going," she says. "There must be some reason why y'all aren't dating now."

"Yep, there is." I tell her all about Jermy's awkward attempts to make out with me.

"I'm just seeing a mental picture of that happening!" She gives me a *come on* gesture with her hand. "More!"

"Well, that's it. We didn't *do* anything."

"What?"

"It's the truth."

"So . . . you're a virgin?"

"I guess so."

She pauses for a second. "Do you think you lose your virginity if you give a guy a blow job?"

I have to look into her eyes to realize she's serious.

"No, of course not!"

She's silent again, this time a bit longer. "Well, good," she finally says.

"What about you?" I ask. "You never dated any boy after Marcus?"

"Not in Texas," she answers hesitantly, shrugging.

"But wasn't that two years ago?"

"Yeah, it was." She purses her lips, obviously wanting to change the subject. "I want to know more about *you*. Why haven't you . . . had sex?"

"I guess I'm just not interested," I blurt out before realizing what I said. "Well, what I *meant* was that I just can't seem to find the right boy. I mean . . . well, do you know what I mean?"

"Maybe," she smiles. "Did you ever kiss Jermy?"

"Well, yeah." I really want to add "unfortunately," but don't.

"No, I mean did *you* ever kiss *him?*"

Now I get the meaning of her question. "If you put it that way, then I guess no, I didn't."

"But he kissed you?"

"Yes."

"A lot?"

"I—I don't know." The last thing I want to do is make her think my relationship with Jermy was in any way desirable.

"Was it every day?" She's leaning forward, and her eyes are laser-locked on mine.

"Um, no," I respond, to which she seems to be relieved. "And it didn't mean anything."

"It wasn't romantic?"

"Oh God, no!"

"Then, what kind of kissing was it?" she asks.

"It wasn't making out," I reply, giving her a shake of my head. "Awkward, yes; making out, no. We only dated—if you want to call it that—for three weeks."

At this, she goes quiet. She finally allows a smile to grow across her face. "Awkward? How?"

I look down and smile, then raise my eyes to meet hers. "I guess it's like you know you're gonna have to do it, but it just doesn't do anything, and you want it to end."

"Like you're eating a raw oyster for the first time!" she laughs.

"Exactly!"

She gives out with a long peal of laughter, but finally comes to rest with her eyes back on mine. "Show me," she whispers.

I catch my breath. "*Show* you?"

"Yeah. Show me." She leans in. I can see her eyes darting back and forth to mine.

"H-how?" I feel caught off guard.

"*Kiss* me," she says. "Kiss me like you kissed Jermy."

Uh-oh. I didn't expect this.

I freeze up big time. My mind races with the mental image of me kissing a girl. I don't even know what that would feel like. I'm not sure how to do it. Yet, the idea of kissing Robin now somehow seems exotic, and more so by the second. I feel tiny shivers running up my spine. She inches a bit closer. I take a deep swallow. It's the moment of decision. I can't believe this. I'm actually going to do it.

I turn more toward her and lean forward—just a little. She does the same but holds her position. What the hell. I close my eyes and go in, delivering a quick peck at first. When she doesn't recoil, I do it again, but this time longer. It's a closed-mouth kiss, yet I breathe in an intoxicating fragrance about her mouth before slowly pulling back.

It's that second kiss that leaves me breathless.

I've *never* felt anything like this. If I've ever wondered what an earth-moving experience was, this is it. When I open my eyes, I see that Robin's are still closed. I breathlessly study her face. Through the window behind her, I see a flash, followed by the low rumble of thunder.

She holds her position for what seems like a long time—as if reliving it over and over. "That was nice," she says after finally opening her eyes.

"I liked it, too." I can't believe I just said that.

We slowly melt into smiles, and finally, she gives me a grin.

"That didn't feel awkward. Are you sure that's how you kissed Jermy?"

I smile and let out my breath. "No, that's definitely *not* how I kissed Jermy."

"I didn't think so!" she laughs. She locks eyes with me again, this time with noticeably more intensity, and then shakes her head.

"What?" I say.

"We just *kissed!*" she says.

"I know . . . it was *your* idea!"

"Doesn't that sound *gay* to you?"

Her question makes me squirm. "Yeah, I guess it does."

"Well, I don't know about *you,* but *I'm* not gay!" she says, trying her best to hold a straight face.

"Me, either." We're silent for a few seconds, then we both laugh again—but it's a nervous laugh.

"Let's talk about something else," she says, to which I agree.

She gestures me over to her vanity where she pulls open a drawer to reveal about a half-dozen bottles of perfume.

"Which one is your favorite?" she asks.

I stoop over and spend a minute or so reading the labels. I don't recognize the names of any of them. "I don't really know," I tell her, doing my best to act like I know of them, but just can't decide which one is my favorite.

She lets out a delightful giggle. "Go ahead!" she says. "Try them! Tell me which one your favorite is!"

One by one, I sample each. All of them smell nice, but there's one that captivates my senses. I examine the label. It's something called "Wildwood Vanilla."

"This one," I say, smiling at her.

"Wow!" She clasps her hands. "That one's *my* favorite!" She picks up the bottle, sprays her wrist, and holds it out for me to savor. The sweet fragrance of vanilla is instantly familiar, and I know why I picked it.

We somehow end up sitting on her bed as the conversation becomes animated and covers every school topic we can think of. It's only when Grams calls to tell me that dinner is in forty-five minutes that I realize the time has completely gotten away from me.

"Are you leaving?" she asks as I rise from the bed to look for my book bag.

"Well, I have to," I moan, letting her know I'd stay if I could.

"I'll give you a ride," she says. She starts to pull herself up, but I playfully push her all the way back down, leaving her sprawled haphazardly across the bed. She smiles at me, a wide-eyed look of mischief on her face.

"Nope! I can walk!" I tease, returning her smile with a wink.

"It's *raining!*" she says, pointing to the window.

I had totally forgotten that little detail. "You're right."

She gives me a smile. "I'm *always* right!"

"No, you're not!" I assert, giving her my best coy expression.

I see her brow raise ever so slightly, and she pauses for a second or two before extending her right arm.

"Help me up."

Laughing, I take a step forward and grasp her hand. She makes no effort to help pull herself up, forcing me to strain. At first, there is no resistance, but then she smiles and gives me a forceful tug. There's no avoiding it: I land squarely on top of her with my left arm awkwardly hanging off the bed where I tried to break my fall and missed. My right arm—my hand still in her grasp—is pinned between the two of us.

I'm startled, but she's lost in convulsive laughter. I can feel her breasts against mine, and something about that physical contact zaps my brain with electricity. Then, she parts her legs ever so slightly, causing my body to sink in closer to hers. Neither of us tries to untangle. Suddenly, we're both quiet, and she extends her left hand to slowly caress the right side of my face. Then, she moves her hand to the back of my neck and slowly draws me in until our mouths are only an inch apart. I feel like I'm about to explode.

"Tell me 'no,' and I'll stop," she whispers. Her breath kisses my face, causing my head to spin with a giddy anticipation I've never felt before in my life.

Her eyes are so wide I feel like I could fall in. I breathe in the smell of her breath and find it intoxicating. After a long second, she gives a slight pull against the back of my neck. Closing my eyes, I sink in and surrender my mouth to hers.

I actually hear bells ringing in my head, and there's a strange sensation pulsing in me like I'm falling. Like a runaway carnival ride, I feel out of control. I'm sure that every single atom in my body is on the verge of breaking through my skin and escaping into space.

The kiss is intense and open-mouth—and nothing like I ever imagined kissing would be. I can't get enough. Both of us eagerly explore each other, touching and tasting, writhing in the quest for the perfect angle, only to move on to the next. I find it unfathomable that the sensation of a girl's soft lips on mine is able to bring out this kind of passion in me.

Finally, she pulls back just a little, breaking contact. Our lips are almost touching and remain so for another long moment. I'm out of breath and on the verge of gasping. After another few seconds, I slowly push myself up to sitting.

And then reality comes crashing in. What just happened?

"Why did you do that?" I lightly touch my forefinger to my still-moist lips.

She says nothing at first, and there's an almost imperceptible change in the expression on her face as she looks up into mine.

"I don't know," she says at last.

The sight of her still sprawled on the bed, making no attempt to sit, keeps my eyes wide open and my brain on overload. My throat is so tight I can barely breathe. Finally, I take a deep breath and stand.

"I've gotta go." My voice is shaky and hoarse. "I'll just—"

"I'll drive you home," she says, getting up as I rise from her bed.

"N-no! I mean, I'm just gonna walk home. It's not far." I look around and find my book bag. She gives me a strange look as I hoist it over my shoulders. A sudden inner conflict has me trembling. I have to get out of here. Now.

"Ash?"

"I'll let myself out, okay?"

Everything is awkward as I open her bedroom door and descend the staircase. I don't even turn to see if she's there. At the bottom, I quickly exit through the front door and then jog down to the road before slowing to a walk. I don't look back, but I know she's watching me. I can feel it.

It takes me just twenty minutes to walk home, and I sweep right past Grams on my way up to my room, where I look at myself in the mirror for a long time. I towel-dry my hair, brush my teeth, put my phone on silent, and join Grams at dinner, where we eat in almost complete silence. I can tell by the way she's looking at me that she knows something is amiss.

That evening I find it hard to get started on my homework. All I can think about is Robin—and what happened between us. I don't think I'll ever be the same, and I'm trying to decide if that's good or bad. It takes a long time to finish my assignments, and afterward, I'm completely exhausted. I don't even get ready for bed, and instead just plop down and stare at the ceiling until sleep finally overtakes me.

7

I'm lying in bed, fully awake for at least an hour now, my mind racing a million miles an hour to a million different destinations.

I can't get Robin off my mind. What does it say that I willingly and passionately kissed a girl? And what the hell am I feeling in my gut? Am I gay?

I remember in ninth grade when Kenna Lowell pulled me aside before school one day and said, "My mom told me that gay girls suck each other *down there.*" The idea of doing that had been immediately repulsive to me. And now that I think about it, there was Gracie Wilson in tenth grade who told me that on a dare she had kissed a girl, and that had unsettled me for some reason. Still, it didn't make me think she was gay.

My head is really spinning. I need Orm. I raise my phone and tap out a text message:

Come sooner today.

The reply is immediate. *How much?*

30 min?

It's obvious I've caught him off guard. But just when I'm about to follow up, he answers.

You okay?

Yeah but I need to talk.

A thumbs-up emoji appears. I force myself out of bed to get a head start on my now-accelerated morning routine. I'm on the porch when he arrives.

"So, what's going on?" he asks before I'm even settled into my seat.

"Just drive." I take a deep breath. If ever there was a secret to share—one that *needed* sharing—this is the one. "I went over to Robin's after school yesterday."

"I know," he shrugs, giving me a *keep going* expression.

I open my mouth, but suddenly have difficulty forming the words that need to come out. But who am I trying to kid? This can't be dressed up.

"Robin and I made out."

I see his right eyebrow immediately go up. "You did?"

"Yes."

"And you're telling me this because?"

"Orm! I kissed a *girl!*"

"Okaaay."

"Well?"

"Well, what?"

"Don't you have anything to say about that?"

"If you want me to tell you that's disgusting, you're gonna be waiting a long time."

"Really?"

He chuckles but says nothing.

"But . . . th-that's . . . it's—"

"A sin? Is that what you're trying to say?"

I nod. "Something like that. It sort of is, isn't it?"

"Well, I guess if you listen to Reverend Barncastle long enough it is," he replies sardonically.

"Wait, so *you* don't think it is?"

"I don't think so. I mean, what do *you* think?"

I lean forward and massage my temples. "I don't know," I moan. "It's deeper than just being a *sin.*"

"What else is it, then?"

"Well, does this make me gay?"

From his reaction, I can see that Orm understands how worrisome this is to me. His voice is gentle and reassuring.

"I have no idea, Ash. I think it's for *you* to say. And *only* you. All I know is you're my friend. That's all that matters to me."

We're almost at school, so I hurry it up.

"Orm, she just pulled me down on top of her and started kissing me!"

"For how long?"

"I don't know! Maybe a couple of minutes? I mean, if it was *her* idea, maybe *she's* gay, but not me?"

Orm stares straight out the windshield.

"What?" I say, after a long minute of silence.

He turns back toward me. "And how hard were you fighting her during those two minutes?"

"I couldn't fight her, she was holding me down!" I can't believe I just lied like that.

Orm sees right through me. He raises an eyebrow. "Lame."

"Okay, you got me. But it was *her* idea!"

"Ash, you were on top of her, and it lasted for a couple of minutes?" He lets out with a sigh. "I get this is a big shock to you, but don't start lying to yourself. You don't want to go down *that* path."

My shoulders sag, and my throat tightens. "Okay, you're right . . . as usual." I search his eyes. "God, Orm, I'm so confused!" I'm about to burst into tears—something I don't do very often.

"Maybe you're overthinking it," he says in his calm voice. "You don't have to figure out all the answers right now, you know?"

"Y-you think so?" I manage, after regaining a bit of composure.

He gives me a smile. "Well, let's look at this way. Do you want to do it again?"

I'm stunned into silence. His question hits the nail right on the head. It's exactly the burning issue that's got me so tormented. *Do* I want to do it again? Do I want to feel Robin's lips on mine? Do I want to feel that fire inside? The heat of her body against mine? The smell of her skin . . . her breath? The taste of her mouth? And what does it mean if I do? I'm tortured about something that's so beguiling, yet terrifying at the same time.

"That's what I'm trying to figure out! Right up until it happened, I would have never thought something like that would even happen. And just a couple of weeks ago, I never, ever thought I could have these . . . well, feelings. For a girl! What do I do?"

His expression doesn't change. "Do you want to do it again?" he says, this time more slowly.

"Okay," I confess, after a long pause, "maybe I do. But Orm, she really did something to me. I'm not the same person. She literally rocked my world."

"Is that really so bad?"

I face straight at him. "I'm not exaggerating when I say that I felt the ground move when she kissed me." He says nothing. "No boy ever did that to me! I mean, what do I *do* about that?"

"Maybe you don't *do* anything."

I think about it for a minute. Maybe he's right. All I know is that something that feels so right has me feeling like I never even knew myself until now.

"Walk me in?"

He gives me a wide grin. "Sure!"

For the few minutes it takes to get to the entrance, I take several deep breaths and somehow get to a calm place. But after he leaves, I know who I'm going to find at my locker.

I could easily avoid her. But I don't. And as I round the corner, I see her. The sight of her is actually comforting in a way I can't explain. Now I'm right back to butterflies in my stomach and the fear that I'll say something stupid. I'm not sure I can breathe.

"Ash?" She's somehow different this morning. Or is it me?

"Robin?"

"Yeah," she says in a barely audible voice. She eyes me up and down. "I was waiting for you," she adds.

I let out a soft but forced laugh.

"Well, I have to get to class."

As I close my locker and take a step back, she steps forward and peers deeply into my eyes—and I have no defense for that.

"Are you okay?" she asks.

"I'm fine."

She steps another few inches closer, and I feel faint. I recognize the fragrance of her perfume—the exact fragrance I picked out as my favorite. My eyes lock onto the lips I tasted just yesterday.

"Are you upset with me?" she whispers. I tear my eyes away from her lips and look up, and the expression on her face is one of . . . well, *fear*. I don't know what to say.

"I-I don't think so." That part is true. It's me I'm worried about, not her. She sighs and glances around as if checking for eavesdroppers.

"We need to talk," she announces in a firm whisper. "After third period. Behind the lockers in B wing."

Her take-charge display calms my nervousness a bit. Both her time and location are perfect, as it's an out-of-the-way-area, and the break between third and fourth period is longer than usual because it's also the start of the first lunch period.

"Okay," I manage to whisper. It's obvious she trusts me. Now I feel guilty for making her worry. What the hell is the matter with me?

I'm utterly useless through the first three classes of the day. All I can think about is the talk we'll be having. Is she going to confess that she's gay? Will I be expected to make the same confession? It's been a long time since my palms were this sweaty. Yet after third period finally ends, I can't wait to see her, and rush to B wing.

I slow down before rounding the last corner. She's not there. I feel a sudden ache in the pit of my stomach. I'm about to assume the worst—that I've somehow scared her away—when I hear her voice behind me. I whirl around to see her shushing me with a finger over her mouth. Without saying a thing, she takes me by the hand and leads me into the alcove between the school office and the back side of the row of lockers. It's kind of cramped in here, but at least it's private. We take a seat side by side on the bench, and for a minute, neither says anything.

"You wanna start?" she finally says.

"No, you go ahead."

"Okay," she nods. She takes a deep breath and lets it out. "About yester-day. It's . . ." She's gesturing with her hands, but it's clear she can't find the right words. She looks like she's rehearsed her speech, but at the moment of truth, lost it to stage fright. I open my mouth, but she raises a palm and then starts over. "What we did yesterday . . ." She lets out her breath in a loud *whew*. She looks away for a second but then makes strong eye contact. Her eyes are brimming with tears. "Ash, did I do something wrong?"

Before me is the suddenly fearful and timid, yet most popular girl in school. And in her eyes, I see a vulnerability I've never seen before this mo-ment, the kind of vulnerability that brings me into perfect emotional sync with her.

I feel an unexpected confidence welling up inside. Seeing her in distress gives me clarity of thought I didn't have only moments before. As I search my heart, I'm sure of it. There's no confusion, now. The only thing I can compare to this realization is when I'm working on a really hard math prob-lem and suddenly, what should have been an obvious solution just appears in my brain and I wonder why I didn't see it from the start. And that's exactly what's happening now. I see the events of yesterday in a whole new light, and wonder why I didn't from the start. I feel my insecurity melting away—and now all I want to do is reassure her.

"No," I whisper, "I'm pretty sure you didn't."

She lets out with a long sigh of relief and wipes her tears as a familiar smile returns to her face.

"Thank God I didn't," she says. "When I saw your face this morning, I started imagining all kinds of horrible things, like maybe you didn't want to be my friend anymore! All through—"

"No—"

"— first and second period I couldn't think straight." She's looking down now. "And in third period—"

"No, Robin—" I say, in a stronger voice.

"— Mr. Thompkins gives us a pop test, and Asher, I swear I almost—"

"Stop." I clasp the top of her hand and give it a squeeze—and it feels so right. "You didn't do anything wrong." She looks up into my eyes. A couple of tears are running down her cheeks. I reach up and wipe them away.

"Are you sure?" she squeaks, glancing down at her left hand in mine.

I want more than anything to quiet the fear and uncertainty within her. In fact, *all* I want to do is comfort her. And I realize that in comforting her, I am comforting myself.

For several minutes, time seems to freeze. Finally, she gives me a hesitant smile and turns her hand palm up to interlace her fingers into mine. The soft touch of her hand warms me, causing me to squirm ever so slightly. I visually trace the outline of her mouth, then the outline of her eyes. With a mind of its own, my left hand cups her cheek and lightly caresses her. Taking the initiative on an intimate touch like this surprises even me. She squeezes my hand in return but doesn't move her head. I steal a quick glance behind us, then face her and speak in a whisper.

"Robin?"

"Yes?" she whispers in reply.

"Look at me."

She turns her face up to me so I can see her eyes and mouth. I feel her body shudder. With my thumb, I give her a reassuring stroke along her cheek, which provokes a tentative smile. Then, with newly-found confidence, I pull her in until our lips are barely touching. We hold this position for a few moments until suddenly, our mouths melt into one.

The feeling inside me is intensely satisfying and settles once and for all Orm's question of whether or not I want to kiss her again. With her mouth on mine, I'm a million miles away from school in a secret universe with just her. And I don't want to come home. It seems forever before we slowly disentangle. For another long moment, our eyes are locked onto each other.

I lean forward and whisper into her ear, giving it a soft kiss.

"Does that help?"

She quickly wipes her eyes and returns her gaze to my face. I see a smile beginning to form.

"Yes," she says in a soft voice, once again giving my hand a squeeze.

"Okay, then!" I give her another quick kiss. "Now let's get outta here. Bell's gonna ring any second now."

Fourth period is a blur. I'm not sure I heard a single word from anyone. All I can think about is Robin and how she makes me feel. Finally, in the lunch line, I see her again. She's with Dill, and it irks me. This time, I know why.

Both Orm and Robin are waiting for me when I arrive at the table. Dill is next to Robin, appearing as clueless as ever, with no inkling I was passionately kissing his girlfriend just an hour before. Robin is pretty much back to normal, and she gives me a sideways look as if to acknowledge the secret we share. From there, the ambiance of lunch is as typical as ever.

All is right in my world. I settle into a routine centered around Robin. She's in every thought, at the top of every priority, and the reason for every hope. She's consuming me, and I'm not complaining.

On Thursday, almost in answer to a prayer, she suggests we meet at "the place," which sends my head into another tizzy. With the feverish anticipation of once again feeling Robin's mouth on mine, I rush to our secret hideaway and find her there, but so is some boy who's reclined on our bench, reading a book and obviously skipping class. I'm not sure who's the most startled, him or us. His eyes follow our arms all the way to our hands, which I only now realize are clasped. We simultaneously let go, turn, and walk out.

"He saw!" I say as we arrive at the hallway intersection where we take different directions to our next classes.

"I know!" she whispers.

Her eyes have a strangely worried look about them, yet she seems okay by lunchtime. And on Friday afternoon she pulls me aside in the parking lot. Orm smiles over his shoulder and keeps walking.

"Have you heard?" she asks. There's a confident smile on her face.

I give her a shrug. "Heard what?"

"You seriously haven't heard?"

"No, I haven't heard anything. What is it?"

She gives me another one of those smiles—the kind that makes my head swim. "I broke up with Dill today."

I hear what she says, but it refuses to register in my mind. I'm stupefied. She reaches out and pushes my chin back up into position.

"W-why?" I manage to ask.

She gets a puzzled look on her face. "What do you mean *why?* I would think you of all people would know *exactly* why."

The true nature of *us* is suddenly apparent. It's more than physical. Much more. And for a moment, it startles me. But then I get a grip on reality and remember I've never been one to worry much about what other classmates think or say about me. I hold on to that, and in a few seconds, all is normal.

"Hey, you okay?" she asks.

"Yeah, I'm okay." I lean in slightly and speak in a lower voice. "Better than I've ever been, actually!"

Her eyes brighten.

"Ash . . . um, would you like to . . . um, come over on Sunday afternoon?"

That perks me up. I knew she'd eventually ask. I've wanted her to ask. I've been waiting for her to ask. In a way, it tells me she thinks I'm worth having around.

"Sure!"

"You would? Okay, I'll text you!" She touches my hand before walking away, but this time it's more personal, and I can tell she meant it to be. I'm beginning to really enjoy her affectionate gestures.

Saturday passes in a blur, and Sunday dawns bright and sunny. I'm out of bed at seven. My anticipation quotient is off the charts, and it isn't hard to see that Grams notices something is up as I skip down the stairs to breakfast with a smile on my face and a tune on my lips.

We sit across from each other as always. She's already dressed for church, and as I pull myself up to the table, her blue eyes are fixed on mine. I can tell she wants to talk.

"Are you and Robin O'Leary good friends?" she asks, smiling and taking a sip of coffee.

I almost choke.

"Mmhmm," I utter, swallowing a bite of biscuit and honey.

She nods in response. "You know, their family owns a lot of land around here! That house they live in must be big."

"It is," I reply, after a long pause trying to figure out where she's going with this. I swallow a long sip of my coffee.

"Well, I hear they're good Christian folk, even if they're Catholic," she smiles. Then she gets a serious expression and leans in. "God smiles on His own."

What? She's never said anything like that to me before.

I give her a tentative nod, then shovel the last bite of scrambled eggs into my mouth and push away from the table before she says something else about God. I'm not thinking about God. I'm thinking about Robin—and what's in store for the afternoon up in her bedroom.

After Sunday School, and while waiting for the Sunday sermon to begin, I'm completely preoccupied in reliving the sensation of kissing Robin. Suddenly, Reverend Barncastle snaps me out of my daydream by slapping the top of the dais and opening his sermon. "Today," he thunders, "I want to talk about homosexuals!"

I think my heart just jumped into my mouth. I've heard a couple of Reverend Barncastle's "anti-homo" sermons in the past and breezed right through them with no concern at all. That he is going to preach one *today* is downright terrifying.

"They call themselves gay! They say they are proud!" he spits out, this time pausing for effect. "I ask you, *what* exactly do they have to be proud of? I'll tell you what!" he growls, in response to his own question. "Nothing!" He holds up his Bible and glares at his audience as a few "amens" float up.

Without warning, he suddenly pivots in my direction. As he holds his silence for dramatic effect, I can not only see, but *feel* people turning to see the object of his attention.

That's when I notice his eyes are locked directly onto mine.

8

I'm suddenly faint and feel exposed, as if I'm out in public completely naked.

A fierce snarl spreads across Reverend Barncastle's face, almost as if he's accusing me of being Satan right here in church. I gasp so loudly that Grams turns her head to me.

"You'll see disgusting displays of men kissing *men*, women kissing *women*, and other behaviors even viler!" he spits, his eyes boring holes in mine as he continues nonstop. "God calls it an abomination! Brothers and sisters, we must never tolerate this perversion in our midst!"

I can feel a pang of nausea in the pit of my stomach that claws for release. It's only after what seems an eternity that he looks away. I'm so lightheaded I have to bend forward and rest my forehead in my hands to keep from fainting. I thought I was at peace with myself about Robin, but not anymore.

Does he somehow know I kissed Robin? And if he knows, who else knows? Everyone? I finally look around to see if anyone is staring at me, but get only three or four return stares. Still, I avert my eyes and spend the rest of the time during the sermon with my head down, not daring to show my face, and hoping Reverend Barncastle doesn't see me.

I don't know how I make it to the end of the service, but with panic coursing through every vein, I'm finally in the car with Grams and headed home. Then, out of the blue, Grams remarks on how "godly" Reverend Barncastle is. Then she says, "I pray you'll marry a man with that same godliness in his soul."

"What?"

"I said, I pray you'll—"

"Never mind, Grams." She gives me a strange wide-eyed stare. When we get home, I immediately go up the staircase to my room, close the door behind me, and plop facedown onto the bed.

I've been taught all my life that God loves me. I've *believed* all my life that God loves me. It feels different now, and for the first time in my life, I feel spiritually lost. Am I an abomination? Or, could he just be wrong about it? Maybe I'm not gay. Or, if I am, maybe it's not too late to stop. I know I don't want to go to hell. I'm completely helpless and in tears an hour later as I pick up my phone and tap out a message:

Something's come up. Can't come over.

My thumb hovers over the Send button for a long time, but I just can't force myself to hit it.

And I don't know why.

I toss the phone to the side in frustration. I can't get the look of Reverend Barncastle's angry face out of my mind. For the first time in my life, I feel like I'm in free fall toward a nervous breakdown.

Yet—I crave seeing Robin. I *really* crave seeing Robin.

I just can't get around that one, simple fact. So, *not* seeing her is out of the question. But what am I going to do if she wants to kiss me? Do I have the strength to refuse something I've been so wanting to do again?

It's only twenty minutes shy of two in the afternoon, I'm a disheveled mess, and I'm out of options. Panic gets me up and on my feet. I hurriedly fix myself up in the bathroom and grab my camera before setting out. When I turn into Robin's driveway, she's in the front yard to greet me. She smiles and excitedly runs up to my car and opens the driver's side door.

I love how happy she looks. Why can't I just be like her? Before I know it, she's pulled me out of the car by my arm and has me in a bear hug with my feet off the ground.

God, I wish I hadn't gone to church this morning.

"I'm so glad you're finally here!"

I've never seen her smile so radiantly. Inside, I say hello to her mom, after which Robin takes me by the hand and pulls me up the stairs to her room. Once inside, she closes the door and puts me against the wall.

"Wait!" I manage to gasp before she has her mouth on mine. We're only an inch away from each other. The sight of her lips are driving me insane with lust. It's all I can do to not give up and just pull her the rest of the way in. But then her eyes open wide and her jaw sags.

"I-I'm sorry!" she splutters, as she pulls back and places one hand over her mouth.

"No." I have to take a deep breath. When I see the wounded look on her face, I hurriedly add, "You didn't do anything wrong."

I don't think she's even breathing. For a moment she says nothing, but then she whispers a response.

"You don't want me to kiss you."

I place my camera on her school desk next to a book bag, take a deep breath, and look straight into her eyes.

"Robin, yes, I do . . . I'm just kind of confused."

"About what?"

"I-I don't really know. It's so complicated."

"I don't get it. Are you mad at me?" Her chest is heaving.

"No." Suddenly, my eyes are brimming, and I use my sleeve to wipe a tear.

"Then why? Behind the lockers, *you* kissed *me!*"

She's right. What in the hell is wrong with me? Robin breaks her eye contact and looks around. When she thinks I'm not looking, she quickly wipes her own tears. I let my gaze fall to the floor as an unexpected guilt rips me. I feel so conflicted. Something's not right, and I can't science my way out of it.

"Are we still friends?" she asks.

"Yes!" I nod. "If you'll still have me, that is." At least I know *that* much.

"Okay," she replies, as her eyes dart around the room and then finally settle on me. She doesn't look quite as panicked anymore, as if she's halted a dangerous freefall.

We turn to random conversation. She starts it, and for the next half hour, we engage in small talk about school, but it's awkward and we both know it. The big issue remains in the air between us. We run out of things and people to talk about and the room gets silent for a long time. I can't allow that. I feel like it's my problem to fix.

"Hey, you wanna take a look at my portfolio?" I ask. "It's online."

"Yeah," she replies, gesturing to the laptop on the desk.

Finally, something to do. Within seconds, I'm logged on, and I pull up my "Museum Exhibit" folder. I turn the laptop screen toward her and let her take control. For the first time since she tried to kiss me, she smiles and moves the stool up even closer to the desk—which means she's very close to me again. For the next few minutes, she studies the images on the screen.

"Ash . . . you truly have a gift! You have to do something with this. You simply have to."

"I am. I've applied to the Winston."

She snaps her head toward me, her eyes huge and her mouth agape. "Seriously?"

"Yes, last year."

"Oh my God, so have *I!*" she squeals. "So, we might be going to the same college?" She reaches over and grasps my hands. "Can you imagine? Us at the very same college?"

She's contagious. I can't help but smile and squeeze her hands in return. The awkwardness of the past few minutes seems to be almost gone. Both of us are giddy and smiling. But then her joyful expression quickly melts away and she's quiet.

"Robin?"

"Ash, what if we don't both get in? They only accept one out of every thousand!" Then, her eyes come to rest on our clasped hands. After a moment or two silence, during which I feel myself tremble, she looks up into my face. "Is this gay?"

I clear my throat. "I-I don't think so."

She considers this response for a second. "So, we can hold hands?"

Wow. I get that fluttery feeling in my stomach again. I *want* to hold her hands. I *really* want to hold her hands. I mentally picture her slender fingers entwined with mine. I hear a voice that sounds like mine saying "Yes."

"Can I ask you a question?"

"Yeah, sure." I think I know what she's going to ask.

"Are we ever gonna kiss again?"

Just mentioning it makes me short of breath. I simply can't take my eyes off her lips. I'm sure she sees it.

"M-maybe we talk about it later?" I force out.

She thinks for a moment and then voices an uncharacteristically flat "Okay," after which she withdraws her hand, stands up, and plops down on her bed, behind my chair. I turn to face her. "Did I tell you what Dill said when I broke up with him?" she asks, completely changing the subject.

"Tell me."

Seeing her on her bed, in *that* place—the exact place where we kissed—seizes my every thought. I allow my eyes to follow every curve of her face. I'm sure she sees what I'm doing. I'm weak. In fact, I'm *very* weak. It takes only her gesture of patting the bed to bring me over.

"Well, he said I would regret it."

"And?"

"That's it. He said he could get *any* other girl."

"So he's gonna start dating one of your friends or something?"

She shrugs and looks off to her left out the window.

"He can do whatever he wants."

Her brooding manner has me puzzled.

"You're acting like maybe you regret breaking up with him."

"Not really."

"What's up, then? You're acting strange."

"Ash, we're both acting strange. You know?"

She has a point. "I guess so. But I don't want to be."

"Neither do I," she says, making eye contact.

"So, do you regret breaking up with Dill?"

She doesn't answer right away, and when she does, I can see it's difficult for her. Whatever it is she has bottled up inside, it's enormous.

"Well, you do some things, right?" She turns to me and locks onto my eyes. "And then, you hope for . . . other things . . . to happen."

"Yeah, I guess."

She holds her gaze on my eyes for a long time. Finally, she swallows and looks away.

"Well, I guess that's that."

"Wait, what do you mean? Do you blame me for—"

"No, not at all!"

She turns back to me and I study her face, trying my best to figure out what she's saying.

"So, you *don't* want to go back to him?"

"No, Ash, I already told you. I broke up with him because I wanted to. Because I . . ." She leaves the sentence dangling, but then finishes it with, "nothing."

"What's 'nothing'?"

She closes her eyes and exhales. "You just don't get it."

"Well, help me out, then."

Her chin quivers for a split second, but then she purses her lips and looks into my face. "Okay." She uses her hands to gesture. "I said you do some *things*. Right?"

"Yeah," I nod.

"And then, you hope . . . *other* things will happen." She nods as if encouraging me to guess.

"Okay, other things, then. *What* other things?"

She freezes, and for what seems forever, we stare into each other's eyes without saying a thing. Finally, a single tear emerges from her eye and trickles down her face.

"You just . . . hope," she whispers.

Just then, I get it.

My God, do I *ever* get it. She turns her face away and wipes at a few more tears.

"Robin?" I feel my own eyes brimming up. The enormity of what she's done simply stuns me. Why was I so blind to it all? And wasn't it what I really wanted?

"I just feel so *stupid,*" she manages, choking back sobs.

I pull her in and she immediately nestles herself into me. For a long time, we slowly rock back and forth as my own tears drop onto the bed between us, mixing with hers. After several long minutes, I can take a deep breath.

"*I'm* the stupid one," I whisper into her ear, kissing it softly.

"No," she says, trying to stifle the last of her sobs, "I assumed way too much."

I pull her closer and kiss the side of her neck. There's a strength inside me now—one I didn't have in me this morning. And with it comes the realization that this is my life, and I really do have control of it. I've had a few "aha!" moments in my life before now, but this one makes all the others trivial. With my blinders removed, I'm horrified of the damage my words and actions have inflicted on Robin.

"No, you didn't assume too much," I assure her in a soft voice. "It was me. It was all me. And I'm so sorry!"

"Yeah?"

"Yeah. Things just kinda got crazy and moved really fast. And somehow I lost track of what's really important." I pull my face back and stare into her eyes only an inch or so away. "I now know that what *we* have together is what's really important."

She takes a deep swallow, tilting her head ever so slightly to one side, and gives me a weak smile. "Really?" she whispers.

"Yes, really."

My eyes are drawn to her mouth. Like a child reaching for candy, I lean in and press my lips to her mouth. And once again, it's like I've stepped out the door of an airplane into open space. The taste, the fragrance, the smooth-ness . . . all of it overpowers my senses. I'm almost out of breath when she stops me.

"Wait," she whispers, holding up a finger and giving me a smile.

She wipes the last tear from her cheek, then rises, and with her hand, pulls me up from the bed. I watch as she takes the top sheet and comforter and folds them back. Then, she sits back down on the bed and slides under the covers. She scoots over a bit, pulls the covers further back, and with a smile, gestures for me to join her.

The sensation of being next to her body while lying down is just inde-scribable. I nudge over as closely as I possibly can, turning on my left side to be able to face her.

"Now, kiss me again," she whispers, turning on her pillow and raising her mouth to meet mine. My heart is racing and on the verge of leaping from my chest. Everything feels so right. I'm so into kissing I can hardly breathe, and every few minutes we have to come up for air. When we finally break contact, I see her face, and she's smiling ear to ear.

"What?" I ask, a smile of my own spreading.

She gives me soft caresses on the side of my face with her fingers. "You've just made me forget every guy I've ever kissed, that's what!"

I grin and lean in for a quick kiss. "Well, I would say you've made *me* forget every guy I've ever kissed, but you're making me think I've never even *been* kissed."

She smiles all over again. I wonder if she knows that the shape of her mouth makes me crazy. She once again pulls me in, and we twist around each other in a mad frenzy. I'm mostly on top, and I can feel her hands groping and caressing the back of my head, then neck, then back, and then almost all the way to my butt. I feel like I'm going to explode. Then she spreads her legs just enough so that my right leg, which has begun to wrap itself around her legs, finds a cove of new warmth. Almost immediately, my knee and lower thigh contacts forbidden places. Even though we're kissing, I can hear and feel her reaction.

I pull my mouth off hers and look into her eyes as I move my knee back and forth, watching how each movement brings forth a new expression. She breathes in an out in a staccato.

"You like that, don't you?"

"Oh, God, yes," she moans.

I cup her face and watch the pleasure written across it as I slowly move my knee up and down in a slow rhythm. My eyes come to rest on the lips I was devouring just seconds ago, and I'm struck by the fact that if I never kiss anyone again for the rest of my life, I can die happy knowing that I've kissed *those* lips.

"God, you are so beautiful," I whisper. I kiss her ear very softly, then her neck, and follow around to her cheek. Everything about her smells delicious, and I can't get enough.

Just barely at first, but then increasing in intensity, I feel her shudder. Her fingers dig into my back, and her breathing becomes a series of shallow pants. There's a sudden gasp, then she relaxes and lets out a long breath.

I snuggle down to rest on her shoulder, and she cradles my head as her labored breathing gradually quietens. For what seems a very long time, we silently bask in this sensual closeness.

"Guess what?" I say.

"What?"

"I can hear your heart!"

She laughs softly, sending her chest up and down as she giggles. Everything is perfect. I've never experienced this kind of intimacy. I never knew intimacy like this even *existed*.

"What does it say?" she whispers.

"Um, it says thump . . . thump . . . thump!"

Once again, a laugh erupts from her, this one a bit loud, but she shushes herself when I raise my head.

"Silly, that's not what it's saying!"

"Oh yeah?" I reply. I kiss the side of her neck and then nestle into her bosom. "Then what *is* it saying?"

She pauses for a moment and caresses my face. "It's saying . . . don't leave."

I turn my face up to meet hers. For a long minute, we're eye-to-eye, almost as if drinking from a fountain. And as my eyes dart between hers, an incredible warmth spreads within me. She uses a finger to trace my lips.

I give her finger a slow kiss.

"I won't," I softly breathe.

9

I feel good. *Really* good.

It's morning, and I'm awake much earlier than usual. I'm snuggled up under my covers and completely tangled up in thoughts of Robin. It's like little jolts of electricity are shooting up and down my body, and I can't get this smile off my face. Over and over, I mentally replay every single detail of what happened yesterday. I can still feel the incredible sensation of her lips on mine, the taste of her mouth—even the scent of her body.

My entire being feels alive, and what Orm told me a few weeks ago is really starting to hit home. I *do* hunger for her touch. I *do* want to make her happy. I can't wait to see her every day at school. Am I falling in love? Maybe! Do I want to fall in love with Robin? Yes! The thought of having her in my life, all to myself, every single day, sounds like heaven to me. Everything is so perfect.

Once out of bed, and as I begin putting myself together for the day, I impulsively sing out in a barely contained whisper, "I kissed Robin Cierra O'Leary!" She's a narcotic, pure and simple, and I'm desperate for more of her. All I want is to get to the next opportunity to kiss her. But where?

Her house? My house? In the locker area at school? I've never had as great a need for privacy with someone else as I do now. The need to feel her soft, warm lips on mine spins my head into a mad frenzy of desire.

"It happened again with Robin!" I confess through a smile, as Orm gives me the second double-take. We've barely gotten out of my driveway.

"Like I can't tell?" he replies, holding back a grin.

I take a look in the visor mirror. "Does it show?"

"Like a train headlight on a moonless night," he replies in a matter-of-fact voice.

"You know what? I don't care! I don't care if everyone can see it!"

"Hey, you're not the first to show up at school on Monday with a fresh-fucked look all over your face!"

"We didn't fuck, you moron!" I giggle. He gives me a big grin.

"So, what *did* y'all do?" he asks, after a minute or two of silence.

"We . . . kissed." I break into a broad grin. God, I love talking about it!

He gives me a *keep going* look.

"Okay, then. Yes, we kissed, but we were kinda lying in her bed next to each other." I try to hold a serious expression, but he says nothing. "And . . . I guess we kissed for a lot longer than ever!" I can't repress a smile.

"And?"

"Maybe we fell asleep next to each other."

He nods his approval. For some reason, I can't wipe the smile off my face. After he pulls into a parking spot, he turns to face me.

"I've never seen you like this, Ash," he says, giving me a huge grin. "And I'm happy for you. Seriously!"

"I found out something!"

"What's that?"

"I found out that I like kissing!"

"Yay for you!"

"In fact, I like it a lot!" I see his brows go up as his smile widens. "I'll be honest, Orm; I think I'm falling in love."

"I believe you! You're different now—in a good way."

I find Robin standing right next to my locker as I turn the corner into C wing. My eyes widen with anticipation, and I don't really care who's watching. Her face is bright and expressive, as if eager to tell me a secret. When I get to her, she laughs and focuses her eyes straight on me.

"Hey, girl!" she chirps. Her lips have a high-sheen lip gloss on, and the sight of it makes me want to devour them.

"Hey!"

"I wanted to call you last night!"

"Why didn't you?"

"I don't know. Maybe I was afraid."

"Of what?"

She smiles down to her feet, then twists her body back and forth before looking up. "I was afraid you regretted . . . after you went home." Her eyes are searching mine. I feel horrible that I ever made her unsure about me. In fact, it disgusts me that I did.

"No!" I lean in and whisper. "I have no regrets. None. And I want you to feel safe with me. Because you are."

She surreptitiously reaches in and touches the back of my hand, causing me to have an immediate shudder.

"Well, then I'll call you tonight," she says in a low and sultry voice while giving me that coy smile of hers that simply blows me up every time.

"I'd like that!"

She quickly glances around, then says, "Wanna meet . . . at the place?"

It's exactly what I wanted to hear.

"Yeah!"

The warning bell sounds, and she turns to leave. "See ya!" she mouths to me, before hurrying off to class. I watch her as she disappears from sight.

I'm no good for any of my classes. Time has slowed down just so it can torture me. My mind is fixed on one thing, and one thing only: the end of third period. And when it finally arrives, I check the hallway before slipping into the narrow corridor in the back of the locker bay. Robin is already there and she steps toward me. We straightaway clasp each other in a torrid kiss, but then, afraid of being found out by some lurker, we pull back.

"God, I've been waiting for this all day!" she says.

"I didn't think it would ever come!"

For a minute or so, we drink in each other's faces.

"Are you sure you don't regret it?" she says.

"More sure than anything ever in my life," I reply, giving her hand a squeeze.

"Wanna hear a secret?"

"Sure!"

She hesitates and swallows. After a few seconds, she briefly looks away, and I can see she's struggling with whatever is on her mind.

"What is it?" I prod.

She turns back to me. "I'm about to say something," she says, "and it's something I've never said to anyone else."

"What?"

I think I know, and if it's what I think it is, I'm about to be the happiest girl in the world.

She takes a breath, smiles at me, and says, "I love you," in a soft whisper.

I want to jump up and down for joy. It's all I can do to not scream out in delight. I don't care who's watching. I use my free hand to caress her face, then her lips. Then I gently pull her closer and plant a soft kiss on her lips.

"Well, guess what?" I whisper.

"What?"

I give her lips another caress with my thumb, and she kisses it as it passes over. "I love *you*, too."

For a few magical moments, it's as if the rest of the world has ceased to exist. The fourth-period warning bell sounds, finally breaking our trance. We both know this area will be flooded by students within a minute, so we gather our books and walk out into the hallway as if nothing has happened. I'm about to turn away when she stops me.

"Can I give you a ride home today?" she asks through an impish grin.

It suddenly occurs to me that she won't be riding home with Dill anymore. I can't help but allow a smirk to cross my face.

"You sure can!"

She smiles and turns to leave. No one is in the hallway yet. On impulse, I call out her name. She turns to face me. I mouth a silent, "I love you!" She grins, looks around, then mouths in return, "I love you too!"

After school, as I settle into her car's passenger seat, I realize that she could be my new ride home every day. As she drives the car out of the parking lot, she reaches over and takes my hand, being careful to keep it below window level.

"I have a question," she says.

"Go ahead!" I'm almost giddy with anticipation of whatever word candy she has for me this time.

"Do you think you're gay?"

Strange, but a question that just a few weeks ago would have provoked an indignant denial now doesn't even faze me.

"To be honest, I don't care if I am. What about you?"

"I don't know," she says, "but I know I love you."

"And I love you, too!"

"I've thought about it before," she continues. "About being gay."

"Really?"

"Yeah. I had a girl crush a year ago. It was when I was living in Texas."

Her confession literally stupefies me.

"Wait, you've had a *girlfriend* before?"

For just a fraction of a second, she hesitates, but then she looks over at me. "Yeah, we sort of dated . . . secretly."

I don't know what to say.

"Anything wrong?" she asks, her eyes now fixed on mine. There's a hint of panic in her voice.

"Were y'all in love?" I ask, after a long pause to search my thoughts.

"I don't think so," she replies.

I feel a sudden shortness of breath.

"Do you miss her?"

She looks in my eyes without moving, but after a second or two, she shakes her head.

"Not now."

"But you did?"

She nods plaintively. "Yeah. She was an unfinished story."

Wow. It's almost too much information.

"Ash, she was just a crush."

I finally let out my breath. "Am *I* just a crush?"

"No, you're *much* more than a crush."

I replay that statement several times in my head, allowing it to calm me. I'm actually a bit surprised at my sudden panic attack over something that happened before I even knew her. I breathe in deeply, then slowly let it out.

"I think I got a little jealous there," I whisper, letting out a nervous laugh. "But I get it now . . . that I don't have anything to worry about. It just caught me off guard."

"And you're right . . . you have nothing to worry about." She tightens her grip on my hand. "So how about you? Any girls?"

"I don't have *any* girl history," I manage to say.

"Good." We stay silent awhile until I notice we're far past the cutoff to my house.

"Hey! Where are you going?"

"Anyone expecting you home right now?"

I shake my head. "No, why?"

"Wanna see my secret place?" she asks, giving me that disarming smile again.

"Sure!" The fact that it's secret doesn't escape my notice.

"Okay, then, let's go!"

She flips a switch on the ceiling, causing the sunroof to completely open. The immediate inrush of wind blows our hair out of place, me more than her since my hair is long. I can't help but laugh as her red hair flies in the wind, revealing all the contours of her face.

"Give me your hand back!" I call out over the sound of the wind. She gives me a smile and slides her fingers into mine.

"I *love* your hand!" she gushes.

I feel completely liberated. Without even thinking, I pull our hands in and give her forefinger a soft kiss, and she does the same.

After a few more minutes, she gently pulls her hand back and turns the steering wheel. We drive down a long country road. I can see a lone house in the distance. She takes another turn, and this road is beautifully landscaped on both sides by trees and shrubbery adorned with newly emerged leaves. Every second or third tree has a wisteria bush along side it, and the effect is stunning.

"Where *are* we?"

"You want to know? For real?"

"Yes!" I look around, and off to the right my eyes are drawn to the most gorgeous small lake I've ever seen. Its waters are blue, while the vegetation around it is green, lush, and inviting. My senses are kissed with the delicate fragrance of wisteria. A few places on the shoreline are nothing but grassy knolls that gracefully slope down to the water's edge.

"That," she declares, "is *Robin's Lake.*"

"Whaaat?"

She nods.

"You're serious?"

"Yep!"

"So, wait . . . how is it this lake has *your* name?"

"My dad named it."

"You mean, your family *owns* this lake?"

"Yes!" she smiles. "It's been in our family for decades. It's why we moved to Sagebrush."

I focus my attention on the lake as more and more of it comes into view. It appears to be maybe a couple of hundred feet across, but almost double that in length. The far shore is densely populated with trees right down to the shoreline. On the shore to the right, I see a mother duck and her ducklings, and hummingbirds dart to and fro within the wisteria blossoms. I pull my eyes away and face toward Robin. It's obvious she's been watching my reaction, and she has a bright smile on her face.

"It's so beautiful!" I gasp, immediately turning back to the window.

She brings the car to a stop. The road is barely wide enough for two vehicles to pass by each other. We're far out of sight from the country road that took us here.

"This place, right here, is my secret place," she whispers. "It's my favorite place in the whole world."

The vista is spectacular. It's the spot where the lake comes closest to the road we're on. And there's something magical in the combination of Robin and this landscape that I can't quite put my finger on.

"Do you come here a lot?"

"At least once a week!"

"Do those people mind?" I ask, pointing toward the house in the distance.

"That's actually *our* house," she says. "It's a vacation house."

"Hold on," I smile, raising a forefinger. "You guys have a *vacation* house?"

"Yep!" she nods. When I don't immediately respond, she places her hand on my shoulder and gently allows her fingernails to stroke my neck for a few seconds. "You're the first person I've ever showed this place to."

I smile and place my hand on hers. "I guess that makes me special?"

She gives my neck a gentle squeeze. "Hey, guess what the name of this road is?"

"Um, O'Leary Road?"

"Nope! But you're warm!"

"Does it have your name?"

"Yes!" she shrills, through a smile.

"Robin Road?"

"Close! It's Robin's Lake Road."

"This is trippy," I say, looking into those to-die-for green eyes. "I mean, you own a lake *and* the road!"

"I know, right?" She gestures toward the lake. "Years ago, when I was a little girl, my dad named this Robin's Lake. So when the county took over maintenance of the road and asked him to name it, he named it Robin's Lake Road."

"Aww," I say, "that's special!"

"And I'm here with you . . . that's what's *really* special!" After a minute, she follows with, "Are you really sure you love me?"

"Robin, yes!" I take a breath. "Although . . . I have to admit I was afraid at first. But hearing you say you love me today made me realize how much I love you!"

"Good! Then I'm glad."

"I love you, even if it makes me gay."

I see her eyes get wide. "Seriously?"

"Yes, without a doubt," I nod. "If this love I have for you here"—I lightly touch my chest over my heart with the fingers of my right hand—"if that's what being gay is all about, then I'm gay."

She silently eyes me for what seems a long time. "My God, you're so brave," she sighs.

"Well, what about you? Do you feel the same thing? About being gay?"

She purses her lips. "It's scary."

"How?"

She turns away, and I can see her swallow. "It's my dad," she says, turning back to make eye contact. "He's Catholic. And when I say he's Catholic, I mean he bleeds Catholic blood. It's his Irish ancestry. All of his family is from Ireland, and they're all religious like crazy."

"Let me guess. He doesn't approve of gay people?"

"He thinks they should burn in hell."

"Burn in hell? Why?"

"It's just how he feels. It's why I'm in Sagebrush."

"Huh?"

"Okay, I'm going to tell you something no one in Sagebrush knows," she says. "We didn't leave Texas because of any job or because our vacation home is in Oklahoma. We left because of me and the girl crush I told you about. My dad moved us here to get me away from *her*." She turns her head away as if she's afraid to see my reaction.

Damn. I'm beginning to wonder if there's any more secret stuff she has to share. Still, being made to feel the object of her own family's shame is pretty heavy shit. I lean over, pull her in close, and softly kiss her ear. After a minute in this position, I feel her arm on my waist, pulling herself closer to me. The center console is a formidable obstacle, but somehow, we nestle into a comfortable position.

"So, we have to keep all this from your dad?"

"Yes," she whispers, "and basically everyone because he'd find out."

"Okay, I get that. But I'm thinking back to that song you sang at the talent show."

"Oh, yeah." She lets out a soft chuckle. "He didn't know I was going to sing *that* song. He wasn't too happy about it."

"You looked pretty enthusiastic! Are you sure you weren't maybe saying something?"

At this, she laughs softly. "Maybe!" she replies. "But no one would suspect, because I was also dating Dill."

"Kinda like flying under the radar, eh?"

Again, she laughs. "I guess so!" After a second or two, she adds, "But we still have to keep this on the down low for now."

"Sure."

"I mean, do *you* want other people to know?"

"Seriously, Robin, I don't care who knows. But, not if it makes you unsafe," I reply.

"I like that," she says, in a voice barely above a whisper. "*You* make me feel safe." I feel her snuggle in even closer. We spend a long time nestled up to each other. Finally, as we're shuffling a little to get more comfortable, she lets out a sigh. "Kiss me," she says while stroking my cheek and neck.

I pull her head up to my mouth and kiss her. She continues to caress me, and then I realize that her left hand is under my shirt. Smiling, she breaks lip contact and looks up to see my reaction.

"Does that feel good?"

I can barely catch my breath. "Yes."

She withdraws her hand and pulls herself up. "Lean forward."

I comply, to which she slides her hand under the back of my shirt and unfastens my bra. When she moves her hand back to the front, I feel myself gasp. She lightly drags her fingernails over my midriff for a minute or so, causing it to spasm, and then she starts up toward my breasts. She cups my right breast in the palm of her warm, soft hand, and gently squeezes.

"How about that?" she asks, before giving my cheek a soft kiss.

"Mhmm," I moan. I pull her in for a long, sensuous kiss while she continues to fondle my breast to the point that I feel like I'm going to explode. Without even knowing it at first, I become aware that my pelvis is moving in and out in a slow rhythm that is matching the tempo of her caresses.

"Do you want to do that to me?" she whispers.

"Yes," I gasp.

"You can do anything you want," she smiles, with a twinkle in her eyes. I don't have to be told twice. I slide my hand beneath her blouse and release her bra. In another second, I have her left breast in my hand.

It's incredibly soft and warm. I notice it's not as big as mine. Caressing and squeezing it causes her to sigh ever so softly. After a minute, and almost in tandem, we both pause just long enough to climb into the back seat. I'm almost on my back when she resumes her tender caresses.

"Spread your legs," she says.

My heart begins to race. I'm game for anything above the waist, but I find myself strangely hesitant about *down there*, even though it's no surprise to me we're here. She senses my hesitation and looks into my face.

"You okay?" she asks.

"Umm . . ." I don't know what to say.

She gives me a reassuring smile. "It's okay," she whispers. "Do you trust me?"

I swallow, then give her a nod.

"You sure?" Of course, I trust her. What's the matter with me?

"Yes, I'm sure," I say in a hoarse voice. "I've just never done this before."

"Neither have I!" she giggles.

Something about her willingness to admit her own inexperience is instantly disarming, and it makes me laugh along with her.

"Come here," I say, to which she moves her head up next to mine and looks in my eyes. We share a long kiss, and instantly, the awkwardness of the past few moments vanishes as if it never even existed.

She gives me a smile, then lays her head on my shoulder. I know what's next. The anticipation of what she's about to do leaves me breathless. Very deliberately, she places her hand on the crotch of my jeans and begins to massage very slowly. I hear myself moan, and my pelvis seems to get a life of its own. Only a minute or two later, I'm on the verge of telling her to go underneath, but she's a step ahead of me and is already sensuously unbuttoning my jeans. When she slides her hand beneath my underwear, my entire body reacts with a head to foot shiver.

"You're wet!" she giggles.

"What?" I fight the impulse to pull myself back up. I feel messy all of a sudden.

"Relax," she purrs, picking up on my near panic. "It's really nice!"

I take a deep breath, and then feel myself relaxing once again in surrender to her. For the life of me, I can't figure out how she's able to relax me like this, especially since we're in a car on a public road where anyone could walk up and see us. Even the fear of discovery doesn't faze me. I'm completely vulnerable, but I've never felt safer.

"Just close your eyes," she soothes. I comply without protest. My abdomen convulses as if it has a life of its own. I fact, I feel like a bomb on a short fuse. It takes her only a few minutes to bring me to the most mind-bending orgasm I've ever experienced—or thought possible.

She puts her face up to mine and kisses me.

"Well," she says, "did you like that?"

I have to struggle to get enough air into my lungs to even say something.

"Holy shit, Robin," I gasp, "I think you blew up my brain!"

She lets out with a soft chuckle. "Good!"

That a *girl* could so easily do this to me, or even that I could enjoy it so much, becomes another milepost of self-discovery on a path I never once in my life anticipated. One thing's for sure now: the revulsion I felt at Kenna's description of "gay" girl sex has been completely replaced with a hunger for anything Robin wants to do.

As we settle into the quiet of the moment, I see how right this is. I feel her snuggle her head even deeper into my embrace, and I want with all my heart to pull her inside me and never let her go. I could stay like this forever and still want more. Here in her loving arms, I find a quiet peace that's the answer to all the greater truths about myself I seem to be uncovering as of late. In fact, I'm in a new country, where every spoken word is a beautiful truth.

And I never want to come back.

10

The hardest thing about being in a secret romance is acting like you're not.

When you're totally blotto over someone, people can just *see* it. And so it is with Robin and me. Although we take precautions with public displays of affection, I know some people are putting two and two together. It's frustrating—not that people might know, but that we have to hide. It's no secret to Robin that I want to shout our truth from the rooftops, or less than that, just to enjoy the simple pleasure of walking hand-in-hand in the hallways at school like all other in-love couples do.

I'm not complaining too much, though. Each day at school, we say hello in the mornings, secretly meet in the back of the locker bay after third period, sit with each other at lunch, and then Robin drives me home. Except for the last few weeks or so, that is.

Nearly every day after school, she drives us out to Robin's Lake where we sit in her car and enjoy each other. And make out. And all the other things that come from making out. We seem to have it all—except the privacy to go even further.

When I wake up this morning, I know something's wrong. My throat is on fire, and I'm lightheaded. Grams sees it, too, when I show up for breakfast, and she hurries up to me, places her hand on my forehead, then helps me into my seat.

"You're not going anywhere today," she announces. "Soon as you eat, you're right back up those stairs to bed."

I know not to argue with that tone of voice, and I don't have the energy for it anyway. Once I'm back upstairs, undressed, and in bed, sleep mercifully reclaims me. When I wake up again, even my head is throbbing. I hear a voice to my side.

"Here, take these." A hand with a couple of pills appears in my face. After taking them, a glass of water appears. I pull myself up just a little before taking the glass, but when I do, I see that the person beside me is Robin. She's perched in my chair and has a school book and a stack of papers in her lap. "Go ahead," she says, gesturing to the pills and water glass. "Down the hatch."

I obey and swallow the pills. "Robin," I manage, instantly igniting the fire in my throat. I want to ask her why she's here, but she shushes me, a finger to my lips. Motioning for me to scoot over a bit, she sets her book and papers on the bedside table and then lies on the bed beside me.

"Don't give me any grief," she says, through a mischievous smile. "You don't want me to have to go get Grams!"

I pull the neck of my nightshirt all the way back up. "I hope she didn't see *that,*" I say in a hoarse whisper, smiling into her face and pointing to the mark on my neck.

"Oh, did I do that?" she grins. "Well, the one you gave me is still there, too!"

I open my mouth to say something, but I'm too exhausted to carry our silliness any further. I'm just glad to see her face. She positions herself where she can finger comb my hair and gently massage my scalp. When I wake up again, she's back in her chair and speaking softly to Grams who is in the room beside her.

"Honestly, Mrs. Norman, I don't mind. I'll be fine right here."

"Okay, honey," Grams says. "Just come get me down the hall if you need anything."

"What time is it?" I ask, forcing my words out.

Both direct their attention to me. Robin looks around, picks up a glass of water, and hands it to me. "It's almost eleven," she says. "Here, drink this." After I take the glass, she strokes my forehead with the back of her hand, then turns to Grams as I sip. "She's still got a little bit of fever. I'll keep an eye on her."

When I next wake up, I feel better. I turn to see in the window that it's just now dawn, and to my amazement, Robin is slumped in my chair next to me, asleep, her school textbook still open in her lap. God, I love her so much. I reach over and nudge her.

"Hey!"

She immediately opens her eyes, then leans forward to study me. "You okay?"

"Yeah, I'm better," I smile. "How long have you been here?"

"Since fourth period yesterday," she nods. "Orm told me."

"You always seem to be in just the right place to take care of me!"

"I wanted to," she smiles. "I told mom I was gonna be here to take care of you for at least a day. So, I'm gonna be right here with you until you can get up and around." With that, she straightens my pillow and then settles back into my chair with a smile.

With Robin taking care of me, I don't just feel cared for—I feel loved. When I'm thirsty, she has water for me. When she sees me wiping my forehead, she immediately fetches a cool, damp rag and lovingly bathes my forehead and face with it. Later in the day, I'm able to get up and walk around without feeling weak, so we gather at the dining room table and work on our homework together. There's something very comforting about her being right there with me, even if we're both heads down and not saying much to each other.

By that evening, whatever bug I had is pretty much gone, so she gathers up her stuff to leave. "I'll see you tomorrow at your locker," she whispers, then steals a kiss when Grams isn't looking.

As I face the ceiling in bed that evening, I realize my contentment is off the charts. I could never feel more safe and loved than how I feel right now.

It's as I'm finishing up preparing for school the next morning that I admit to myself that I'm hopelessly in love with Robin. There's no turning back. Without her, I'd be lost. She completes me in a way that gives a joyful purpose to every single day. As I search my heart, I realize I want to be in love with her forever. Yeah. It's that serious. She's my everything.

At school, I count down the minutes to the highlight of the day: the end of third period. And as we slip into our secret area, I hear Robin gasp. It's Jermy McIvers. He's loosely holding his smartphone in one hand and lounging on *our* bench.

"Jermy, what the hell are you doing here?" I move to stand directly between him and Robin.

He lazily pulls himself up, and by the smirk on his face, it's apparent he intended to catch us here.

"Oh, I reckon I'm just tryin' to get some privacy," he answers in a slow drawl. He keeps his eyes on me as his mouth forms a sardonic grin. "Long as we're playin' twenty questions, whatch *y'all* up to?"

"Let's just go," Robin says to me.

"Naw!" Jermy replies, as he places his phone into his pocket and hitches up his jeans. "Y'all stay right here. *I'll* leave."

I watch as he makes his way out through the locker corridor. He gives me one more glance over his shoulder before disappearing from sight.

Robin raises an eyebrow. "So, *that's* your Jermy?"

"Unfortunately, yes. What a creep!"

We exchange looks and decide it's too risky, so we turn to leave. Now, I'm pissed, because these few precious minutes I get with Robin mean a lot to me. But then I get an idea.

"Why don't you come over to my house today?"

She stops, looks at me, and gives me a grin. "Sure!"

Now *that* brightens my mood. I smile while caressing her face with my eyes. "I just love you!" I whisper.

"I just love the look in your face right now, you sexy thang!" she whispers in return. My heart skips a beat as she gives me a quick kiss before leading the way out.

Our escape is clean. After a long afternoon, the final release bell of the day comes not a second too soon. I practically sprint to the parking lot where Robin is already waiting. In no time at all, we're at my house.

"Should we hold hands going in?" she asks in a low voice as we make our way to the front door. I look up to see her grinning, and I have to put my hand over my mouth to keep from bursting out in laughter.

"You're so gonna get me in trouble saying shit like that!"

Yet, we do hold hands as we go in—for at least the first ten feet. There's a sweet aroma wafting through the house, so I know Grams is in the kitchen. Robin follows me, and we find her putting the finishing touches on a tray full of cupcakes.

"I thought the two of you might show up and could use an after-school snack!" she beams.

"Aww, Grams, thanks!" I put my arms around her neck and give her a big hug.

"You girls enjoy yourself," she says, heading out of the kitchen. "I've got some laundry to attend to."

The cupcakes are German chocolate with dark chocolate frosting, and they're delicious. But it's not long before Robin and I can barely keep our hands off each other.

"C'mon, let's go up!" I say, giving her a sideways smile.

Halfway up, I encounter the squeaky step, and its groan takes Robin by surprise. "When I want to sneak in, I always step over that one."

"Why would *you* need to sneak in?" she asks under her breath, but then she loses it with a snort as I take her by the hand and pull her into my room. It's all she can do to keep from laughing aloud. I close the bedroom door, then turn around to her. To my surprise, she's walked over to my display wall, where I've hung my favorite works of my photo art. She stands silent, her attention focused on them.

"You like them?" I ask, joining her at the wall.

"I was looking at them yesterday. These are awesome!"

"You really think so?"

"Hell yes! Did you take these with that camera you brought to my house?"

"Actually, yes, I did."

"Ash, this is seriously, freakishly good."

"Thanks!" I move up beside her and take her hand.

"People need to see these," she says, continuing her observations. That feels good, especially coming from her. Her attention is riveted on a landscape in the center of the wall collage.

"That's one I took last year." It's a view over a stock pond and into a wheat field with a rusty old windmill in the background. "It's the very first piece in my portfolio that I submitted to the Winston last year."

A look of excitement spreads over her face. "Baby, can you imagine if both of us end up at the Winston next year?"

"I know!"

"Oh my God, I'd be *so* happy! We could do anything we want to, anytime we want to!"

"That would be nice. But . . ."

"But what?" she says.

I let out a sigh. "Let's get real. You're gonna get in easy. But, me? I'm not on your level. I'm just trying to get in on a wing and a prayer. I'll probably end up at some community college in Kansas."

She tilts her head, and a forlorn expression appears on her face.

"I think you're wrong. I, for one, believe in your abilities."

"That really means a lot, coming from you."

She gives me a smile—yeah, *that* smile—then slowly walks over to my bed and takes a seat. "Come here," she says.

I walk over and stand in front of her, whereupon she leans forward and wraps her arms around me, snuggling her head into my bosom.

"Can I tell you something?" I ask.

"Sure! What?"

"Before I met you, I was worried because I'd never been in love!"

"Really?" She looks up and holds my gaze for a few seconds, then laughs softly. "I bet you never guessed you were destined to fall in love with a girl, did you?"

I grin from ear to ear and nod. "Never in a million *years!*" After a moment or two of reflection, I add, "You know, once we're out of high school and out of this town, we can come out, right?"

A smile spreads across her face. "Sure!" But almost immediately she follows that with an expression of consternation. "Sorry I'm so much trouble."

"Hey, forget that! Meeting you was the most awesome thing to ever happen to me."

She snuggles in tight and is in the process of playfully wrapping my free arm around her when the unmistakable sound of the squeaky step sounds off.

"What's that?" she says.

"Quick! Get up! It's Grams!" I say in my loudest whisper.

We both leap to our feet. "No! You stay seated, I'll be standing over here!" I tell her as I back away. Everything's a flurry. But after a few seconds, I realize Grams merely is headed to her room.

"I think she walked past," Robin says.

"Yeah." I laugh. "Just a close call."

But later, as she's leaving, I notice her nervousness, and stop her before she gets into her car. "Are we okay?"

She gives me a reassuring smile. "Yes, baby, we're okay." As I watch her drive away, though, I remind myself of how much more she has on the line than I do.

As the days and then the weeks peel away, we become public fixtures in tiny Sagebrush. It's not uncommon after school to find us at any of the half-dozen or so fast food eateries on the main strip in Sagebrush, whooping it up with each other as if there's only us in the entire universe. I don't think I've ever had as much fun in my life as I have in the last few weeks. Yet we refrain from public displays of affection, and that's hard—at least, it is on me. But in private, we're moving closer together than ever. And I know where that's going to lead.

On a warm Saturday morning in April, she pulls into the driveway and honks, instead of getting out to come in. Once I climb in, she says we're going shopping, but won't say where. Along the way, she holds an almost constant smile, caresses my hand, and even reaches across to cup my breast just as a trucker passes on the left—leaving us crumpled in laughter when he honks his air horn in response.

I know where we're headed. But honestly, I don't care where we're going, so long as I'm going there with her. When we arrive at a mall in Dalhart, nearly an hour away, we loosen up. Robin seems to have no problem being public with our affection—and the deliciousness of that freedom to be who we are is intoxicating.

Everywhere we go, it's hand in hand. As I soak up the closeness, I recognize within myself that I've needed this freedom. There are no gawkers, no harassers, no people staring down their noses at us. We even chance across another girl couple in the lingerie store. After playfully browsing the more intimate apparel in the store, we follow them to a sandwich shop on the north end of the mall where we all sit and visit. It turns out they're from Omaha and just passing through. After an hour, we give them a fond farewell before heading back to Sagebrush late in the afternoon.

On Thursday morning, back in "no PDA" land, Robin greets me at my locker—and it doesn't take but a second to know she's up to something.

"I bet I can make you smile," she says, unfolding her hand. It's a key ring with a single key on it. "It's obvious we need our privacy," she grins, "and now, when we go to the lake, we can go *in* the house!"

I feel a shiver of excitement. "Wait, won't someone know?"

"Nah! No one but my dad goes out there this time of year, so we'll just wait until he's out of town!"

My imagination is immediately flooded with exotic possibilities. I move closer and whisper, "I love you, baby!" It's a pretty bold gesture here in the locker area, but somehow, I don't care as much.

She breaks into a coy smile, then leans in. "So . . . guess who's out of town for the weekend?"

"Are you kidding me?" I can barely contain myself.

She raises both eyebrows and smiles. "Baby, we're gonna spend the *night* there!"

"Oh, shit!" I squeal. "But what about your mom?"

"I'll tell her I'm staying with you! She doesn't go out there without dad, anyway."

"I can't *believe* this!"

"What about you? Will your Grams let you?"

"Of course! I can go wherever I want!"

"Perfect! Just be sure to bring your overnight tomorrow so we can leave from school. And, oh yeah, don't forget your camera!"

"Okay!"

"*And* your jammies!"

"Okay!"

"But you may not need them!" she adds in a sultry whisper, after which she daringly mouths me an air kiss.

The next afternoon as I walk into the parking lot, I see her standing next to the passenger door of her car. As I get closer, she gives me a smile with that sexy face of hers, and I feel like the luckiest girl in the world. That this awesome girl is mine simply blows me away. As I settle into her car and we get started down the highway, I find myself contemplating everything that makes me love her: her excitement with life, her beauty, her sense of adventure, her raw sensuality—in short, I love *everything* about her. She seems to know what I'm doing and holds up her palm to me. I slide my fingers between hers and clasp her hand.

"I love you so much, baby!" I gush. She tries to lean over for a kiss, but I have to point her head back to the road as we break down in laughter.

"C'mon!" she says, parking in the home's driveway, "I can't wait to show you around!"

As I get out of her car, I smell it again. It's the now very familiar fragrance of wisteria. It's strong, and it puts me in a magical mindset like I was the first time we came out to Robin's Lake Road. I stop and turn toward the lake to drink it in.

"You really do like that, don't you?" She brushes my hair aside to give me a kiss on the side of my neck. I find her hands on my midriff and entwine my fingers with hers. She turns me around and kisses me. "Let's go in!"

The first thing to greet me inside is an ominous-looking business portrait of her father on the entranceway wall, staring down from on high at any and all who enter.

"You're absolutely sure your dad won't show up?" I ask, moving past the portrait without taking my eyes off it. "That portrait's creepy!"

Seeing my reaction, she reassures me as we walk further in. "Trust me, he won't. He's out of town. Besides, Mom practically has to drag him out here."

We turn a corner into the living area, and I can see right away that this house is not as opulent as their house in town. Still, it's nothing to sneeze at. The furniture is classy, the living room is large, and as we approach the dining area, I can see through a wide bay window to a large deck out back that edges up to the lake itself, where the soft breezes are pushing the waves up in small laps of water. There's a short pier jutting out maybe ten or fifteen feet.

"Well, what do you think?" she asks. She's smiling *that* smile again, stirring my imagination.

"It's really nice!"

"I'll show you around. C'mon!" She takes me down a hallway. "*This*"— she pauses to turn on a light—"is the master bedroom."

I'm not surprised she takes me here first. The size of the room takes my breath away. It's huge, maybe even half the house. There's a sitting area off to the side that's probably larger than my entire bedroom at home. A king canopy bed occupies one wall, and across from it is a massive oak dresser beneath a large mirror. Lavender curtains almost hide a set of French doors just to the side, no doubt leading out to the deck area. The adjoining master bath is almost half as large as the bedroom. She sees me looking at it and tugs me in that direction.

"What do you think?" she asks, as we step into the bathroom.

I'm speechless. The floor is tiled in mauve with a design that mimics sand on a beach, complete with seashells. On one side I see two side-by-side sinks in front of a large mirror, and the walls all around are adorned with a mauve wallpaper pattern of a seascape that perfectly complements the tile. The tub is ginormous. I'm thinking three people would easily fit in it. Next to it is a double shower encased in clear glass. On the far end is a built-in hot tub.

I shake my head slowly back and forth. "Oh shit!"

Robin giggles and gives me a coy look. "Think we can find something to do back here tonight?" she says. God, I love her flirtations! She leads me back through the bedroom, through the main living area of the house, and into the kitchen. "Take a look at this!" she says.

The kitchen has a super large island that contains the most ornate and elaborate gas range with built-in grill I've ever seen. "Now this," I say, gesturing to the stove top, "is where I could spend a lot of time."

"You cook?"

"I know a few recipes," I tease.

"Good! We'll cook tonight!"

She grabs my hand once again and leads me to the second living area, toward the back. There's a huge sectional sofa that dominates the center of the room. On the wall to the side of a huge marble-hearth fireplace is the largest television I've ever seen. Quick as a cat, she has me on the couch beside her, both of us leaning back into the lush decorative pillows.

My mind is suddenly racing with the thoughts of what will inevitably happen between us tonight. I can tell she's thinking the same exact thoughts. Our hands find each other and she rolls to her side to face me.

"Nice movie theater, right?" she whispers.

"Um, yes, to say the least!"

She rolls over on top of me and gives me a deep, sensual kiss.

"You like that, don't you?" she asks, giving me a smile.

I smile, then pull her back in. When we break, she whispers, "you can have more, later!"

We both laugh, and then she motions for me to stay put. She glides her way into the kitchen, returning with a bag of tortilla chips and a bowl of salsa—and an impish grin.

"Oh my God, yes!" I hear myself, as I sit up.

We find ourselves cross-legged on the couch sideways, facing each other with the chips and salsa between us, and gorge ourselves while laughingly discussing any and every gossip topic we can summon. When we finally run out of those, the discussion turns to our favorite songs, then favorite movies, and it's a long one.

Our ability to feed off each other's brains is incredible. It doesn't surprise me that she likes musicals, as she can easily name more than fifty. I guess it doesn't surprise her much that I'm a sci-fi fan. I look up to notice that just like that, nearly four hours have passed, and the sun is down.

I shake my head in amazement at the intimacy that so naturally comes to us when we're together. It makes me think that before I found her, I wasn't alive. She makes me love *her*—but along the way, she makes me love *me*.

"Can you believe it's dark?" I say.

She springs up and hurries to the kitchen. I can barely see her in the darkness when she comes back in, but as she draws near, I see she's smiling and has a couple of wine glasses.

"Follow me," she says, giving me one of the glasses and offering her arm to help me up. As expected, she leads me to the master bedroom, where she adjusts the dimmer switch on the wall to give only the faintest glow from the overhead lighting. Before even taking the first sip of wine, I feel a familiar warmth spreading through me. She picks up a remote, and with a few clicks, music can be heard from built-in speakers in all four corners.

"Cheers, babe!" she says, smiling while holding up her glass. I wonder if she knows how much I love it every time she calls me that.

"Cheers!" I respond, smiling ear to ear.

We clink glasses and take the first sip. It's delicious, and its fragrance completes a perfect setting—just me and my Robin.

"Check this out," she says, retrieving another small remote from the bedside table. She points it toward the curtains and clicks a button. Immediately, the curtains part, revealing the French doors that lead to the outside deck area. The deck is rimmed by soft electric lighting that reminds me of tiki torches.

We stand hand in hand while sipping our wine, and in no time, our glasses are empty. Seemingly out of nowhere, she produces the bottle and fills both our glasses. I'm feeling *really* good. We toast each other again, this time sealing our toasts with kisses. It isn't long before I turn up the glass and get nothing.

"I'm kinda lit!" I say as she fills my glass yet again.

"Me, too!" she laughs. "I have an idea. Follow me!"

She opens the French doors and pulls me outside onto the deck. At the far end of the deck, just feet away from the lake, she slides her left arm around my waist. Together, completely exposed to the night air, we stand and breathe in the scent of wisteria from the soft night breeze and listen to the chorus of about a million frogs. I want to melt into her arms and never come out.

After a few minutes, we find ourselves staring into a pale-yellow full moon emerging from behind the clouds and hanging just over the tops of the trees on the far side of the lake. I catch her staring at the deck. Looking down, I can see two complete figures in silhouette, illuminated by nothing but moonlight.

"Moon shadows!" I exclaim. The music from the bedroom is still audible, and I realize at that moment that the song being played is "our" song. "Let's dance!" I whisper, setting my glass of wine down on the deck off to the side.

"Okay!" she smiles, setting her glass down.

I take her hand and we walk to the center of the deck and turn to face each other. It's our very first dance, and the scene couldn't be more magical.

I place my left hand on her waist as she puts her right arm on my shoulder. With our free hands clasped, we begin a slow two-step to the romantic strains of the ballad. When the last chorus starts, we instinctively move closer, placing our arms around each other, mine at her waist, hers at my neck. We gently sway in each other's clasp, and as the song ends, I drink up her lips in a long, steamy kiss. I'm drunk on the sensation of her body against mine.

"That was so fucking romantic," she whispers.

"We danced in the moonlight!" I whisper back.

She looks deep into my eyes and gives me that coy smile again. "Have you ever danced in the moonlight before?"

Her question makes me smile. "No, baby."

"Neither have I," she says, pulling me in closer.

"You know what?"

"What?" she says, looking down into my eyes.

"I don't *ever* want to dance in the moonlight with anyone but you."

"Neither do I, baby, neither do I," she breathes.

All is right in my world, and I want nothing more than to hang onto this moment for eternity. I feel cocooned within the safety of her love, and nothing can hurt me. Closing my eyes, I savor the kisses she plants on my neck and ears.

"Let's go back inside," she whispers. Arm in arm, we end up back in the master bedroom, where we finish off the last few sips of the wine.

"Are you trying to get me drunk?" I ask, as she drains the bottle into my glass. I use my left hand to softly trace the contour of her ear.

"Maybe!"

I can't help but grin. "Who knows what could happen, then."

"Well . . . we could make love," she says, giving me a coy expression.

I knew it was inevitable we would find our way to this milepost. I've had plenty of time to think about it, fantasize about it, and get ready for it. I can feel an inner anticipation rising at the thought of it. My hands are trembling as I take a sip and then set my glass on the bedside table before turning back to her and stepping in close.

"You don't have to get me drunk to do *that*," I whisper.

She pulls me in and plants a soft kiss on my lips. After a minute, she pulls back just a little, leaving our lips barely touching, and then uses her tongue to gently caress the tip of mine. I hear myself gasp softly as she cups my face and plants tiny sensual kisses on each lip, then dives in for a torrid open-mouth kiss. I'm going mad with this frenzy as we both grope each other's breasts when she suddenly pushes me back onto the bed. Quick as a cat, she climbs on top and starts working my shirt up and over my head. I'm doing the same with hers while on my back, and it doesn't take long for both of us to be completely topless with our hands all over each other. Then, after a couple of minutes, I try to unbutton her pants but our positioning isn't right.

Fuck it. I switch to helping her with my pants, and once she moves off me, I'm able to slide them right off, underwear and all. She immediately lies on her back, and together we get her pants and underwear off. We breathlessly stare at each others' naked bodies. It doesn't take but a few seconds before we're groping each other all over again, and there are no off-limits.

I'm on top of her, exploring all I can with my hand while drinking up the wildest kissing imaginable. Every few seconds, I come up and look into her face, and each time, I'm overcome by her raw sensuality and beauty. Her eyes, her mouth, that tongue, even the scent of her vanilla perfume—all of it is driving me freaking insane with lust. I move down to her breasts and feverishly kiss and suck them until she's moaning.

Suddenly, she pushes me over and gets on top of me. Now it's her using her mouth to drive me insane. With her hand and fingers on my crotch, I'm so wet I know I must be leaving a spot on her sheets.

And then she starts moving down.

I know what's coming. She's the teacher, and I'm the student. I surrender my body to her. It's not long before she's on her stomach between my legs. Knowing what she's about to do pushes me to the edge of madness. Then, I see her face go down.

The sensation I feel is nothing like I could have ever imagined possible. I'm involuntarily gyrating in rhythm with the movement of her tongue. She applies a combination of gentle suction and forceful flicking. It's more than I can hold in, and within seconds my entire body explodes in a seismic orgasm that seems to last forever.

For the next few minutes, I struggle for breath as my body shudders. I reach down to find her face as she plants soft kisses all over the insides of my thighs. Eventually, she starts working her way up my abdomen until she's at my breasts, and then my lips. The warmth of her body is so stimulating that I try to make every square inch of my skin be in contact with her somewhere.

"Well," she says in a low, sultry voice through another of her irresistible smiles, "did you like *that?*"

It takes several tries just to catch enough breath to be able to speak. "You're so incredible," I finally gasp.

After a few minutes of closeness, and with my mind racing with the anticipation of a reciprocal act, I make my move. Quite contrary to everything I learned from Kenna Lowell, the idea of performing oral sex on Robin is incredibly erotic and gets more so by the minute. I gently roll the two of us over so she's on her back.

Following her script, I begin at her breasts. By the time I get to her thighs, she's already positioned her legs apart. I'm absolutely delirious with the thought of applying my new knowledge. Finally, I go straight in, savoring every sound she makes as I tease her with my tongue and use my hands to gently squeeze her breasts. To my delight, and after only a couple of minutes, her abdomen shudders with release, which continues until she uses her hands to still my head.

"My God!" she exhales, her body heaving up and down.

"You liked it?"

"It was incredible!" she manages to get out, as she continues to catch her breath. "Come up here."

I pull myself up and turn my head, laying it on her shoulder. I wish I could stay like this forever. I'm overwhelmed by a level of emotional fulfillment that permeates every atom in my body, and I feel tears welling up in my eyes that then spill down the side of my face past my ears. I hope she doesn't notice, but within a minute, she does.

"Are you okay?" she asks, raising her head.

"It's okay. I've just never been this happy." She smiles and gently wipes my tears before laying her head back down. I place my arms around her neck and hug her in close, but after a few minutes of silence, I raise my head and look up into her eyes.

"I love you so much, baby," I force out in a crackly voice.

She pulls me in tight. "And I love you so much, too," she whispers.

I give her cheek a soft kiss and savor the ambience of the moment, praying I'll never forget it. After another few minutes, I raise my head.

"Sing me a song, baby."

I hear a soft giggle. "You really want me to sing you a song?"

"Yes, I do," I reply, giving her cheek a kiss.

"Okay, then! I know just the one. Are you ready?"

"Yes!"

Taking a deep breath, she begins in perfect pitch with a melody I immediately recognize.

"It's our song!" I blurt out, to which she smiles, but keeps on singing. I close my eyes and immerse myself in the beauty of her voice. The lyrics she sings are the sweetest sentiment I've ever had directed toward me. I hang onto the verses as if they are life preservers on a stormy sea. It's when she starts the last verse that she strokes my cheek with her fingers. I open my eyes and watch the words come out of her mouth:

Since we met on Monday, no day is complete without you,

No joy is worth remembering without you,

No life has meaning without you,

So, with you I'll stay, living a passion every day,

Singing every joy, down this path I've chosen,

Hand in hand, my darling, my one and only love.

As she sings the last five words, directing them straight into my eyes, it's too much. Tears well up again and I can't even see straight. Ever so gently, she wipes them away, and then she leans in and gives my cheek a lingering soft kiss.

"I meant every single word I just sang to you," she whispers.

I'm opening my mouth to reply when the explosion occurs.

Blam!

The sound of the door slamming open is so loud it causes both of us to convulse. I jerk my head around. And there, standing in the doorway with the look of hell's fury in his eyes, is Mr. O'Leary.

11

The darkness is so complete that it's all I can do to see where to put one foot after the other.

It takes Grams forever to find me out by myself on the lonely country lane that connects to Robin's Lake Road. The ride home is deathly silent. She keeps looking over at me and then shaking her head. I'm doing all I can to contain my crying. My tears have nearly been depleted, but I can't stop shaking. Once we're in the driveway, I bolt from the car, go inside, and sprint to my room, where I close and lock the door, and then lie down across my bed.

I bury my face into my pillow. I don't want Grams to hear me. After another ten or fifteen minutes, I raise my phone to my face to see if I have any messages from Robin. Nothing. I message her with a terse query:

You there?

After five minutes, I tap out another text:

???

Still no response. Possibilities race through my mind. Battery could be dead. Nope, not likely. She doesn't want to talk to me. Nope, not likely. She's preoccupied with her own family drama at the moment. Yep, that could be it, but I have no idea how long that will play out.

At least I was able to escape my tormentor. I can only imagine what she's going through right now. The misery of not being able to get in touch with her is unbearable. I drag myself from my bed and then it hits me. I left my camera at Robin's vacation home.

I've been in my room for about an hour when Grams comes knocking. I take a deep breath and sigh. There's no escaping this conversation. Might as well just get it over with. I trudge over to the door and open it for her. She has a forced smile on her face.

"Hi, sweetie," she says. "You want to talk?" She takes my hand and gives it a squeeze.

"I'm not sure, Grams," I reply, looking down to avoid her eyes. I'm sure she can smell the alcohol on my breath, but she doesn't mention it.

"Okay, sweetie, then remember this. Maybe it'll help. Whatever trouble you're having, you just gotta let it go and forgive. That's what Jesus would want you to do." She pauses and searches my face. "I'm sure Robin's ready to do the same thing."

"Sure, Grams."

She eyes me for a few seconds. It's almost as if she realizes that she's missed the mark, but doesn't have any idea what the real issue could be. As I'm waiting for her to leave, I hear my phone beep from behind me. Grams hears it, too.

"I'm sure that's Robin, so you two make up, okay?"

"Okay, Grams." I can barely contain myself. The door is shut for only a microsecond before I have my phone in my hand. It's a message from Robin, and I feel my heart leap. I open it and read.

This is Mr. O'Leary. Robin will not have her phone for the time being. Do not contact her, or I will be forced to speak to your grandmother.

I read the text again. My throat is suddenly so tight I can barely breathe. It's just about my worst nightmare—her father is trying to separate us now that he knows the true nature of our relationship. What if he's already planning to move again? That scares the hell out of me. I want so bad to speak to her, to hear her tell me she loves me. I want her to tell me that nothing will ever separate us.

What only an hour ago was so beautiful is now the single worst experience of my life. I would literally give all I own to have her safe with me right here, right now. It's the not knowing that's killing me. I try to tell myself that I'll see her on Monday at school, but that's two, torturous, unbearable days away. Might as well be next year. My agony is too much to bear. I need Orm. I raise my phone and tap out a quick message:

Come over.

Even though it's late, his reply appears on the screen within a few seconds. I have to wipe my tears away to see clearly.

Now??

Yes!

On my way.

As of right now, Orm is my lifeline. Actually, he's always been my lifeline. It's just that I've never needed a rescue like I need one now. I go downstairs to wait for him. Grams is cleaning up the dining room and sees me.

"Feeling better, sweetie?"

I try to give her a smile, but only manage to sniffle. "Better. Orm is coming over."

He doesn't live that far away. I lie on the couch turned to my side so I can watch the driveway through the living room window. As his car turns into the lane, I surprise even myself by how fast I bolt through the door and get to his car. He's barely out of his car as I throw my arms around his neck and start crying all over again.

"Ash?" He's hesitant, but then puts his arms around me and pulls me in close. "Hey, there!" For several minutes, all I can do is sob and heave. Orm must think my Grams has died or something. Finally, I pull away. He softly wipes a tear I missed.

"Thanks for coming, Orm."

"Sure, but what's got you so upset?"

"Can we just sit in your car?"

"Yeah, sure thing," he answers, with a look of concern on his face. He opens the passenger side door to allow me to take a seat, and he sprints around to the driver side and joins me. I'm still composing myself. He's patient as I pull myself together. Finally, I'm able to take a deep breath.

"Oh, God!" I sigh.

"It's Robin, isn't it?"

Of course Orm would know. I nod my head yes.

"I'm guessing y'all had a fight."

"No," I reply, shaking my head. "I wish it was that simple." I turn sideways to face him and try to figure out where to begin.

"She rejected you?"

"No, no." I take a huge breath and let it out. "It's her father."

"Okay," he says, allowing a thin smile to appear. "Her dad doesn't want his daughter to . . . um, be with you? Is that getting close?"

I nod. "Sort of," I reply. "Actually, it's worse than that."

"Okay, I give up. You're just gonna have to tell me."

It's now or never. "Her father . . . he, like, caught us."

Orm's eyebrows go up. "*Caught* you? Like, together?"

"Yeah. Like, together. But worse."

"Y'all were holding hands or something?"

"Orm, it's worse than that."

He scratches his chin, then makes another run at it. "Kissing?"

"Okay, stop." I take another deep breath. "Actually, at the time, we weren't *doing* anything." Orm is really confused now. He opens his mouth to speak, but I shush him with a raised finger. "We actually just got through fucking. And we were completely naked on her bed."

"Holy shit!" he whispers. "Her dad caught y'all fucking? Where were you? At Robin's house? Why would y'all do that there? Was he—"

"Geezus, Orm! Hang on, will you?" I pause and then try to sum it all up in just a single sentence. "We were at their vacation home, and we both thought her dad was out of town for the weekend. But yeah. We fucked. And then got caught."

Orm's eyes are as wide as saucers as he studies my face. "How much did he see?"

I roll my eyes. "Orm! We *fucked!* Her dad walked in on us while we were still naked in her parents' bed!"

"What did he do?"

I have to turn away to gather my wits. I just hope I don't start another fit of uncontrollable crying.

"It was horrible," I reply, my voice cracking. "He said the most vicious things to both of us, then he threw me out of the house without a ride back home."

"How did you get home?"

"Grams. But honestly, Orm, that's not the issue. Her dad caught me and Robin naked. On a bed. Can you get that through your brain?"

Orm sighs and nods. "Yeah. I get that. Wow. Doesn't get much worse than that. At least he didn't catch a *guy* in bed with his daughter."

"Oh, *fuck* you, Orm!"

He raises his hands in defense. "Bad joke—sorry, Ash!"

"He knows his daughter is gay! Actually, he already knew that. But now he knows it again. And now—"

"Stop, Ash," Orm says, shaking his head. "Too much, too quick. So, he knows his daughter is gay. Maybe some shit hits the fan. Maybe he's mad as hell. But he comes around, right? I mean, that's his *daughter.* You're not little girls! You're both eighteen!"

"No, he *doesn't* 'come around'!"

"Why not?"

"The problem is that he's straight-up Catholic!"

"And . . . ?"

"Orm, it means he thinks gays are going to hell and he doesn't want his little girl to go to hell. That's what it means, okay?"

"But she can do what she wants, Ash!"

I'm hanging on Orm's reply. It's what I desperately hope is true, more than anything.

"Technically, yes. But, he took her phone away, so I can't call her. And he told me to stay away from her, or he's gonna call Grams."

"Like he can keep y'all away from each other? C'mon!"

"I hope not, but it's a possibility. When they were living in Texas last year, Robin had a crush on a girl at her high school there, and he found out. He moved the family all the way here to get her away. And to keep people from knowing."

"Shit! So he's really determined to get her away from you?"

I give it a moment or two of thought. "Yeah, I think you're right."

"What I don't get is why she was dating Dill."

"Don't you get it? Dill was her cover. She dated Dill to get her dad off her case and make him think she wasn't really gay. I'm telling you, this is way sketch. I just wish I could talk to her right now!" I fight the urge to cry.

He senses my mood and does his best to reassure me.

"You will," he soothes.

"It just hurts so bad, Orm!"

"I know. But, Ash, you've covered a lot of ground in the past month! Things are gonna seem . . . well, hyped up and exaggerated in importance, if you get what I mean."

After a few moments of reflection, I see he could be right. I *have* come a long way. We sit in silence as the song playing in the background finishes.

"To be honest, I might still be thinking of myself as straight if Robin hadn't come along."

"So, you now think of yourself as gay?"

"Oh, yeah. I'm not that dense."

"Some might say Robin *made* you gay."

"She might have *awakened* me, but she didn't *make* me gay. I mean, when I really think about it, I've known for a long time I'm different. Remember all my boy trouble? I guess I know what that was all about now."

He gives me a smile. "Hey, at least you're in touch with yourself, now."

"You know what's strange? With her, I feel more alive and in touch with myself than I've ever felt in my whole life."

"That's so great, Ash!"

"And, you know what else? I know I have the right to be whoever I want to be."

Orm gives me a fist bump. "I'm actually envious of you. I think you've got something most of us don't even know we're missing."

We both face to the front and gaze upward in the direction of the full moon.

"Robin and I danced under that moon just an hour ago." I feel myself starting to tear up again. "Oh God, this hurts so bad!"

He steadies me with a hand to my shoulder. "Ash, I think you really *are* in love."

We listen to a couple more songs before I leave his car. Thanks to him, I'm way settled down, but once in bed, I have a hard time falling asleep. Waiting two days before I see Robin is going to be hard. Now that I think about it, that's the longest time we've been out of touch since our first kiss over a month ago. God knows I could certainly use another first kiss from her right about now.

I'm apprehensive as hell as I walk the hallway to my locker Monday morning. Robin is nowhere in sight. That's alarming, and makes my stomach tighten up with worry. What if she's already gone?

First and second period go by in a fog. I'm just hoping I can hold myself together. After third period, I cautiously make my way to our secret meeting place, and I'm relieved beyond all description to find her there waiting for me. And even though the air is permeated by the faint but foul aroma of the chemistry lab across the hall, it's *our* space, and at least for the time being, everything is right again.

I look around to make sure no one else is there. I don't know why, and I know it's irrational, but I'm afraid her dad, or even Jermy, might just appear out of nowhere. I practically throw my books onto the bench and rush into her arms. For what seems a long time, we hold on to each other in silence.

"Baby," I manage to finally say, "I knew you'd be here!"

"Baby," she whispers in return, now stroking my hair, "I missed you!"

"Me too!"

"I would have called you, but my dad took my phone away! He won't even let me drive my car. He's taking me to school and picking me up."

"He texted me and told me to stay away from you, or he would call Grams."

"Fuck!" She stamps her foot. Then, she looks straight into my face. "Okay, we're not going to panic. What we have is a lot stronger than his bullshit. I love you with all my heart! And I know you love me, right?"

"Yes, baby," I whisper.

"So, we're going to outlast this. School will be done in a few weeks. We'll both move out and go somewhere together. Maybe Chicago! Or anywhere but here!"

I give her a smile. "Anywhere, baby, just so long as you're with me."

"So, no getting down about this. We're gonna be strong and come out stronger! The future is ours, you know?"

Her words are the sweetest comfort imaginable.

"You're right. We're not gonna lose the good thing we have." I want to snug myself into her embrace and never come back out.

She sighs as she wipes away a tear. "What would I do without you?"

"It's gonna be okay. C'mon, let's sit." I gesture to the empty bench beside us. We sit in silence for a few minutes, both of us regaining our composures.

"My dad was just so out of control!" She takes a deep breath and looks toward me before facing forward again and gesturing with her hands. "We had the worst fight you can possibly imagine!"

"I think I can imagine."

"You can?" She sniffs and then forces out another weak smile. "I'm just so sorry he had to see you like that. I swear, I hate him! I'm just so glad you're still talking to me."

"I don't blame *you*, baby." I give her hand a squeeze, which she returns.

"We're gonna have to find another place for after school," she avows. "That's just it. He's not going to ruin the best thing that ever happened to me. I won't let him."

"I love that about you," I whisper, "that you're willing to fight for us. Just know I'm right in there with you."

She turns to me and opens her mouth to speak. "Ash, can I ask you a question?"

"Sure, baby, anything."

"Are you ashamed of being . . . well, being with a . . . a gay girl?"

"No, baby, I'm not ashamed of you at all. Not even possible. I don't care if you're a Martian!"

"Even if . . . well, you know?"

"Yes, even if you're gay." She gives me a tentative smile. "You think of yourself as gay now?"

She doesn't reply right away. I can tell she's struggling. "I do," she finally replies, looking straight into my eyes. "I have to accept that."

"I'm proud of you, baby. But, I know that's hard for you."

"It's *very* hard. Back in Texas, after my dad found out about my crush, everyone, like, tried to 'cure' me. And Ash, I really thought I needed to be cured. I *wanted* to be cured—so my family would love me again . . . so I wouldn't be the family *project* anymore. I wanted my family to be *respected* again." Her voice trails off into that of a little girl on the verge of helplessness.

The sight of her being defenseless like this infuriates me.

"*Cure* you? Like you've got a disease? How dare they! You're the most wonderful person I can possibly imagine!" I pull her close, and she lays her head on my shoulder.

"Sometimes it's so hard to just face another day," she says, her voice cracking. "But from this point, I'm accepting who I am, because if I can't accept myself for who I am, I really don't have much."

"Damn straight, baby! We're getting out of here as soon as we can. Fuck all this shit. From now on, it's me and you against the world."

She closes her eyes and smiles again, snuggling up to me. For several seconds, we remain in this position. I don't care if someone sees us. My girl needs me.

"Wanna see something?"

She smiles and nods. "Sure!"

I reach into my hip pocket, retrieve a sheet of bright yellow stationery, and slowly unfold it. "Take a look!"

She holds the sheet and reads. "It's our song! You wrote down the words to our song!"

"Yes, I did, last night. I'll always keep this close!"

She takes it from my hand, gives me a smile, and plants a kiss on the face of it. "For you, baby," she says, handing it back to me. The imprint from her lipstick is perfect.

"Oh my God!" I take the sheet and fold it up and clutch it to my bosom before carefully sliding it back into my pocket. Without warning, she stands, straddles my legs, and sits down on my lap facing me, her face only an inch from mine.

"I love you," she says. "You better know that. For all time, I'll love you, Asher Kendall Robinson."

Hearing her say that to me, I'm unable to hold back. I cradle her face with my hands and pull her in for a kiss, which lasts several seconds longer than I intended. We part very slowly, and then, still maintaining eye contact, she rises and pulls me up with her hand. She leaves the locker area first. I'm gushing internally with new confidence. To hell with the world, I've got Robin O'Leary!

Fourth period happens. I know this because here I am, leaving that class and heading for lunch. All I can see and hear in my mind is Robin O'Leary telling me she'll love me for all time. As we sit at lunch, side by side, I feel her solidarity, her closeness, her electricity. Every few minutes, we manage to find each other's eyes. Despite yesterday, everything's perfect now.

When the final bell rings, it suddenly hits me that I won't be riding with her, which makes me angry all over again. I tentatively approach the parking lot and look around. The last thing I want to see is Robin's father. Thankfully, he's nowhere in sight. I head for Orm's car. He's about to leave without me when I raise my arms to signal him. He stops long enough for me to climb in.

"I guess I'm back with you," I mutter.

Orm looks at me with a puzzled expression. "You okay?"

I clench my fist, then make myself relax. "Sorry. This is normally our time together."

"Oh yeah. Sorry, Ash."

"I saw her today, and at least we're in a good place. I just need to chill."

"That's great! Shows me y'all are strong."

Once I'm home, Grams greets me.

"Did you and Robin settle your differences?" she asks in her cheery voice.

"Yes, we did."

It's not a lie. But it's not the complete truth, either, and I wonder when I *will* be truthful to her about Robin. Later that evening I realize I didn't remind Robin to bring my camera to school. I'm not concerned, as I have another couple of days before my Photography class assignment is due.

My journalism homework requires me to answer a quiz online, so I open up my laptop and sign on, figuring it will take no more than a half hour to finish. I set my phone off to the side and out of the way. About ten minutes later I hear an alert from my phone that I instantly recognize as Orm's text tone. It can wait. I resume working, but then Orm texts me again. I know he's just checking up on me, but I have a train of thought going. I keep working and am almost done when Orm texts me once again. I let out a sigh of exasperation.

I shake my head and begin the last question of the quiz. It's a tough one, so I have to search my textbook, and I'm determined to wrap it up without interruption.

Just then, my phone rings, and it's Orm's ringtone. Geez! I turn to the bed, retrieve the phone, and answer.

"Orm, for God's sake, I'm trying to finish my homework!"

"Chill, okay? Just wondering if you've been on your phone."

I hesitate before answering. He knows about Robin losing her phone.

"Don't get me started."

There's a long pause. "So . . . you're okay?"

"Yes. I'm okay."

"Okay, bye." And with that curious sign-off, he ends the call.

Something about the call is weird, but I return to that last question again, determined as ever to get it finished. Just as I finish, I hear a car pull into the driveway. That gets priority attention. I peek out my window, and I'm surprised to see Orm's car and him striding toward the front door.

I let out a long sigh, close my laptop, and rise from my chair to go downstairs. Just then, Orm comes through the door into my room with a worried look on his face.

"Orm, what the hell?"

"Ash," he says, looking directly into my eyes. "Are you *okay?*"

"You came all the way over here to ask me the same question again?"

He takes a deep breath. "Have you been on Twitter today?"

"Twitter? Not since fifth period at school. Why?"

He thrusts his phone at me. "*This* has literally gone viral."

I look closely, and there's a photo displayed on the screen. It looks instantly familiar. My heart skips a beat when I recognize what it is. The picture is of me and Robin kissing each other.

And it was obviously taken while we were in our secret place earlier today.

12

I break out in a cold sweat.

It's apparent from the angle of the photo that whoever took it was standing very close to us, probably between the last two locker rows.

"That's on *Twitter?*"

"Yep, and on Instagram, Snapchat, and Facebook. It's everywhere."

I feel myself sinking fast. "Who posted it?"

"It doesn't matter," he replies tersely.

"Yes, it does!" I fire back. "If this gets back to Robin's father—"

"Ash, this isn't the only tweet! Everyone is retweeting, sharing, reposting. It's viral."

It takes a minute for the implication to settle in.

"Oh God, Orm!" I stagger back and sit down at my desk. "Oh, shit! Oh, shit!" The recollection of Jermy hanging out in the secret area last week suddenly pops into my head. "I know who took that photo!"

"Who?"

"It's your creepy cousin, Jermy!"

Orm's expression melts into incredulity. "You sure about this?"

"Yeah. I'm pretty sure. We caught him hanging out in our secret meeting place last week, acting all weird! It was almost like he was expecting us to show up."

"Secret meeting place?"

"Yes! That's not the point, though. He was—"

"Yeah, yeah, I get it, but is this someplace that people would normally be in?"

Suddenly I get what he's angling for. "No, it's not a place where people normally go. It's pretty out of the way, in B wing behind the locker rows near the cafeteria."

"Okay, yeah, I've seen that area," he nods. "It *is* out of the way. Tells me that whoever did this was expecting you and Robin to be there."

"Orm, I'm so scared for Robin!"

"Take it easy, Ash, I'll get to the bottom of it."

"No, you don't understand! When her dad gets wind of this—"

"Look, I get that it's gonna be bad news, but you can't unpost that photo. It's gonna have to run its course."

My phone suddenly alerts … it's a retweet from one of my friends, Christine, who apparently received it from someone else. The word "lezbos" has been added across the front of the photo. I show it to Orm.

He takes a look and then shakes his head. I toss my phone to the bed.

"The worst part is I can't even call Robin!" Another alert from my phone. This time, I don't bother to look.

"Okay, maybe you stay home from school for a few days?"

"Orm, I don't give a shit if people know I'm gay. It's *Robin* I'm worried about! Anyway, I'm sweating out a college admission. My grades really do matter right now."

He hangs around giving me moral support until I finally convince him he can leave. He gives me a side hug. "Okay, then, see you in the morning."

I lie in bed on my back facing the ceiling for the longest time, mired in fear and uncertainty. I *know* her father will see it. And I know that a phone call to Grams is coming. Even though she doesn't have her phone, I'm sure Robin already knows about the viral pic, and I'm sure she's absolutely crushed, not to mention terrified. Me, I'm just a nobody, but she has a ton of social standing she's gonna lose. I want to be with her so bad.

Tuesday morning dawns cloudy, and the air is dank with dread. I don't really feel like dressing up, so I grab a random pair of jeans and a brown tee. I spend maybe two minutes putting on some blush and a little bit of eyeshadow and mascara. I don't even bother with lipstick.

Walking in from the parking lot seems quite ordinary. It's when I get inside that I get the first inkling that I'm the big news story of the day. A couple of girls off to my left stare at me and then whisper, before walking away—one of them giving me a last look over her shoulder as they disappear down the hallway. I don't get another twenty feet before a couple of guys let out with a snicker as they pass in the opposite direction.

As I turn the corner into my locker area, I see heads turn toward me. Not a good sign. The noise level seems to be more hushed than usual. And although I expect it, I feel my stomach sink when I make the final turn to my locker. Robin is nowhere to be seen. This hits me worse than I thought it would. I turn completely around to scan the area, and as I finish my turn, a boy that I hardly know, standing next to my locker, says, "Guess your bitch didn't show up today." He high-fives a guy next to him and walks off.

I want to throw my books at him. I hear more whispers and see people pointing. Just then, I feel a hand on my shoulder. It's Orm.

"C'mon, Ash, just get your books and let's go." I look up and do my best to smile, but I realize my eyes are teary. He gives me a smile and then warns off a guy walking toward us who, from his expression, has something snarky to say to me. Together, we walk all the way to my first-period classroom, after which he gives me a quick hug and watches from the doorway until I'm in my seat.

If I thought I was distracted by Robin before this, I'm totally dismantled now. The teacher's voice is nothing but a dull drone in the background. I can't even get my textbook open. I keep my head down, but two or three times I look around as surreptitiously as possible. A girl on the next row over gives me a smirk when she catches me sneaking a peek.

Where is Robin? I *need* to know. I put my forehead into my palms and prop myself up. I'm in this position when an aide taps me on the shoulder and hands me a note. It's from Principal Lowrey. "Please come by my office after first period," it reads.

I know I'm not guilty of anything, but I'm sweating bullets as I enter the principal's office. There are two other students in the seating area just inside, and they give me the once over as I close the door. I'm sure they know why I'm here.

Principal Lowrey sees me through her office door which is slightly cracked open. She immediately opens the door and calls me in, bypassing her office assistant out front. I'm shaking as I take a seat across from her desk.

"Asher, we're aware of a certain photograph of you and Robin O'Leary that is making the rounds on social media." She pauses for a response but I don't have one. She takes a deep breath and then leans forward in her chair. "I'm disappointed that you chose to engage in this behavior with Miss O'Leary. We teach better values than that. I can only imagine how disappointed your grandmother is. Did you ever stop to think about her?"

I'm entirely knocked off dead center. "N-no, ma'am."

"I don't know what kind of agenda you're pushing, but in this school, there will be no such evangelizing. Do I make myself clear?"

Evangelizing? I'm so confused, and in my emotional state, I don't even know what to say, or what question to ask to clear up my confusion.

"I asked you a question, young lady," Principal Lowrey says.

I force myself to swallow. "I don't understand," I manage to say. "What kind of evangelizing are you talking about?"

"The gay agenda."

"W-what's that?"

"Miss Sullivan, it's clear you have been influenced by some proponent of homosexuality into believing that such behavior is normal. I, for one, will not allow you to spread that immorality in this school! Do you understand?"

My head spins. What the hell is the "gay agenda?" It doesn't matter. I feel my anger stirring, and I'm tired of being lectured. I lean forward and make firm eye contact.

"I haven't been brainwashed by anyone, and I'm not trying to spread any kind of immorality." She's got maybe one more bullshit accusation before I lose it.

She points a finger into my face. "Yes, you are, because I know your grandmother, and she wouldn't allow this kind of disgusting behavior."

Welp, she just used up her last bullet. Now I'm pissed.

"Shut the hell up about my grandmother!" I shoot back. "That so-called disgusting behavior was nothing more than a kiss shared by two consenting people who just so happen to be in love with each other! You moron!"

I think I just knocked *her* off center. Her eyes get big, and she freezes. After a second or two, she comes at me again.

"So, you admit to being a homosexual? And accuse Miss O'Leary of the same?!"

I'm just about at the boiling point. "I think I admitted to being in love!"

"Not in *my* school!" she fires back. Her eyes are narrowed, but she manages to keep her voice under control. "Public displays of affection are a violation of the Student Code of Conduct! And I won't have it! It's immoral, indecent, and wrong!" She rises and leans over the desk toward me.

I'm on my feet in an instant, facing her down. "Well, you must stay pretty busy, then," I reply before she can say anything further, "because we both know that boys and girls are kissing every single day in this school!"

Her voice lowers in pitch, but its volume increases to a snarl. "You had better get that attitude under control, Miss Sullivan! You're lucky I don't call your grandmother in on this!"

My hands are trembling with rage. I lower my voice but match her intensity. "You know what, Principal Lowrey? You and people like you make me sick! I just realized that! So, thank you for that lesson. Is there anything else?"

She slaps both hands onto the desk in front of her. "Miss Sullivan!"

I turn and stalk out of her office, brushing past her office assistant who is right outside the office door, no doubt listening in on everything. As I enter the hallway, I hear my name again, but I ignore it and continue on my way.

I'm so mad I can barely find my way back to class. I wonder if Robin has been called in for the same lecture. And then there's that creep, Jermy McIvers. I can't believe I ever let him touch me. I'm willing to bet money that no stern lecture on morality awaits *him*.

Somehow, I make it through second and third periods, fighting down nausea every minute. With third period at an end, I make a beeline for the secret meeting place. I realize the mistake of that decision the second I round the corner in B wing.

There, congregated at the exact location of the entrance to the locker area, is a group of about fifteen students, Jermy McIvers being the obvious ringleader. All are staring in my direction as if waiting for me to show up. They break out in laughter and pointing as soon as they see me. Jermy, slimy coward that he is, quickly slinks off down the hall. The rest of the group hangs around, some of them snapping photos with their phones.

I've never in my life experienced this degree of shaming. Robin is nowhere in sight, so I have to think she either didn't even come to school today or knew not to show up here. I cast my gaze downward and turn slightly to the side, hoping no one else can see my embarrassment. The laughter of the crowd dies down, but I still hear them talking, and I know what they're talking about.

Just then, out of nowhere, anger rises within me. To turn and walk away would give these morons precisely what they want. No more. The shaming stops right here, right now. I raise my head and square up to them, then start walking toward them. That takes a few of them by surprise. A small group of them immediately averts their eyes and leaves. By the time I get to where they were standing, all of them have dispersed. In the distance, I can still hear a few snippets of their talking, but it's quickly fading away.

Sick with worry over Robin, I head to fourth period, even though I'm a good ten minutes early. I want so desperately to see for myself how she is and to comfort her if she needs it. After a few more minutes of wallowing in my distress, I realize that it wouldn't matter much if she were here at school, because all opportunities for privacy have vanished into thin air.

The class passes in a blur. I'm hurrying down the hallway on my way to the cafeteria—even though I'm not really hungry—when Orm comes up behind me and puts his arm around my shoulder to walk me the rest of the way. Together, we enter the cafeteria and take our place in line. I immediately notice that Robin is not at our usual table, nor is she in line.

"We're gonna eat the biggest, nastiest pizza they have today," he announces with a grin.

"Sure." I take a quick look around. Quite a few are staring at me, but I don't care anymore.

"Just ignore them," he says. "We'll sit by ourselves." At the end of the line, he pulls out his wallet and pays for my meal as well as his. I look in the direction of our usual table, but still no Robin.

He leads me to an unoccupied table on the far side near the windows. The sun is out now, and it paints the table with a bright orange swath. We unload our trays, and I stare at the slice of pizza on the plate in front of me. Orm is busy wolfing down his slice while keeping his eyes on me. I'm keeping a lookout for Robin.

"Eat," he says.

He means well, but I shake my head. I don't even feel like talking.

"Hey, I'm here for you, Ash."

We sit in silence for another five minutes. I don't think I've ever been this helpless.

"My day basically sucks."

He stops chewing and stares at me for a long time with a frown on his face. "I get it. I guess I never knew how unfair . . . well, how *cruel* some people can be to gay people."

I nod, then stare out the window. There's another long period of silence. I take out my phone and see over twenty text messages from people whose numbers I don't recognize. After opening a few, I get the gist of it. One fellow student's Instagram post reads, "What is every guy's secret fantasy? To cure a lesbian!" I show the offending message to Orm, who gets an angry look on his face.

"Report that!"

"For what purpose?" I shoot back. "I just have to get through the next few weeks, and I'm out of here! I'll be out of this bullshit school, out of bullshit little Sagebrush, and believe me, I'm never coming back!"

"Aww, c'mon, Ash, you don't, umm . . ." Orm's voice unexpectedly trails off, his eyes wide and fixated on something behind me. I turn to see, and am instantly elated. Everything is right in the world again.

Seated about thirty feet away—at a table in the far corner with a girl I don't know—is Robin. My heart practically leaps into my mouth. Did she not see me sitting here? I stand and walk quickly to Robin's table. The girl sees me approaching and alerts Robin, who turns to look up.

"Hey!" I smile, as I arrive beside her. "I'm so glad to see you! I was sitting right back there with Orm!"

She turns to face me, but there's no smile on her face. Instead, her expression is one of annoyance.

"What do you want?" she says, in a tone that is flat and emotionless.

I'm caught completely flat-footed. I've never heard that voice or seen that expression on her. She raises her brows, as if impatient. I take a deep breath.

"I . . . well, I looked for you this morning."

She gives me a shrug. "So?"

"Robin?"

I hear the girl snicker.

"If you have something to say, say it," she says, in a matter-of-fact voice.

"Why are you talking like this? Did I do something wrong?"

"Like what?" she sneers.

My ears are ringing. I can barely believe this is Robin.

"Can we talk in private?" I ask, in a lowered tone. I search her face for any sign of affection but see nothing except coldness and contempt.

She pauses ever so slightly, then responds by shaking her head. "Nah."

"What do you *mean*, nah?"

"What does it *sound* like it means?"

My eyes are suddenly flooded with tears, and I have to quickly wipe them away. "Who's th-that?" I ask, pointing to the girl, who now has a smirk on her face.

"No one *you* know."

I can feel my lips trembling. The sudden coldness and distance, only one day removed from a declaration of undying love and steadfastness, has my

125

head spinning.

"I'm really busy, okay?" she says.

"Am I g-going to see you later?"

"Nah, I don't think so," she says, shaking her head, then turning away.

My brain is about to melt and I wish I were a million miles away. It's the fact that she sees what her cruel indifference is doing to me that really stings. Yesterday, she would have taken a bullet for me. Now it appears she'd just as soon be the one firing it.

I feel like a zombie as I retrieve my books from my lunch table and walk out of the cafeteria, wiping my eyes as I go. A boy coming in stops and stares as I rush past him. I don't stop walking until I'm at my locker, where I bury my head against it and sob. The tears come like a river. I replay Robin's cold apathy over and over in my head. Why? Has she stopped loving me? Did she ever love me?

I open my locker and stuff the books I'm carrying into it with all my might and then slam the door shut. The shoulder of my T-shirt that I've been using to wipe my tears now has a large wet stain on it. I head for the girls' restroom. When I enter, there are two girls in there I don't know, but *they* seem to know who *I* am. I don't care. I close myself into a stall, bunch my tee to my mouth, and sob uncontrollably. Nothing about the last five minutes of my life makes any sense at all. And the only person who could explain it to me is the person causing it.

I wish I was dead.

I don't know how I make it through the last two classes of the day, but one thing's for sure: I'm ready to escape. Wiping my nonstop tears along the way, I let Orm lead me out to his car. Once seated, I allow all my books to slide into the floorboard. He gets us out of the parking lot faster than I've ever seen him do it. After a few minutes of driving down the highway toward town, he looks over, then squeezes my shoulder.

"How're you now, Ash?"

I close my eyes and shake my head, trying hard not to dissolve into un-controllable sobbing again.

"I'm not good."

"I saw what happened in the cafeteria. That must have been hard."

"Is this normal, Orm? Is this just a relationship issue? Is this how the relationship game is played? Is everything going to be okay tomorrow?"

He turns into my driveway and parks.

"Whoa, hold on." He takes a deep breath before continuing. "No. That's not normally how the game of relationships is played. You don't go from *in love* one day to kicking your lover to the curb the very next day. There's something going on here. It's not good."

I choke back another sob. "You don't think she loves me anymore?"

"I didn't say *that.*"

"Well, what do you mean?"

"She could be reacting to something, but doing it in a destructive way. Didn't you tell me her father moved their family out of Texas because of a relationship with a girl?"

"Yeah."

"Well, maybe he's on the verge of doing it again, and she's doing whatever she can to convince him not to, even if she has to give you up."

I bunch up my tee at the shoulder and wipe my eyes.

"We were going to be college roommates."

"Well, guess what? Plans don't always work out. The best you can do is just try to land on your feet."

"Are you telling me to forget about Robin? To move on with my life without her?" I know Orm's trying to help, but my emotions are just too raw to hear it.

He exhales with a long sigh. "No, I'm not. Things are really crazy, so give her some space. Let the drama settle down."

I fight with myself to keep my composure. "She's *all* I want, don't you see? I would give up *college* for her!" For a few minutes, I try my best to calm myself, but then, I get angry all over again. "I hate her father," I finally mutter aloud.

"Yeah," Orm says, "maybe *she* hates him, too! Maybe she's trying to find a way to be with you."

For a couple of minutes, my mind races with that possibility. "If that's really true, it would help if she told me, you know?"

He grimaces and nods.

"Do you think she loves me?"

"I don't know. Do *you* think she does?"

"She loved me yesterday."

"How do you know?"

"Because she told me. Because she showed me. Trust me, I *know!*"

"Then why did you ask *me?*"

I turn and stare out the window. "Maybe I need to hear you say it."

There's a long pause. "She loves you, Ash."

"How do you know?" I shoot back, facing him.

"Because she loved you yesterday. You can't turn it on or off like a light switch. The only part of that equation you get to control is what you do about it. If she loved you yesterday, then she loves you today."

I wipe one more tear with my tee shirt as I soak up the comfort of his words. "You're the best, Orm," I say, as I exit his car.

Grams is in the living room seated on the couch when I come into the house, and she lights into me before I can say anything.

"May I speak to you?" she asks, gesturing to the couch beside her.

For a moment, I freeze. Then, I slowly put my books on an end table and take a seat in the recliner off to the side. She takes a deep breath, and I can see the tissue she has in her left hand. So she's been crying. I keep my head down.

"Robin's dad called me and explained what happened over there," she says, her voice carrying a tone I've only rarely heard. "He was furious, and I see why. I'm very disappointed that you behaved in that manner, especially in someone else's home."

Her words sting. Hard. I can count on one hand the number of times Grams has ever told me she's disappointed in me. It almost moves me to tears once again. When I look up, I can see she's waiting for me to respond. But, I'm not sure what Grams has been told. I'm not even sure Robin's father knows the complete story of what happened there. One thing's for sure—I'm not about to fill in anyone's blanks.

"I don't really want to talk about it."

"You were naked in bed with Robin!" Her voice falters. "I thought I raised you better than that! I thought I raised you to be a decent and honorable Christian girl!"

"You don't think I'm decent and honorable, Grams?"

"Not by being like that with another girl!" I haven't seen her worked up like this since she and my mom got into an argument about Harley being drunk in front of her nieces over ten years ago. "God only knows what that poor girl is thinking about you—and going through because of you!"

"Huh?"

"I'm talking about Robin! God only knows what you've put her through!"

"*I* put her through something? Is that what you think?"

"Were you in her bed on top of her without your clothes on?" Her eyes bore into mine.

Wow. "Grams, let's drop it, okay?"

"Yes, or no?" she says in a raised voice. "You should be ashamed of yourself!" She uses her tissue to blow her nose. "I've asked Reverend Barncastle to speak with you, young lady!"

"I won't do it!"

"You will if you know what's good for you!" she shoots back. "If anyone needs a good dose of Christian morality right now, it's you!"

I can't take it anymore. I *won't* take it. I'm about to tell Grams off when I notice the reflections of sunlight on the wall caused by a car pulling into the driveway. I rise to take a peek through the window.

"It's Mr. O'Leary and Robin," Grams says. "He says he wants you to hear something from him so that there's no mistake about it."

Now I'm panicked. "Grams! Why?"

"It's for your own good, Asher," she replies, getting up to open the front door. Before I can object, there's Robin in the front doorway, her father right behind. Her face is completely blank. There's no expression. I'm not sure I even know this Robin. She remains rooted to the spot until Grams beckons her inside and to the couch. I retreat from her as if she were a walking plague. Mr. O'Leary comes through the doorway searching for me, and having located me, fixes a cold stare on me. Once again, Grams gestures to the couch.

"No need to sit, Mrs. Norman," he says, his eyes remaining fixed on me. "What we have to say is short and to the point, and I'll go first, after which my daughter will have something to say." I steal a glance at Robin, but her gaze is fixed downward. "In light of what occurred at my family's vacation home while I was away, I asked Asher to not have any contact with my daughter. Just two days later, she chose to disregard that request, resulting in a certain photo being taken and circulated all over the Internet." Grams dabs at her eyes again. "What happened as a result has torn me and my family apart. We've always enjoyed a good name. Asher, you've taken that good name and stomped it into the ground." He stops and looks to Grams as if having made an irrefutable accusation. Then he turns back to me. "I hope you're satisfied," he hisses.

My blood is boiling, and I step forward to respond, but Grams suddenly shushes me.

"Young lady, hold your tongue!"

"I can't, Grams!"

"You'd better!"

"You'd be wise to listen to your grandmother," Mr. O'Leary growls. Grams arrives at my side and takes my arm in restraint, just as I'm about to light into him. He raises an eyebrow, then nods to Robin. "You have something to say?"

Like a robot, Robin looks up at me.

"I can't be your friend anymore," she recites. "Please don't call me. And leave me alone."

Her voice is hollow and lifeless. I want to say something so bad, but it's only for her ears, so I can't say it right now. Having spoken, she returns her gaze downward. Mr. O'Leary turns to leave.

"Good evening, Mrs. Norman," he says as he opens the front door. At this moment, Robin suddenly looks up to me, and our eyes meet. For the faintest fraction of a second, I'm sure she's going to say something, but she doesn't. Then, suddenly, they're both gone.

Grams looks at me and dabs her eyes with the tissue. "You heard them, Asher. You stay away from that girl!"

Just when I thought it couldn't get any worse, it just did. My stomach feels as if it has sunken through my body and out onto the floor. It takes a Herculean effort to unstick my feet from the floor, but when I do, I turn and race up the stairs to my room. This is as bad as last Friday evening. Actually, it's worse.

Like a zombie, I sit at my desk and stare at the wall in front of me. After another hour, I force myself to get up and get ready for bed, and then cocoon myself under my bed sheets. With my phone in hand, I browse my photos of Robin. The Robin, that is, who loved me just yesterday.

The next morning, I walk into school with Orm, who sees me to my locker and then promises to meet me at lunch. The stares aren't as bad as yesterday. But then I find out why. Crammed under the door to my locker is a folded sheet of paper. When I open my locker, it falls out onto the floor, where I pick it up and unfold it. It's a printed copy of an email that apparently went out to every parent regarding the viral photo. There's a quote from the student conduct policy about bullying and discrimination. Lastly, there's a warning about the disciplinary measures for violating the "student conduct policies." And it's pretty obvious which student conduct policy is being referred to.

I wad up the sheet and drop it. Enough of this bullshit. I grab my books and scurry off to find Robin. In light of her curious glance in my direction, as she was leaving yesterday, I have to know if she's still acting weird. I pull up next to a support column adjacent to her locker area and position myself behind it. By leaning out just a little, I can clearly see Robin's locker, while at the same time acting like I have a legitimate reason to be there.

In less than a minute, she walks up. The same girl is with her, and they're engaged in an animated conversation. Robin suddenly laughs, and the girl does the same. It's clear she's not distraught like me, and that hurts. Then I see Robin reach out and touch her shoulder. I'm about to step out to confront her when the two of them quickly turn and disappear down the B hallway.

At lunch, she once again sits in the corner with that girl. I can see that they're sharing laughter. It's something she did with me just a few days ago. Once Robin finishes her lunch, she gets up without saying a word, busses her tray, and leaves—again, with the same girl in tow. She makes no effort to look at me.

On the drive home, I ask Orm about the girl, and he nods. "Never seen her before. But everyone is posting about Robin's strange behavior, and that she's avoiding everyone. And oh, by the way, I did find out who took that photo. You were right: it was Jermy."

"To be honest, I don't even care anymore."

"I asked him why he did it, and he said he was just trying to have some fun. I told him if he wasn't my cousin I'd punch him out."

"Fun?" Now that pisses me off all over again. "So, it's funny that my life is basically a shit storm? What's he doing for fun today? Sitting on his back porch pulling the legs off grasshoppers?"

Orm nods his understanding. "I told him how it's affected you."

"Do me a favor, Orm. Don't ever mention that piece of shit's name to me again."

The following day sees a repeat dose of misery. At least the staring is almost nonexistent. When I get home, though, I find a letter on my desk, and I can see it's from the Winston Institute for the Arts. I'm not expecting anything from them, so I assume the worst. This must be rejection week. With trembling fingers, I open it and read:

Dear Asher Sullivan,

It is our pleasure to inform you that your application for enrollment at the Winston Institute for the Arts has been accepted by our admissions committee. Congratulations, and welcome to the Winston family!

Your admission entitles you to a full scholarship. As such, all expenses of your enrollment and attendance are fully covered. You can expect a formal admission packet to arrive by registered mail in the next two weeks. In it, you can specify your preferences for housing, schedule your course advisement, and sign up for healthcare coverage.

Once again, congratulations! We look forward to having you on our beautiful downtown Chicago campus next fall!

I have to read it twice to believe it. Then, I check the envelope to make sure it really was addressed to me. I'm suddenly elated, and my joy at being accepted at the college of my dreams goes a long way to diminish the sour turn of events between me and Robin. Under the assumption Robin got her acceptance letter as well, there's a renewal of hope for us to end up together as we wished. Whooping, I go downstairs and show it to Grams, who smiles and congratulates me, thus ending two days of awkward coexistence.

"Your mom would be proud," she manages to eke out.

I turn and walk away, going upstairs to my room. My thoughts immediately go back to Robin. I want to call her, but I can't. Instead, I call Orm to tell him the good news, which is strange because I always thought Robin would be the first one I would call in the unlikely event I was accepted to the Winston.

"I knew it!" he crows. "I *knew* you'd get in, Ash! I'm so glad for you!" But, my silence tells him there's more on my mind. "Oh, wait, does Robin know?"

"I don't know."

"Well, you can ask her at school tomorrow, right?"

"Orm, she and her dad came over yesterday after you dropped me at home. She told me we couldn't be friends and not to contact her."

He's momentarily speechless. "But . . . this changes everything, doesn't it? I mean, there's a light at the end of the tunnel. All y'all have to do is tough it out until you're both in Chicago!"

"It's that *y'all* part that I don't think applies anymore. And I don't even know if she's received her letter yet."

He's silent, which tells me he's making some kind of plan. "I'm sure she did, but tell you what," he says at last, "I'll have someone I know ask Robin if she got hers."

I give him the go-ahead, and the next day at school Orm hunts me down after second period. "She hasn't yet," he reports. "That's all I have."

By Monday morning, I've had enough of being told what I can and can't do. It's right after third period when I nail her coming out of the girls' restroom. The mystery girl is nowhere in sight.

"Hey!" She says nothing and tries to go around me. I step into her path. "Stop! Please!"

When she sees the determination in my eyes, she looks around then moves to the side. "I'm not supposed to be talking to you!" she whispers fiercely.

To be this close to the hollow shell of someone I loved so much just a week ago is eerie. But things need to be said.

"I just need a minute. Are we really done?"

She exhales and stares me in the eyes. "Next!"

"I'll take that as a yes. Did you get your acceptance letter to the Winston?"

I can see I caught her off guard. "So, *you're* the one who wants to know?" She doesn't wait for a response. "No, I didn't. It's not really time yet."

"Yes, it is."

"I think I know a little more about the Winston than you do!" When I don't respond, she says, "How would *you* know if it is?"

I look her straight in the eyes. "Because I received mine."

She lets out with a barely perceptible gasp. "What?"

"Last Thursday." I pull the letter out of my purse and hold it up to her. I see her eyes scanning it. When she's done, she's silent for a minute, like she's replaying it in her mind. "Maybe you'll get your letter today, Robin."

I look for any sign in her face that she's hopeful, and that our dream is still within reach, or that she even still wants that dream. She pulls her books in with one hand and uses the other to wipe her eye.

"Think so?" she says in a soft but hoarse voice. Her facade has crumbled. She's in pain, and that makes me want to comfort her.

"Yes. There's no way I got in, and you didn't." She's searching my eyes. "We can still make our dream come true, baby."

She tilts her head slightly and gives me a look that makes me think she could kiss me at any moment. Her fingers are in motion on the back of one of her books, and she fidgets slightly from side to side. I'm about to reach out to her when the coldness suddenly emerges once again.

"Why am I talking to *you*?" she says, brushing past me and off into the distance down the hallway. "Just leave me alone!" she calls out before disappearing into a classroom. My jaw is on the floor.

After two days, I receive word from Orm that Robin was not accepted. I'm crushed. Now I don't care about anything anymore.

"I don't know if I'm going to Chicago," I tell him, as we sit in his car in my driveway after school.

"Oh, you're going! If I have to drag you up there, you're going! You don't turn down a scholarship to the Winston."

"What use is it, Orm? I don't have *her*. She'll be left back here in Sagebrush all alone with her father."

"So?"

"Do you think I have it in me to leave her like that?"

"We all make our own beds."

"Do we? From where I stand, it looks like someone else made hers."

Monday morning, I'm determined to try again with Robin. I'm waiting by her locker when she arrives. Seeing me, she immediately turns and walks away. I walk up behind her.

"You don't get to run, Robin!" She tops and turns. "I didn't put my heart out on my sleeve for someone to cut me and laugh while I'm bleeding. I'd never do that to you, so you owe me an explanation."

"I don't owe you anything." Impatience is written across her face.

"I hear you didn't get in. I'm sorry."

For a split second, I can see a glimpse of the old Robin in her eyes. And there's the pain, once again. I want to take her into my arms and console her so bad it makes me ache. But then she changes. Just like that. A horrible and ugly anger wells up in her face.

"You just love rubbing that in, don't you!" she says in a sudden, loud voice, apparently with no regard to anyone overhearing. It's so loud I flinch. "Why can't you just . . . leave! Get out of my life! Go somewhere and die! Being your friend was the worst mistake I ever made! Don't you get it? I hate you!"

13

In fourth grade, my best friend was Roshanna Malone.

We were inseparable. But one day, we had a fight—the only one we ever had—and in anger, I cut her out of my life, refusing to even speak to her again. I'll never forget what happened. She spent the rest of the day crying, and was never the same again. Her suffering meant nothing to me. Her family moved away at the end of the school year. It was only then that I felt any guilt over what I had done. Even so, I never apologized or even spoke to her again. That's because in my childish ignorance, I never really understood what I had done to her.

But, I do now.

So, I guess I had this coming. That's life for you, always making you eventually eat your own dog food.

I'm in really bad shape. It's almost bedtime, my eyes are still crying, and my head is still spinning. With everything in me, I'm hoping Robin will call me to say she didn't mean any of it. But I know that's not gonna happen because I'm pretty sure she doesn't even have her phone back.

What really kills me is how she told me in such a vicious way that she hates me. Everything in me tells me you don't walk that back. I get that she's stressed by her father, but he wasn't there forcing her to say *that*.

Orm's advice on all this is simple. "Get a life. Find someone else. You don't need that kind of shit."

But, I can't do that. I don't *want* anyone else. I want *Robin*. I'm in love with *Robin*. Yeah. Even after what she said. I find myself fantasizing that she's desperately searching for a way to tell me that she didn't really mean it and that if I can just catch her away from school and her family, she'll let me know.

But she doesn't.

And my week turns into a blur of crushing depression. I've never been this low. Each morning finds me waking up to a crying jag and curled under my blanket in a fetal position, with no desire to get up and go to school.

Even Saturday is bleak and lifeless. This would normally have been a day that Robin and I went out and had fun. But it's two in the afternoon, and I'm still in bed. There is no energy in my body at all. At least I'm not crying every ten minutes. I pull the covers up over my neck to try to fall back asleep. Then, I hear a knock at my bedroom door. It's Grams.

"Sweetie? Are you in there?"

"Sure, Grams, hang on." What I really want to do is just stay in bed all day. But there's no sleeping late on Saturday by Grams' rules.

I struggle out of bed and into my jeans, fighting down the urge to cry while pulling on the first T-shirt my hands find in the closet. I don't bother with shoes. I have no appetite, even though I've barely eaten over the past few days.

My hair's a tangled mess, so I finger-comb it as I descend the staircase. I stop about halfway down and stoop to peer into the living room. There's a strange aroma in the air that I recognize as a man's cologne. I can see the legs of someone sitting on the couch, so I immediately turn to go back to my room. I'm in no mood for company. As I start back up, Grams calls out to me.

"Sweetie, come on down here. Reverend Barncastle is here."

It just got worse.

Again.

I stop, wipe my eyes, and take a deep breath. I would give anything to be on the other side of the planet. Even though I look like hell warmed over, I pull the neckline of my tee up in front and descend into the living room. Reverend Barncastle is smiling, seated on the near side of the couch closest to the stairs. Grams is sitting across from him in the recliner, and she, too, is smiling up at me.

Here we go. Reverend Barncastle's presence confirms that everyone thinks I'm in need of repair. And who else to "fix" me than the homophobe pastor of my church? Is this a taste of what Robin's going through? I remain rooted to the spot, looking first at Grams, then over to Reverend Barncastle.

"Hello, Asher," Reverend Barncastle says through a smile that resembles more that of a used car salesman than a preacher.

Every strand of hair on his head is perfectly in place. He's in a navy blue suit with trouser legs almost up to midcalf while seated. His patent leather dress shoes are perfectly polished. I see a Bible in his left hand. He gestures with his right hand for me to come into the living room.

"Please, sit with us. I won't be long."

Cautiously, I move toward the other recliner that's across from the vacant side of the couch and take a seat. I want to be as far away from him as possible. Once I'm seated, he adjusts his posture to face me.

"Do you know why I'm here?" he asks, still smiling.

I look at Grams, then back to him. "No, sir," I lie.

He nods as if expecting my answer. "Well, Asher, your grandmother asked me to come visit you, saying you've had a tough time with a friend of yours—a girl named Robin, I believe?"

I don't say anything. Seeing my silence, Grams speaks up. "Yes, Reverend, that's her name."

He nods rapidly while smiling to Grams. When he turns his attention back to me, his face is somber.

"Asher, I've known you and your family for many years. I just want to let you know God loves you, and God forgives sin."

I knew that was coming. Again, I don't say anything.

"Don't you have something to say to Reverend Barncastle?" Grams asks.

I turn to her and shake my head. Reverend Barncastle fidgets very slightly as if sensing that the power dynamic isn't playing out as he expected.

"That's okay, Asher. I tell you what. I'll just say a prayer, and then I'll be on my way. Do you mind?"

"No, sir." Anything to get him out of here.

He smiles, then bows his head and begins, holding his palm out toward me as if dispensing some kind of power in my direction. "Father, we pray for Asher and her family, that they might have peace in your divine love. We pray that she finds healing and that by your grace, she is forgiven of all sin. We pray that you will fill her soul with your love and promise of salvation, that she might be cleansed of impure thoughts and the desires of the flesh. Help her to—"

"What?!" I bark out. It's too much. The room falls instantly quiet. Reverend Barncastle freezes, his eyes as wide as saucers, his arm hanging in midair, and his mouth wide open. I hear Grams gasp.

"Pardon me?" he says, regaining his composure.

"Asher!" Grams follows, to which Reverend Barncastle stops her by directing his raised palm toward her.

"I'm not going to listen to you basically telling me I need to be healed and that I have impure thoughts, and whatever you said about sins of flesh!" I say, looking him straight in the eyes.

"Asher, all of us have impure thoughts that compel us toward—"

"What? Each other?"

"Well, er . . . umm, yes, that can happen. What I'm talking about, Asher, are impure thoughts that some people have that lead to . . . well, an unhealthy attraction between two people of the same sex."

I've reached my limit. I stand up and start for the stairs. Reverend Barncastle's eyes are about to bug out, and I hear Grams call my name. I stop and turn as I get to the landing.

"Don't worry, Reverend Barncastle. I only have *healthy* attractions to females." I can hear Grams gasp as I sprint back up the staircase. It's not long before I hear the front door open and then close, signaling that Reverend Barncastle has left the house. I may have been dead to the world ten minutes ago, but now I'm wide awake—and mad as hell.

After a fast shower, I half-dry my hair, get dressed, then rush out the door, saying nothing to Grams. On a hunch, I drive by Orm's house. He's home.

"Hey, Ash!" he says, opening his front door.

"Can you go for a drive with me?"

"Umm, sure!" I turn and quickly walk to my car with Orm in tow. "What's up?" I head back out onto the highway.

"Grams thinks I'm going to hell!"

"What? She told you that?"

"No. But she called Reverend Barncastle over this morning."

"Why?"

"I think it's obvious. I need to be fixed so that I'm not attracted to Robin."

He leans back and places a hand to his forehead. "Shit!"

"You know the best thing I've realized since I got my acceptance letter? It's that soon I'll be out of this redneck town and in a big city where people won't take a look at me and decide I'm a defect."

"I don't think you're a defect."

"That's because you're my best friend. But what if you knew a gay male? Would you distance yourself? Would you think *he* was a defect?"

He doesn't respond right away, and I can tell I've hit a nerve. "Umm . . . no," he says, finally, clearing his throat in the process.

"See? That hesitation is exactly the kind of attitude I want to get away from, where people pass judgment on others out of pure fear and ignorance."

"I'm learning, Ash, okay?" We ride in silence for a few more minutes before he speaks up. "Where are we going, by the way?"

He's peering out his side window. It's only then that I realize I've been mindlessly driving toward Robin's Lake. In fact, the cutoff for Robin's Lake Road is just up ahead. I move over to the shoulder of the highway as we approach it and point straight down its narrow lanes.

"See that little road way down there to the right?"

"Yeah?"

"That's Robin's Lake Road."

"No shit?" His expression lights up and he stares in the direction I'm pointing.

"See that house way over there?" I slow to a stop. He squints his eyes in the direction I'm pointing.

"Yeah, but just barely. That's what? A couple of miles off the road?"

"Sounds about right."

"So, this is where it all happened," he muses, turning back to me.

"Well, it's not much more than a far away place now."

I crane my neck to have a last peek. Seeing it again gives me mixed emotions. Still, it's all I can do to resist turning in. A fleeting fantasy image of me chancing upon Robin down by the lake invades my mind.

"Have you driven out here a lot?"

I have to work to focus myself on the here and now.

"This is actually my first time driving here. I always came here with Robin after school. The house you see is actually right up against the lake. Robin's Lake."

"Sounds romantic, I'll give you that."

"It is." I close my eyes, reliving every minute of the one time I was at the house, especially the magic of dancing in the moonlight with *her*. It makes me remember that I've lost the best thing I ever had, and I feel myself sinking again. He notices.

"Let's get out of here," he says, extending a hand to my shoulder.

We ride around for another hour or so, mostly in silence, until finally he suggests we go get dinner, which is fine by me since I'm finally hungry for the first time today. There's a Dairy Palace right on the edge of town, and we set up in a booth in the corner away from the foot traffic. We each order a burger and fries but combine the fries into a single pile, doused in ketchup.

"Orm," I say, gesturing to him with a fry, "do you remember what you told me way back when I asked you how it felt to be in love?"

"Mhmm. What about it?"

"You said you knew you were in love because you felt more alive than you ever had before."

He nods and settles back, taking a sip of his soda. "Yeah. And it's true."

"Well, *now* I see what you meant."

"You do?"

"Yeah," I sigh. "Robin made me feel so alive that I could only have been dead before I met her."

At this, Orm gives me a hesitant nod. "Yeah, that's how you know."

"And now that I've lost her, I *really* feel dead."

His reply is hesitant. "I know you're hurting."

"Robin's killed me, Orm. She literally has. It's not just that she broke up with me, it's how she did it."

"I know how bad a breakup can make you feel."

"No, I mean she's fucked my life. I've never felt this kind of pain. I don't know if I can get over this!"

"Everyone always does, though. Just takes time."

There's a moment of painful silence, where I have to fight off another urge to cry. We finish our meal with small talk. After dropping Orm off at his house, I head back to my miserable existence. But without warning, tears well up and spill down my cheeks once again.

I pull into the driveway and park, slumping myself forward with my head on the steering wheel. Between sobs, I get angry with myself all over again for all the unexpected crying. The memories of who we were and the moments we shared pass through my mind like a sad movie.

And I want it back so bad.

I want to feel the touch of her lips on mine and smell the fragrance of her perfume. I need her. I need to know she's mine like she was last week. Without her, I am utterly and completely lost. How can she toss me aside like she did, as if I meant nothing to her? Our "I love you" conversation plays out in my head for the millionth time. Was she lying the whole time?

The next morning I'm upstairs in my bedroom walking around like a zombie and trying to figure out what homework is due when I realize that I still don't have my camera. I unlock my phone and am about to call Orm when a Facebook notification pops up. It's Robin. Looks like she's got her phone back. And she's posted something.

With my heart suddenly pounding, I open it. It's a share of an online article about "letting go." I feel a huge lump in my throat, and now I wish I hadn't looked. I toy with the idea of calling her to ask about my camera, but then decide I just can't take the risk of letting her putting another knife in.

Orm is more than willing to help me out. "Give me an hour and I'll have that camera back in your hands." I spend the hour hoping that Robin will call me or text me. Instead, I see a couple of her tweets. One of them is a retweet of an advertisement for a musical festival in Chicago. That's curious. Then, another tweet that's an old photo of her and Dill on Valentine's Day. That one really gets to me.

I hear the doorbell ring, and I run to answer it. It's Orm, but there's no camera in his arms.

"It's not at her house," he shrugs. "Robin says it's probably at the vacation house, and they're not going back there anytime soon."

"What? Did you tell her I *need* my camera?"

"Well, I figure she knows that already. Doesn't she?"

"Did you speak to her father?"

"Umm, no. But he was standing behind her."

"And *he* didn't say anything about getting it back?"

"Nope."

"And Robin didn't offer to go get it?"

He sighs and shakes his head. "I hate to say it, but it looked like she didn't really give a shit."

I'm sinking fast. How can you can love someone and the very next day treat them like they're nothing? It takes me a full four hours to do a couple of assignments that would usually take me only an hour or so. I tell myself there are only a few weeks of school left and then I'm out of here.

By Monday morning, I've got a plan to get my camera back. I know that to do this, I'm risking another dose of cruel rejection, but I've gotta have my camera. I mentally summon the courage and make a beeline to her locker— just in time to catch her.

"I want my camera."

She turns quickly, and our eyes meet. The expression on her face is one of surprise, not scorn, and it instantly takes the edge off my mood. For a long few seconds, our eyes remain locked. "Please," I add, in a much calmer tone of voice.

Without saying a thing, she takes off her backpack, unzips it, pulls out my camera, and carefully hands it to me. As I take the camera, our fingers touch. I look up at her face. She has a sad, forlorn expression, almost like she's trying to stare off into outer space. I try to make our finger contact last as long as possible, but then withdraw before I cross some kind of line.

"Thank you," I say, in my softest voice.

She nods and stoops to zip up her backpack.

"Hey," I say, as she stands back up. "Let's talk."

She says nothing but stands unmoved with our eyes locked. There's no one close by. I can tell she's intentionally letting me see her unguarded. After a few more moments of silence, she parts her lips and whispers, "I can't."

"*Why?*" I plead. "Why can't you just talk? After all we went through . . . the promises, the plans . . . please! Baby, I still love you!"

I hear her sniffle. Then she looks around, shoulders her backpack, and practically runs away from me, leaving me even emptier than ever. After third period, I risk being the butt of another social media explosion by intentionally walking past our secret meeting place.

There's no crowd waiting for me. But neither is Robin. My next opportunity is lunch. I'm practically aching with anticipation as I walk into the cafeteria. But then I'm crushed all over again when I see Robin at the same table in the corner, sitting with the same girl—laughing and carrying on as if I don't even exist. It wasn't so long ago that it was *me* she laughed with during lunch. I just can't imagine sitting with some girl in the same room Robin is in and having a good time.

Orm gently cajoles me back to our usual table, and although I get a few stares, it seems I've been accepted back into the group. He keeps me occupied in conversation, and that helps. One thing I can't help but notice is that no one makes a single mention of Robin. Later, on the way home from school, I tell Orm about my strange encounter with her at her locker.

"Maybe it was because you surprised her, and she didn't have time to armor up."

"Maybe. But maybe I somehow broke through, even if it was just for a few seconds."

"Did she have her disciple with her?"

"No, not this time. But who *is* that girl? And how does she know her?" For a second, a random mental visual of the two of them kissing flashes through my mind, causing me to shudder. Orm sees it.

"What, you think that's her new girlfriend?"

"Honestly, I've considered it."

"Well, I could probably think of her name if you gave me enough time. She's a freshman."

I'm just sitting down with Grams for dinner when my phone beeps. It's an Instagram chat message from a girl I casually know at school, Riley Foster, who's in my English class. I open the app and read the message.

Hey if you need to talk you can call me

Well, I guess the misery grapevine is working. I start to tap out a polite no thanks, but on second thought decide to just ignore it.

Later that night, a powerful wave of jealousy washes over me. It doesn't make sense, but I can't get it out of my head that she and this girl might be doing all the things the two of us were doing just a few weeks ago. I'm wondering if she's over at Robin's house, and the idea of it is making me crazy.

Really crazy. In fact, I can't get it out of my head.

I decide to drive by just one time and see for myself, and if it's not true, I can let go of it. Under the ruse of going to gas up my car, I cruise through the kitchen right past Grams and out the door. Once on the road, I head straight toward Robin's house. It's only a few minutes until I'm on her street.

I drive at normal speed past the house. There's no car in the driveway, which is a big relief. But then I wonder if Robin's close by somewhere, maybe even walking on her street. I could talk to her without that girl being with her. I make the block at slow speed, craning my neck both left and right. Nothing.

As I pass her house, I slow almost to a stop. The lights are on in several rooms, so I assume they're home. My eyes go to a specific second story window that's dark, and I feel a lump in my throat. It takes all my willpower to make it home without crying.

The very next evening, I give in to the same urge, telling myself that I just wasn't there at the right time last night. But this time, my mission changes. Instead of just making a drive-by check for that girl's car, or looking for Robin out and about in the neighborhood, I watch her house for a while to see if anyone arrives. I'm parked three houses down next to the curb where there's no risk of being seen by Robin or her family. And yes, I feel creepy doing this. It's not something I would ever have done in the past. After an hour of seen nothing, I give up and go home.

It's the third evening in a row, and I fight the compulsion—but find myself back at the same spot. This time, there's a car parked in front that I don't recognize, which makes my stomach sink. All I can think about is Robin and that other girl up in her dark bedroom. As I'm craning up to the right to see her window, a man knocks on my car window, scaring the bejeezus out of me. The guy looks to be about forty, in jeans and a tank top, and has a baseball cap on. He leans over and squints in through the window at me.

"You need some help, young lady?"

I let out with a nervous laugh. "No, thanks!" I give him a shrug. "I'm just waiting for someone!"

He stares at me for a few seconds, looks in the direction I was, then returns his gaze to me. He gives me a nod, touches the bill on his cap, and turns to walk away. It's only then that I realize how stupid my explanation was. Thank God he didn't pursue the issue by asking questions. Just to make sure I avoid him, I start the car and move it down a couple of houses, stopping only one residence away from Robin's. I sit in the darkness and bite my lip, waiting to see who will come out and get in that car.

After an hour, my nerves are shot, and I'm tired, so I decide to leave. Just as I start up my car, I'm flooded with flashing red and blue lights from behind. Worse than that, I see Mr. O'Leary, clad only in boxers and an open red flannel shirt, making his way across his front yard straight for me.

And he's carrying a pistol.

14

I let out a tirade of profanity under my breath, all of it aimed at Mr. O'Leary.

There's no doubt in my mind he's behind the police showing up. This is just about the worst, most embarrassing thing I can imagine, and I guess I should have known I'd have it coming.

Mr. O'Leary, his face contorted in rage, comes up to the curb about twenty feet in front of me as the officer approaches me on the driver's side. He shines a flashlight right in my face, causing me to squint, then motions for me to roll down the window.

"You need any help?" the officer asks.

"No, sir." My voice is thick and gravelly, and I have to clear my throat. "Th-that man has a gun!"

"Hell, no, she doesn't need help!" Mr. O'Leary bellows at the officer. "She's stalking my daughter!" His face is puffy and red, and I can faintly hear Mrs. O'Leary calling for him to come back away from the officers. Still, he staggers another couple of steps forward. It's only then that I notice Robin standing next to her mom in the front yard of their home. Now I want to shrink completely out of sight.

The officer turns to Mr. O'Leary and motions for him to back up and stay quiet, which only infuriates him even more. "You better do something, or I *will!*" he froths.

The officer returns his attention to me, asking for my license. I dig for it and hand it over with trembling hands. He returns to his squad car, leaving me completely vulnerable to Mr. O'Leary. Fortunately, Mrs. O'Leary has caught up to him and seems to have him occupied.

If I didn't know better, I'd say he's drunk off his ass. After about five minutes, the officer returns to my window and hands my license back to me.

"Do you realize that by coming out here night after night, you worry these people?"

"No, sir."

"Why are you doing it?"

At this, Robin's father finds new rage and comes charging up to the car. "I already *told* you, she's stalking my daughter!" he thunders.

Suddenly his face contorts, and with the sound of a wounded animal, he doubles over with a sickeningly long and hacking cough.

"She *won't* leave her alone, even at school!" he manages to wheeze out, his voice sounding like someone has his throat in a vise grip. He pulls himself back up with difficulty. "And now, she's watching us at night!"

His eyes are bugging out, and he gestures with his forefinger toward me as he faces the officer. The officer is opening his mouth to respond when Mr. O'Leary lets out another coughing gag, clutches his chest, and doubles over once more. Mrs. O'Leary catches up to him and places a hand on his back as he wretches. With some insistence, she gets him backed away from my car.

My eyes dart over to Robin. She's standing still with her hands over her mouth, observing the scene and making no effort to attend to her father. I wonder if she's seen this behavior before.

"Miss Sullivan," the officer says, after returning from Mr. O'Leary, who has now been seated on the ground and is alternately wiping his forehead of sweat and waving people away from him. "I don't know what's going on between you and this family, but I'm giving you a formal warning that if you show up here again, I'll charge you with stalking. Do you understand?"

"Y-yes, sir."

"You realize that if you were just a year younger, I'd have to call your parents?"

"Y-yes, sir."

"Okay, then. Clear out and be on your way."

"Yes, sir." I feel like I could wet my pants any second.

As I pull out I notice at least a dozen people are out in their yards, some in pajamas and bathrobes, and all watching the spectacle I caused. I hear Mr. O'Leary scream out something about my grandmother. Everyone stares as I drive by, and I want to melt into the floorboard. Somehow, I manage to tap out a *help!* text message to Orm as I make the turn off Robin's street. Grams is waiting for me when I get home.

"Asher Kendall!" she announces as I enter through the side door into the kitchen. "Get in here, now!" She's sitting in the recliner, the end table lamp the only light on in the room. It's obvious she has been awakened after having gone to bed for the evening. I take a seat on the couch across from her.

"I know I messed up, Grams," I say before she can launch into me. After a second, her expression softens.

"What were you doing, child?"

I take a deep breath. "Looking for Robin." I'm not going to deny it.

"But why? You heard her father. You heard *her!*"

I lean forward, trying hard to still my shaking hands.

"Grams," I say, my voice breaking, "I'm in love with Robin. I don't know any other way to say it. I'm in love with her, I lost her . . . and I'm kinda having a hard time with that."

Grams tilts her head as a look of puzzlement spreads over her face. And after a few seconds, she sucks in a deep breath.

"Lord, child, how is it you're in love with a *girl?*"

"I just am, Grams." I've never seen this expression on her face. She simply stares at me like I'm an alien from another planet.

"I don't understand it," she says. "Is that a fad, now?"

It hits me how childlike her question is. She really doesn't get it. But at the same time, I know she's trying.

"Grams, this isn't a fad."

"Then, why?"

"Gee, Grams, I don't know! Why did you fall in love with Gramps?"

She stares at me as if I'm speaking a foreign language.

"Gramps was a *man*. Girls are supposed to fall in love with *men.*"

"Are they?"

"Well, yes," she says.

"Then why did I fall in love with a girl? Did I just not get that memo?"

That response stumps her for a second. But then she comes right back.

"Child, a woman can't love a woman. It just doesn't work."

Wow. Here she is in her seventies and she can't see past a sex act. Was I that clueless a year ago?

"Yes, Grams, it does," I reply, leaning forward.

She clears her throat, which she always does before explaining something sexual in nature to me.

"Child, a woman can't have sex with a woman. Do you get what I mean?"

"Grams," I reply, speaking in the same intonation she just gave me, "yes, they can. Believe me when I tell you this. They most certainly can, and they do."

"Two women have the same plumbing! It won't fit. It's not like a man!"

"It doesn't have to be like a man." This is a curious role reversal. Here I am giving Grams a sex education talk instead of the other way around. "It doesn't matter what plumbing you have, Grams. All that matters is that you're in love and want to express that love."

"Oh, dear," she sighs, reaching with trembling fingers to her chin.

Right that instant, there's a loud knock on the front door. I walk over to answer it, fully expecting to see Orm. Instead, I find a hulking and wheezing Mr. O'Leary who can barely stand. He's wearing the same scrubby clothes he was when I left him just minutes ago. The odor of beer assaults my face. He pushes past me, stumbles into the living room, and bumps the end table at the end of the sofa. The lamp on it crashes to the floor. He immediately confronts Grams.

"You!" he roars into her face, spit flying, and causing her to recoil with a frightened shudder. "*You* had better control your daughter, Mrs. Norman," he growls, tottering over her and shoving a finger into her face, "or I promise you, the police *will!*"

Grams' face reveals stark terror and her eyes well up with tears. It's too much. Nobody treats my Grams like that. Gritting my teeth, I bull rush him, shoving him hard from the side. He didn't see it coming, and with a yelp, he lands hard on the floor. My anger now finds a release. With all my might, I deliver a kick to his exposed abdomen. He lets out a loud "oomph!" and rolls over on his back, his hands clutched to his stomach. Grams springs from the recliner and backs away from where he's sprawled.

"How *dare* you come into my grandmother's house and attack her like that!" He tries to back away from me, his eyes wide. "Get your ass up!" He rolls to his stomach to try to stand, but succeeds only in toppling back down. Finally, he's against the wall in a sitting position. I move in closer. "I said, *get your chicken-shit ass up off the floor!*" Grunting and struggling, he finally pulls himself up, letting out a long hacking cough in the process.

"I'm warning you—"

"No!" I shout. I put my finger in his face. "You sick son of a bitch!" He inhales as if to speak, but I cut him off. "Shut up!" He lets out a breath of foul air and I see his eyes dart over to the open front door. "Get the hell out of here! *Now!*"

Like a simpering dog, he backs up, sidles toward the door, then leaves, but not before yelling, "Stay away from her!" He manages to stumble into the hedges by the door, uttering profanity as he extricates himself. Once he's in his car, I close the door, then walk over to Grams and give her a long hug.

"Lord have mercy, that man sure scared me!"

"Are you okay?"

"Yes, I-I think I'm okay. Thanks to you, it seems."

"I've needed to speak my mind to him in the worst possible way!"

"I'm glad you did," she sighs.

A voice from behind us calls out. "Are you two all right?" It's Orm, who has let himself in. "Who was that?"

"That was Robin's father," I reply.

"Whoa!" He takes a look out the front door, then helps me get Grams settled back into her recliner. I give him a quick recap of what just happened as he helps clean up the mess. Then, I explain my police encounter to both. Orm gives me a *don't do that again look*. Yet, both he and Grams commend me on how I took charge. It's nearly midnight when I urge him home, assuring him my Grams and I are okay.

Early the next morning, I'm buoyed by my newly-found confidence and have energy to burn. With nothing else to do, I decide to finally finish my photography assignment. It's a still life assignment, so I use the flower garden out front that Grams has put so much time into.

I actually feel good taking care of myself like this. This is my groove. Just me and my camera. How did I somehow let "me" get away from me? Two hours and nearly a hundred photos later, I head back inside.

"I see you're taking pictures again," Grams says, as she unloads the dishwasher.

I give her a smile. "Yep! Here, Grams, let me do that!" I get everything unloaded in a couple of minutes, then give her a hug and kiss. This is my best day since Robin turned on me.

"It's good to see you happy like this, sweetie!"

I scamper upstairs to work on the photo processing, but before I can start, social media notices start popping up on my phone. There's an Instagram post from Robin, barely an hour old. It's a gorgeous panoramic view from the top of the Willis Tower, the 110-story skyscraper that dominates the downtown Chicago skyline. I position my finger over the "like" icon, hesitate, then move off it.

After that momentary hiccup, I pull myself up to my desk and get back to work on my photos, hoping I can keep Robin out of my mind. But then, I find that the very first file in my camera is a mystery photo of her—and I'm stupefied. I remove my hand from the mouse and sit back, breathing heavily.

Oh my God. It's perfectly composed. Her face and shoulders are centered, and she is looking straight into the lens with her body turned ever so slightly to her right. The expression on her face, while not a smile, is very expressive, conveying a hint of sadness. I lean forward and zoom in on the photo, making her face fill the frame, and for several minutes, study every feature and every curve.

Finally, I bring up the time and date stamp. I see right away that the photo was taken the evening before she returned the camera to me, meaning it was in her house after all when Orm went over. Is that why she lied about it? So that she'd have time to have this photo taken?

I focus on her eyes. "What are you saying, baby?" I whisper. My face is drawn closer until finally my lips are touching the image of hers. I finally close the photo and search the memory card for more Robin images. There are none. Is she trying to send me some kind of message?

The next morning sees a continuous barrage of rain. With only a small, foldable umbrella, Orm and I find ourselves splashing over rain puddles in the parking lot at full gallop until we make it into the school building. I pop into the girls' restroom to see what can be done with my dripping wet hair. After spending a minute or so combing it out in front of the mirror, I turn to leave, but just as I do, I see Robin at the door, not five feet in front of me. She turns quickly and walks out. It takes a moment to realize, but she was obviously watching me comb out my hair. I almost take out after her, but incredibly, I'm able to fight the urge. I only have to last another four weeks before I'll be done with landmines like this.

Riley Foster stops me in the hallway right after lunch. "Hi, Asher." She smiles, coming to a stop just in front of me. "Hey, how're you doing?"

It's a nice gesture. "Okay," I reply, to which she smiles. Her eyes are brown, almost the exact shade of her hair, which is in a bun that rides high and just to the side. I think she's on the girls' softball team.

"Nice!" she smiles. "I was just wondering if maybe you want to come over and chill tonight?"

The invitation is so unexpected I have to process it mentally before its translation becomes apparent. She's hitting on me. I'm at a total loss of words. But then, I pull myself together and return her smile. "Sure. Send me the address."

"Okay, girl!" she says, giving me a light-hearted smile and backing away before turning and walking away. After dinner, I drive to her house. She seems ecstatic to have me over. Once we're in her room, she produces a bottle of Jack Daniels whiskey.

"You want some?"

"Holy cow, Riley!" I grin. We share a couple of drinks, and being loosened up a bit, the entire Robin story comes out. She then confesses that she's gay, as are a couple of other girls she knows.

"We're a tight group, us gay girls," she explains. "But I would never have thought *you* were, or especially Robin!"

We share a laugh over that "gaydar" misfire and keep drinking. It's after dodging three kisses that she lands the fourth, and I'll admit it's not bad. On the way home, I recognize that I feel guilty for having kissed Riley. But then, I end up kissing her again the very next weekend.

The last few weeks of the school year seem to fly by. I rarely see Robin, and it's easier to push thoughts of her from my mind. Toward the end of May, I receive my notice of graduation rehearsal. This is it. There's hardly any time left. I have to face it: the reality of graduation confirms the finality of the "Robin" phase in my life. I'm actually doing a pretty good job of accepting it.

Saturday morning is graduation rehearsal, and I'm feeling happy. But then, I see Robin and feel a familiar lump in my throat. In the rehearsal, as we're walking two-by-two up the aisle to our assigned seating are, I do my best to avoid staring at her, but she happens to end up walking up the aisle only a few feet ahead of me. I try to avert my eyes, but it's just no use. Right as she turns into her seating area, she turns her head and makes direct eye contact with me.

Her expression is flat and expressionless—as if she's just the shell of a person going through the motions of life. She's a far cry from the confident singer I saw surrounded by her fans on an evening just three months ago.

Soon enough, we're all given our graduation robes and mortarboards and then dismissed. As we're walking out into the parking lot, Orm steals up behind me and places his mortarboard on my head, laughing out loud while snapping a quick photo. I grab his phone away and look at the pic. My expression is too funny, and we both crack up. I'm still laughing when I'm startled by Robin suddenly brushing past me. I stop dead in my tracks, causing Orm to jump to the side to keep from bowling me over. With wide eyes, I stare as she climbs into her car and starts it up. She makes no further effort to look at me.

Unbelievably, she's still potent: without even trying, she's managed to deliver a zinger straight to my heart. But graduation is next week. Once school is out, I'm not sure I'll ever even see her again. And while that realization would have broken me just a month ago, I take it pretty well in stride, now. I'm not bullet-proof, but I'm trying.

Orm says I've learned a lot about love. One thing I find tragic is how some love affairs end. Take mine, for example. You can be entirely in love, thinking you are loved, only to find out that the person you love suddenly doesn't love you back. And there's nothing you can do about it. It's not like you can make someone love you. You can't. When you get rejected, you just have to find a way to make it to the next day, then the next. There have been a lot of those "next days" for me, and I wonder if I'll have to be in Chicago before I get her completely out of my mind.

"What are you doing later?" I ask Orm as he drives us from the school parking lot.

He gives me a smile. "Hey, you wanna come over and look at the full moon on my telescope?"

Just the medicine I need. "Yeah!"

Orm, geek that he is, has one of those telescopes that tracks whatever you point it at and displays it on a tablet. It's pretty cool. We spent an entire evening in July last summer watching Saturn cross the night sky.

He gives me a thumbs up after bringing the car to a stop in my driveway.

"You know, we could go down to Dalhart until it's time to watch the moon. We've got plenty of time."

"Oh my God, Orm, you're the best! But, I need to study for finals."

"No problem!"

I'm almost out of his car when a "what the hell" notion hits me. I lean back in.

"You know what, Orm? I'm gonna go anyway. Can you give me a little time to cram first?"

"Sure," he laughs, "but don't forget you've already got your Winston scholarship!"

"I'll text you!" I call out as he backs from my driveway.

I head upstairs to resume studying for finals that begin on Monday. After a two-hour cram session on physics, a Robin tweet pops up on my phone. I can't help myself. I open it to find a photo of her and Dill. Underneath is the hashtag #*soulmate*.

That crashes my study session big time. I close my books, breeze through the kitchen, and find a bag of chips in the pantry. I grab it and stuff a handful of them into my mouth before texting Orm to come get me.

"You hungry?" he says as I climb into his car with the bag of chips.

"Not really. I'm just bored." I don't want Orm to know I'm still vulnerable to Robin's tweets and am using him to escape.

The sun casts a beautiful golden hue onto an otherwise dull expanse of corn and wheat fields as we head south. We spend the time choosing songs to play and then singing along—one of our favorite fun activities we invented several years ago. We finish up with a rousing rendition of "Thunder" as we pull into the mall parking lot. I'm feeling much better now, thanks to Orm.

"After you, ma'am!" he proclaims, gesturing with a sweeping bow after getting out and waiting for me to come around the car.

"Thank you, sir!" I reply, laughing and trying my best to kick him in the butt as he straightens up and moves just out of range. I catch up and grab his hand, and we laugh all the way to the entrance.

The mall here contains about thirty stores, anchored on one end by an impressive sporting goods store called Big Bucks—the "bucks" referring, of course, to male deer, not dollars. We cruise down the center of the mall's covered area, every now and then stopping to go into a store. After window-shopping and exploring for a couple of hours, we happen to walk up on the women's lingerie store. With no explanation to Orm, I come to a full stop. I can't help but remember the last time I was here, and I feel my throat tighten a bit. I have Orm wait outside.

Near the back of the store, I turn a corner and am dumbstruck to find Robin and Dill together, only twenty feet away. Neither of them sees me. She's smiling and looking over a risqué camisole while he's holding about a half dozen more. When he says something to her, she laughs and looks up into his eyes. I think I'm going to vomit.

I turn and literally run out of the store.

"Let's get out of here," I say to a puzzled Orm as I breeze past him.

"Are you okay?"

"No."

He sprints after me and positions himself in front of me once I've slowed to a fast walk. He's walking backward as I step forward.

"What can I do?"

"Take me home. Please."

I can tell he wants to talk about it, and usually I would, but I'm completely devastated and in no mood for conversation at the moment—mainly because I don't want to cry again. He respects that and is silent the entire forty-five minutes it takes to get back to Sagebrush. But after pulling into my driveway, he turns a worried face to me.

"What's up, Ash?"

It's all I can do to keep my composure as I tell him what happened in the lingerie store.

"Holy shit! What are the odds?"

"I can't seem to get away from her!" I wipe a tear. "She seems to be in my face all the time!" More tears begin to well up. "I just can't wait to get out of this shithole town!"

We sit silently in the car for a long time before he speaks.

"I'm so sorry, Ash. I wish I knew how to make it better for you."

That's Orm for you. I do my best to give him a smile—which he immediately returns.

"We have a date this evening. Full moon. Remember?"

"I'll be there," I sniffle, getting out of his car. "Promise."

Consumed by sadness, I resume my study. After a couple of hours, I get an alert on my phone. It's a Robin post on Facebook. Is there no end to this torture? Against my better judgment, I open it. It's a photo of the full moon that accompanies a newspaper article about tonight's supermoon. In the comment area is the hashtag #loveofmylife.

I would almost give my camera to have not seen that. Does she always have to twist the knife? I tell myself to unfollow her, but I just can't make myself do it.

At Orm's that evening, I find myself strangely attracted to the image of the full moon. And I know why. With all my concentration, I try to push her out of my mind. Hearing Orm describe the astronomy behind the appearance of the moon helps distract me a bit. But just when I think I've managed to work my way through the day's landmines, I find myself off to the side on his patio, staring up into space.

My mind becomes an unbroken filly and prances back to that evening at Robin's Lake where I danced in the moonlight with her. Once again, I'm captured by what should be warm memories of the most wonderful experience of my life—but in reality are nothing more than reminders of the endless torture of not having her.

We had promised to dance in the moonlight with only each other from that point on. Yet, here we are at a full moon, and we're further apart than before we even met. I can feel myself sinking into grief once again. When I notice Orm coming toward me, I try to use my sleeve to catch a tear without him seeing, but he does.

"This full moon means something to you, doesn't it?"

I bury my head in his chest and softly sob. He wraps his arms around me and pulls me in close.

"Yes," I sniff, finally, wiping my tears on his shirt before pulling myself back. "And it's so hard to get it out of my mind."

"It might sound silly, but you *will* get past her."

"You know, I think tonight is going to be the last time I cry for her. Enough is enough."

"Now *that's* my strong Ash!" He give me a fist bump.

It appears my new resolve pays off as the week of final exams hurries past me with hardly a thought of her. Graduation night is the last speed bump, but then she doesn't even show up for her own graduation. As soon as I get home, I unfollow her from all of my social media apps. The finality of Robin is actually a relief.

The first week of summer vacation seems a bit unreal as it settles on me that there is no more high school. And as the first few days pass, I get more and more used to being on the verge of a grand adventure. My freshman admission advisor, a woman from East London, South Africa, is an able mentor who helps me tidy up my admission paperwork and finalize my fall semester course schedule with hardly a fuss.

Riley Foster invites me over again. And again, we sneak drinks of whiskey. But this time, our conversation is a bit more personal. I can tell she's trying to take the intimacy level up. I end up kissing her four or five times before leaving. I feel no guilt this time.

The fourth week in June is Freshman Camp at the Winston. I can't believe how good it feels to be on campus. And it turns out to be even more fun than I thought it would be. I meet a few people that I actually look forward to building friendships with once I'm back at the end of the summer.

On the last day, I exchange phone numbers with a cute girl named Amsra, who has won her scholarship all the way from India, and with whom I shared a cozy walk down Michigan Avenue the evening before. She's willowy and thin, with coal-black hair. And she speaks with a delightful British accent that I can't seem to get enough of.

Emotionally buoyed, and inoculated against Robin, I wish I didn't have to return to Sagebrush and could instead just remain on campus until classes begin. Once back home, though, I savor my improved sense of self-confidence. I'm actually looking forward to the end of summer when I'll leave Sagebrush for good.

I introduce Orm to Amsra over the phone. He loves her right away, which makes me feel good. Every time he hears her British accent, he smiles. Grams is a bit harder of a sell, but she says nothing negative. She knows I see Amsra in a different light than merely a female friend, but at the end of the day, she's happy for me.

Out of the blue, Orm announces that we're going to give a big Fourth of July party at his place for all the people heading off to college. His folks have a large recreation room out back that used to be a barn, so it's the perfect venue. A couple of days later, he shows me a guest list, and the first thing I notice is that Robin's name isn't on it.

"No Robin?" I ask him.

"I thought it was best to not invite her."

"You're right, probably best." I study his face for a few seconds as he peers into my eyes. "You know, I feel like I've turned a corner, this time for real."

"I know. I can see it. You were in bad shape there for awhile."

"Yep, but I'm done with that now!" He gives me a smile and a side hug.

I wake up on July fourth in an excellent mood, looking forward to the party. My confidence is at its highest point since before I met Robin. Together, Orm and I spend the late afternoon acquiring and then icing down a decent supply of beer. The reality is that now that we're high school graduates, folks around here don't say anything about us drinking, even though technically it's illegal until we're twenty-one.

"Orm, let's never lose touch." We're off to the side, watching as the first of the party guests start arriving.

He raises his beer to mine, and we toast the sentiment. "Never!"

"Then let the party begin!" I laugh, after which I chug the remainder of my beer and crush the can.

About an hour later, as I'm mixing with the party crowd of about fifty, I feel a warm hand on my right arm and turn to see Riley Foster.

"Hey!" she says, giving me a toothy smile.

I'm actually glad to see her. We wander outside and off to the side where we can talk without being overwhelmed by the loud music coming from the sound system. After another two beers, we're getting cozy. She suggests we walk further, and I follow her. Once we're in a secluded spot, I turn her around and kiss her. This time I have no hesitation. She's a great kisser, and I definitely am getting aroused.

"You're good," she whispers, as we break.

"You're not so bad yourself!" I reply. We share a laugh before diving in again.

Right about the time we come up for air the second time, I feel a buzzing on my butt. It's my phone. Without even thinking, I pull the phone out of my rear jeans pocket and answer it.

"Hi, Grams!" I'm sure she's calling to tell me she's going to bed.

"Hey," a soft voice replies. "Do you have a few minutes? I really need to talk."

15

The sound of Robin's voice gives me a head rush.

I didn't think it would—if I ever heard it again, that is—but it does. A million thoughts flash through my mind. I'm sure Riley sees that I've been knocked off dead center. I nod to let her know that I need to take the call, then walk a short distance away.

"What do you want?" I ask, in a lowered voice.

There's a slight pause before she speaks. "I guess you must hate me." Her tone of voice is contrite, which heads off my urge to unload on her.

"Hate you?"

"Yeah. I don't really blame you, either."

For a second or two, I toy with just hanging up. I honestly can't think of a response I'd care to give.

"I'm at a party."

"Okay." Her voice is weak. I can hear traffic in the background.

"Where are you?"

"I-I went for a walk." Her voice is barely a whisper.

"Well . . ." I'm at a dead end. My brain freezes up. I hear her take a deep breath and sigh.

"Okay. Sorry to bother you." I can barely hear her.

Without replying, I end the call and put the phone back in my jeans pocket.

"Everything okay?" Riley calls out. I walk back to her and take her hand.

"Yeah. It's all good." I force a smile, but she sees through it.

She squirms a bit, then looks me in the eyes. "Hey, if you like need some space—"

"No," I interject, "seriously, I'm okay. I'm just startled, that's all."

"That was Robin, wasn't it?"

I let out my breath. "Does it show?"

"It always does," she replies. "You'll learn that soon enough."

"It's just that I haven't heard from her in several months, so she caught me by surprise."

She studies my face for a minute, then withdraws her hand.

"I think I'm gonna go back in. You look like you need to figure out a thing or two." When I start to protest, she smiles and shushes me with a finger to my lips. "It's okay, Asher. I'm not offended."

I watch as she walks away. Just then, Orm finds me.

"You okay?" Then he stops in his tracks. He can tell. He can always tell.

"Oh God, Orm, I'm in trouble."

He raises an eyebrow. "It's Robin. She called you."

"Yeah," I nod. I have to force myself to swallow. "She wouldn't really say anything. We only talked for a minute or two."

He gives me the once-over. "Yep, you're in trouble, all right. C'mon, let's get you back to the party and get your mind off it."

I head in and try to mix with the party-goers, but it isn't long before I'm brooding off to the side. After an hour, everyone else seems to be getting drunk, but not me.

"You're not drinking!" Orm declares, after finding me.

"Guess I'm not in the mood for getting drunk."

We make small talk for a few more minutes, and I run out of things to say. "Ash," he says, pointing at my head, "I *know* what's going on in there."

"Geez!" I moan, wallowing in helplessness, "What do I do?"

"You go."

"Go where?"

"Don't play dumb. Put on your big girl pants and handle this."

I stay rooted to the spot for what seems like a long time, not saying anything. Hearing from Robin was the last thing I expected to happen tonight.

"Seriously, go."

I can't argue. He's right. I know what I have to do.

"Thanks, Orm. I'd be lost without you."

"Anytime," he smiles. He escorts me to the door and watches as I walk to my car.

I take a seat behind the wheel, but before I drive, I get out my phone and dial Robin's number. She answers almost immediately.

"Ash?"

"Where are you now?" The sound of traffic is still in the background.

"I'm on the highway in front of Dave's Burgers."

"Wait for me there." I hang up without waiting for a response.

For a few seconds, I lean my head on my steering wheel, wondering what the hell I'm getting myself into. I know it's a minefield. It wouldn't take much for Robin to destroy me again. After months of no contact, she still has the power to reach across time and space and literally separate me from a girl I'm making out with. But, I just can't help myself. I freakin' cannot resist her.

I'm at Dave's within ten minutes and find her wandering around on the sidewalk next to the parking lot with her head down. She's in dark jeans and a white horizontally striped pullover that looks a bit too thermal for the warm temperatures of July. I pull up to her so she's on the passenger side and then roll down the window.

"Get in."

She nervously wipes her palms on the thighs of her jeans and then climbs in. Her hair is slightly mussed—like it was allowed to air dry after being combed out.

"Thanks." Her voice is low and she averts her eyes from mine.

I size her up. It's hard to imagine that this is the once-famous and most popular girl at Sagebrush High School—strong, confident, and capable of bringing a crowd of hundreds to their feet—and someone I once thought of as a social goddess whose attention I eagerly lapped up and considered myself lucky to have.

"Does your dad know you're out here?"

She shakes her head. "He's out of town."

"Yeah, right. Are you sure this time?"

She nods and continues to stare straight ahead at the floorboard. We're both silent for a good minute. I put the car in park and turn off the ignition, then turn to face her. She looks nothing like the cold, efficient executioner who utterly destroyed me a couple of months ago.

"*Why* are you walking around out here?"

"I-I wanted to call you."

"Why?"

"I'm not sure you wanna hear it." She nervously shifts her position just a little. "Maybe I shouldn't have called you."

"I was almost over you. I thought I had finally turned a corner. So, yeah, maybe you shouldn't have."

"I'm sorry," she says, almost under her breath. She reaches for the door handle.

"But, you did. So, let's hear it."

Her hand, already on the door handle, freezes. She gives me a quick glance, then averts her eyes once more as she returns her hand to her lap. I can see her lips tremble, and I'm completely struck by the change in temperament from her stinging verbal barbs and cruel social media postings only a few months ago.

"I-I wanted to say I'm sorry. I know that sounds lame, and I get it if you don't wanna hear it. But there it is."

"Kinda late on that, aren't you?"

She nods. "Yeah. That's fair."

"So, exactly what are you apologizing for?"

"All the bad stuff," she replies, still speaking under her breath. "I wish none of it ever happened, going all the way back to the first time I hurt you."

"That bad stuff didn't just *happen*. Your behavior is your own choice."

"I deserve that," she says after a few seconds.

"Why, Robin? We faced a problem, and we should have solved it together. That's sorta what couples do."

"I thought you *were* the problem," she replies hesitantly.

"See, I don't get that! How could *I* be the problem? I did nothing to you but love you! What about that makes me a problem?"

I can see her struggling to swallow. "You're right. But somehow I felt . . . ashamed."

"Of what? Me?"

"No!"

"Then what?"

"I-I guess maybe . . ." She shakes her head as her voice trails off.

"You were ashamed of what you *had* with me?"

"It's so complicated—"

"I've got all night!"

At this, she turns her head back downward.

"Maybe I thought everything was *your* fault. Maybe I thought I could make everything right by treating you that way." She faces back to me. "I know that's really fucked up, and I see it now."

"So, you somehow justified treating me like shit? You didn't just avoid me. You were hateful! There were days I didn't think I could go on living. You put me through hell, Robin."

"Sounds so horrible when you put it like that," she replies, without looking away.

"It *was,* Robin, and way more than you know. Do you have any idea how much I trusted you *not* to hurt me?"

She takes another breath. "I get it. That's why I'm here. Ash, I swear, it kills me to know I did that."

"You destroyed me. Do you get that? You literally destroyed me!"

She breathes out but doesn't say anything, instead just shaking her head.

"I made you *safe,* Robin. And I lived for *you.* Every second of every day, all I did was live for you. And what did you do in return? You threw me under the bus as casually as you'd toss a soda can into the trash!" I let out a long breath. I've gotta calm down.

She tries to say something, but no words come.

"Damn, that hurt! You were my very first girlfriend. Do you get that? I made a huge leap of faith. When I put my heart into that relationship, I trusted you to take care of me, just as I committed to taking care of you. I trusted you to be honest with me."

"I-I'm sorry. I really am." I notice a tear trickling down her cheek and it enrages me. She doesn't get to cry!

"Are you?" I hurl back at her, my voice raging. "You know what? When I close my eyes, I can *still* see the look on your face that time when you told me that you *hate* me!" My throat is so tight I have to stop talking just to breathe. She fumbles around trying to begin a reply, but I cut her off. "That moment in time crushed what little of me was still alive. I've *never* felt that kind of pain. Just those three words: 'I hate you.' You would have been much more merciful to just put a gun to my head and pull the trigger!" I turn away and let out a long breath. "God! I can't believe I'm even here!"

I hear her choking back sobs, and when I look over at her, she's wiping one eye.

"I know you don't see it, but I wanted us to last," she says, almost so low I can barely hear her. "I didn't want things to turn out like that."

"You're kidding, right? Exactly what part of 'I hate you' is it that tells me you wanted to make us last?"

She bites her quivering lip, and I can see her heaving softly. "Ash, after my dad found us, and then that photo came out, I didn't think I could save our relationship."

"What do you mean, *you*? That's laughable. Well, guess what? That's a *team* effort. As in *both* of us!" I let out a long sigh and lean back. "Geezus, Robin. What the hell happened? We were so strong! Together we could have survived that photo—or any other storm!"

"I-I know," she responds, her voice cracking. "If I had just been brave . . ."

I study her posture and demeanor for a long time, her hands and fingers trembling when she wipes her eyes. The reversal of our roles drips with irony.

"Are you just setting me up for another snotty tirade?"

"No!" she says, this time a bit forcefully. She turns her head toward me and locks her eyes on mine. "Seriously, I'm not. You may not believe me when I say it—and I get that—but I've come to my senses."

"Your senses," I sigh. "Right. Why should I *believe* you? Why should I *trust* you?"

"Maybe you shouldn't," she replies, with a degree of frankness I wasn't expecting. "I admit I haven't earned it. And yeah, maybe what I did is unforgivable. So if you don't want to trust me, I get it. If you don't want to forgive me, I get that, too." She takes a breath and faces me straight on. "But maybe . . ." She freezes up, and I can see her clenching her fists in frustration.

"Maybe what?"

She lets out a long, quivering breath, then speaks.

"Maybe you can give me a chance to prove I mean what I say?"

Recollections of her cold and cruel demeanor during the last two months of the school year suddenly wash over me, and like a volcano, an unexpected anger erupts.

"Holy shit! Do you think I'm a fucking idiot?" She has nothing to say. "I can't take this anymore. Just get out!" She flinches. "Seriously, just get out. Don't call me, don't do anything!"

Her chin quivers and she blinks back tears. "Okay," she forces out in a creaky voice I can barely hear.

She exits the car and begins walking away toward the highway. I'm biting my own lip as I watch her recede into the night. My tears find their release and stream down my cheeks and drip onto my shirt. I wasn't going to cry, yet here I am openly sobbing. Robin is almost to the sidewalk when I see her pinch up the sleeve on her pullover and use it to dab at her eye, after which her hair is tousled by the evening breeze. That's when I lose it.

I can barely see straight as I start up my car, put it in gear, and tear through the parking lot after her. She flinches when she turns to see me speeding up to her. I screech to a stop beside her. In an instant, I'm out of the car and have her in my arms. She throws her arms around me. We both dissolve into a river of tears.

"Damn you!" I sob. "Damn you for making me love you so much!"

"I'm sorry," she cries back. "I'm so sorry for everything! I love you!" She squeezes me hard. "I love you so much!"

For a long time, and despite the stares of patrons leaving the restaurant, we hold each other tightly as if there's no tomorrow, both of us bawling like babies. The raw emotion that flows between us is powerful. And in a way I'll never be able to explain, it makes whole all that was broken, and alive all that was dead. Finally, after what seems like forever, we find ourselves sniffling and able to compose ourselves. She pulls her face back and looks down into my eyes while giving me a wet-eyes smile.

"I love you," she says softly. "It's unstoppable, and always will be."

I can't help but stare back into those deep, green inkwells.

"Are you sure? Like, *really* sure? In your heart?"

"Yes, I'm sure." She pauses to take a breath. "There was a time when I tried not to, but that got me nowhere. I know now I can never stop loving you."

That's it. I'm done. I have no more resistance.

"I love you, too, Robin. And I'll have to admit I never stopped."

And just like that, I find myself right back in the midst of the same burning flame the two of us shared right up to the moment that goddam bedroom door was flung open.

"Strange," she says, as tears trickle from her eyes once more. She tries to clear them by blinking as I place my thumb on one rivulet and smear it away off to the side.

"What's strange?"

"It's so strange that I hurt the person who loved me the most. I-I'm really having a hard time with that. Kinda makes me scared of myself, if I'm going to be honest."

"Well, your dad—"

"Ash, I can't hide what I did behind the excuse of disappointing my dad."

I raise a finger to make a point, but she shushes me ever so softly and continues.

"Somewhere in here"—she points to her heart—"is a weakness that I have to own up to. Because no one says we're guaranteed a smooth road in life. Nowhere is it written that we always get what we want, or that no one will ever make you feel less than you are. You have to deal with difficulty without losing your basic humanity, you know? I failed that test in the worst way possible . . . by hurting the person I loved the most"—she stops to choke down another sob—"and the very person who would have taken a bullet for me."

"Let's just—"

"That won't happen again."

I spend a long minute scrutinizing her words.

"You wanna hear something stupid?" she says, putting her face right in front of mine.

"What?"

"On the night of the full moon, I was outside for the longest time remembering how we danced in the moonlight."

"Are you serious? I was at Orm's doing the same exact thing!"

She smiles, but without warning chokes down another sob.

"I couldn't call you . . . well, I didn't *think* I could call you . . . so I posted the first thing I could find about the full moon. I was hoping you would know I was thinking about you."

"So that hashtag—it wasn't for Dill?"

"Oh, no, baby, um, I mean Ash . . . um . . ." She exhales with a *whew* and fans her face. "That was you all the way."

I smile at her awkwardness. "It's okay. The 'baby' part. As for the post, well, that went right over my head for sure."

She swallows, searching for her words. I can see her wringing her hands in front of me. "I cried a lot for you that night," she says.

"Well, that's both of us then. I wish you had called and told me how you felt."

She gives me a short laugh, then goes silent for the better part of a minute. "I was afraid."

"What exactly were you afraid of?"

Her face morphs into panic for just a few seconds, but she takes a deep breath and calms herself.

"I was afraid of being disowned . . . being shamed. Disappointing my dad." She pauses for a moment, as if in deep thought. "Mostly I was afraid of who I am."

"Are you still?"

"Not anymore. My aunt has been helping me a lot."

"Your aunt? How's she helping you?"

She looks at me and takes in her breath. "Like the most important thing— that if you can't love yourself for who you are, you can't really love someone else, or expect someone else to love you for who you are."

"So you don't have a problem admitting you're gay?"

"No. And I've already told him I'm gay and to just deal with it."

"Your dad?"

"Yeah!"

"What about me? What's he gonna do when he finds out?"

At this question, she allows herself a wry laugh. "Baby, I don't really give a shit!"

"Really?"

"Exactly," she nods. "I'm an adult. It's time I started acting like one. Even about . . ." She gets a sudden, mournful look on her face, but then tries to hide it with a forced smile.

"What?"

"It's nothing," she says, trying to give me a brave face.

"Be honest—no more hiding your feelings, remember?"

"Okay, you're right," she whispers after a long silence. "It's that I can't be with you after the end of the summer."

That one catches me off guard, and I don't know what to say. I find her hand and interlace my fingers with hers.

"Congratulations, by the way," she says, forcing a smile. "I really mean it this time."

"It should have been you."

"Nah. You always sell yourself short. I've seen your work. They made a good decision!" She pulls my hand up and kisses the back of it. "Besides, I'm going to the University of North Texas. They have a music department and all." She smiles, then adds, "Oh, and Mom and Dad are moving back to Houston after I leave for college."

"You know what that means, right?" I give her a smile.

"No?"

"It means we'll have to visit each other in Texas and Illinois! And we'll have to figure out what to do with those summers!" I'm starting to feel up-beat.

Her face is instantly radiant. "I know!" she says. "In the summers, we'll backpack through Europe looking for adventure! Just the two of us!"

"Yes! And visit the great art museums there!"

"And theaters and opera!"

"And ride the bullet trains!"

"And climb mountains!"

"And spend nights under the stars!"

I'm literally alive with electricity, and it's hard to contain. We dissolve into laughter, and after we calm down, she looks deeply into my eyes and kills me with that sexy smile that seems to be so natural for her. Then, without saying a thing, she places her head on my shoulder and her arms around my waist and pulls herself as close as she can get. If the world ended at this instant, I'd die happy.

"Does your mom know where you are?"

"No, she probably doesn't even know I'm out of the house." She glances at her watch. "But seeing it's this late, maybe you can drop me off?"

"Sure, baby." We head for my car. Before opening the car door, I face her. "I like calling you that, again."

She grins and climbs into the passenger seat. "And I like hearing it!"

"Feels kinda strange . . . *me* taking *you* somewhere in *my* car!"

"I know," she replies with a broad smile. "I miss taking you places in *my* car." She pulls herself up and uses the mirror to get her hair back together.

"Well, we sure made a statement the last time you did," I say, giving her a smile.

"Oh, yeah." She exhales and gives me a sad face. "God, how I wish that day had never happened!"

"Not me," I reply, trying to counter the emotional downturn in her voice. "Maybe that last minute, yes, but I never want to change what happened up to that last minute."

She looks at me through misty eyes. "You're right. Neither would I."

I lean in, and our lips instinctively connect for a long, sensuous kiss—our first in over two months—after which she smiles into my eyes and says, "You have no idea how much I missed *that!*"

"Same here!" I can't stop smiling.

"Well, when can I see you again?"

"Anytime you want! In fact, why don't you come over first thing tomorrow?"

"Tomorrow?" She brings her palms together and giving me a puppy-dog look. "Sure!"

I drive her home and pull up next to the curb in front of her house. She takes one look at me and then shakes her head.

"Oh no, you don't!" she chides. "Get out! You're coming to the door!"

She gives me "the look," and once I'm out of my car, she takes me by the hand to lead me to the doorstep. But instead of giving me a goodbye kiss, she surprises me by opening the door and pulling me inside. I immediately feel my pulse race. I wasn't expecting this.

"Mom!" she calls out.

"In here," comes the reply, from the kitchen. I hear her footsteps approaching.

"What are you *doing?*" I whisper.

"Hang on," she whispers, with a smile.

Just then, her mom's in the same room with us. Her eyes get large, and she freezes in her tracks. Robin grabs my hand.

"Mom, Asher found me out wandering the streets and brought me home!" With that, she turns to me. "Thank you so much, baby!" And before I know it, she gives me a kiss on the lips. "See you tomorrow?"

I'm breathless, and somehow, I manage to nod. It sinks in what she did.

"Starting tomorrow," she adds in a whisper, while her mouth is close to mine, "we're going to be out at the lake for the rest of the summer so they can get this house ready to be sold! Just so you know!"

I can't take my eyes off her mom. I don't think I've ever seen a deer-in-the-headlights look more profound than the one on her face at the moment. With a nod, I turn and head back to my car. Halfway there, I glance back over my shoulder. Robin is on the doorstep looking at me, and she blows me a kiss. For an instant, I wonder if I'm dreaming. But I'm not. Thank God, I'm not.

The next morning, as Grams and I have breakfast together, I break the news to her. "Grams, I just want to tell you that Robin and I are back together."

At that exact moment, there's a knock at the door, and I hear a familiar voice. Grams gives me a puzzled look and says, "Is that—"

"Yes, it is!" I scoot out of the kitchen and across the living room to open the door and find a smiling and animated Robin.

"Hiyee!" she says.

I feel a broad smile across my face. "Best day ever!" I reply. Taking her by the hand, I lead her through the living room to the dinette where Grams is craning her neck. There's a tentative smile on her face, which is surprising, to say the least.

"Look who's here! Like I said, Grams, Robin and I are back together!"

"Mrs. Norman!" she says. Before Grams knows what's hit her, Robin bends down to give her a hug.

Grams is rendered momentarily speechless, but then her eyes grow wide. "Well, that certainly is a surprise!"

I take Robin by the hand. "My car or yours?"

"I kinda like letting you drive!"

We go upstairs together to get my car keys. She sees my camera sitting on the shelf above my desk, and a smile lights up her face.

"Did you find my photo?"

"Oh my God, yes! I really liked it!" I pause for a second. "But, who took it?" Damn. I didn't mean to go *there*.

"My cousin! I was so scared for her to be holding your camera, though!"

"So, that girl who was following you around—"

"My cousin, Maddy!"

God help me. All that emotional energy and she was just a cousin. I can't help but laugh at my gross misconceptions. I grab my car keys, and we're still laughing as we leave the house and climb into my car.

"What about Dill at the Dalhart Mall?"

She gets a sudden shocked look on her face. "Wait! How did you know?"

"Orm took me there that day, and I just happened to see the two of you in the lingerie store."

With that, she bursts out laughing. "Oh my God! Such a small world! If Dill had seen you, he would have literally freaked the shit out!"

"So, you and Dill—"

"Hell, no!" she says. "I didn't even go there with him. He ran into *me* in the mall and started following me around."

"But, you posted a pic of the two of you with that 'soulmate' hashtag!"

She rolls her eyes. "Actually, *he* posted it."

"*He* posted it? On *your* phone?"

"Yeah! He picked up my phone while I was digging in my wallet and posted it. I'm surprised you saw it because I deleted it within seconds. I was so pissed!"

"Ho-lee *shit,* Robin, you have *no* idea how much that post crushed me!" She gives me a wide-eyed look. "I mean, it sucked the very life out of me!"

"I'm so sorry!" She seeks out my hand with hers and holds on tight. I can see it's tough for her.

"Hey," I reply, giving her a return squeeze, "it wasn't *you!* Just knowing that makes me want to jump up and down!"

After a few seconds, she nods very slightly.

"Okay, then!" I start the car, and head into town. Her mood is quiet, so I reach over and tickle her in the ribs, which finally gets her laughing. "Lighten up, okay?"

"Okay," she says, giving me a smile.

Seeing Bilkins Park, I gesture and let out a giggle.

"What?"

"You brought our lunch, right?" I try to look as serious as I can.

"Whaaat?" she replies, and for a moment, a look of panic crosses her face until she sees me grinning, and then we both explode in laughter.

"Gotcha, girl!"

"Yeah, you did!"

"But I do remember a certain day when you actually did bring our lunch."

She smiles and laughs softly. "I was so wrapped up in you that day that I couldn't see straight! You were driving me crazy! You have no idea!"

"And you, you little weasel," I reply, "you were just looking for a way to get me to kiss you!"

"Yep!"

We decide we're hungry and drive up to Lamont, Colorado, pull in to the first truck stop we find, and have a greasy meal of burgers and chili fries. I'm on top of the world. I have *so* missed having fun with my girl like this.

The only hiccup in the day occurs when I get an unexpected phone call from Amsra. Robin eyes me as I engage in a couple of minutes of awkward conversation, after which she admirably restrains from asking any questions. I pull her in close and give her a kiss.

"That's a girl I met in Chicago," I say. "A girl who can't begin to hold a candle to you."

"Chicago, eh? I think I'm jealous!" She gives me a smile, and then we both laugh it off.

The next afternoon, she calls me and asks me to meet her at her house. Her voice sounds somehow different, and she says she has a lot to tell me. My first instinct is to suspect the wheels have come off somewhere, but I calm myself and drive over. When I get there, the house is empty, except for her, and I can tell she's up to something.

"Where's your mom?" I ask, looking toward the kitchen.

"We're all moved into the vacation home at the lake, remember?"

"Oh yeah! So . . . your dad won't come walking in?"

"Funny you mention Dad," she replies. "He actually got home last night. And it wasn't pretty."

"Oh my God! Are you okay?"

"Oh, yeah, I'm fine now. He's not, though. The shit hit the fan."

"You told him about us?"

"Yes. Right when he got home, too."

"How did it go down?"

"I just told him that you and I are back together, and to leave me alone about it."

"Whoa! What did he do?"

Robin's eyes get big, and even though she's putting on a brave face, I can tell she's still affected.

"Well, he basically told me that by choosing a homosexual lifestyle, I was going to hell." She swallows hard. I take her hand and give it a squeeze, which she returns.

"That's it?"

"He also said not to bring you around the house while he's there."

"Well, you don't have to worry about that one! Is that all?"

"Umm, no. He started yelling at Mom about it. They were still going at it when I left to come here."

"Why your mom?"

"I think he figured out that she knew. So, that makes her an accomplice. She's used to it. But he'll be on the road again this afternoon for a few days."

"You're so conflicted, you know?"

"I guess you're right. The sooner I get away from that shit, the better. Know what I mean? But hey, I've got you, you're here with me, and that's pretty damn good for now!"

"Yes, that *is* good."

She gives me a smile. "Baby?"

"Yeah?"

"Can we just lie down next to each other for a while?"

"Sure, anything!"

She leads me upstairs to her bedroom. Once in her room, the memory of our first kiss floods back into my mind. Seems like forever ago, yet also like yesterday. After locking her bedroom door, she turns toward me and I can see her swallow. But then she casually disrobes and pulls back the sheets and comforter on her bed. I wasn't expecting this, but that's okay. I follow suit and climb into the bed next to her, after which she pulls the covers back up and snuggles next to me, laying her head on my shoulder. I curl my arm around her and snug her body right up next to mine.

It's absolutely amazing how right this feels. For a long time, I do nothing more than take in every perception that I can, from the softness of her skin, the warmth of her body, the smell of her perfume, the color of her hair, the sound of her breathing. The list is long. I don't think I could be more contented than I am at this moment. It's when I give the top of her head a soft kiss that I realize she's asleep, no doubt exhausted from emotional stress. And that's okay. I thank my lucky stars that I'm right where I am—just me and my girl.

The next day, she picks me up and takes me to her house. We spend the entire afternoon in her bed, and the wait was worth it. All the old feelings of being the center of the universe have returned. For dinner, we go downstairs and drink wine while collaborating on a baked chicken and rice casserole dinner. A luxurious candlelight bath together while sipping wine is the perfect capstone for the day.

Over the remaining two weeks of July, we grow even closer than ever. Her "in town" house becomes our love nest, even to the point that we spend nights there together when her dad's away. I get the distinct impression that her mom knows, but I don't ask.

It's not long before our pending separation is a painful topic to discuss. But we do. And on one particular evening, Robin seems really down about it. We're snuggled on the sofa at her house in our underwear underneath a blanket, having just finished watching some sappy love story that featured a guy having to leave the girl he's in love with to go to war.

"It's gonna be so weird being away from you after school starts," she whispers.

"Same here, baby."

"I'm glad we're leaving on the same day. That helps."

"Yeah, I guess so. But you know, I'd still just like to know why they didn't take *you.*"

She brushes a few rogue strands of hair off my face with her fingers, allowing them to trace the contour of my ear before stopping near my lips.

"We're past that, baby," she says in a soft but reassuring voice. "We'll be apart. What's important is how we deal with it."

Her words fill me with hope for the future. "You're right."

She kisses me softly and then places her head back on my shoulder. "So, what do *you* think is in our future . . . as in, after we finish college?"

"You mean, four years down the road? Well, I don't know, really. If you're asking whether I see an *us,* yes, I do!"

"Then, can you see us getting married someday?"

Oh boy. Even though I've thought about it lately, that question spins my mind. "Yes, I can. It sounds exciting, that's for sure, but it also confuses me a little."

She doesn't reply, so I explain.

"A lot has happened to me since March. Before I met you, I would never have dreamed that I could fall in love with a girl. Or do the things with a girl that we've done. I've come a long way in a short time. I mean I've already lost you once. Maybe I need a little more time to think about the marriage thing."

She nods but says nothing.

"I'll be honest, though," I add, "I really, really like the idea of us being married."

At this, she smiles. "I guess that *is* a long way in a short time. But just for the record, I'd marry you."

The purity of her statement gives me that tingling feeling—again. I love it. She can still evoke the most potent emotional responses imaginable with just a simple word or sentence. The depth of my love for her seems to be bottomless.

As July turns to August, we settle into a good rhythm. It seems more evident than ever that Robin's mom has come to a full acceptance of her daughter's being gay—at least when her husband's not home, that is.

On my side of the fence, Grams truly enjoys Robin's presence in the house. Does she accept the idea that I'm gay? Well, there's been no further lectures on plumbing. That's probably as good as I'm going to get from her.

Halfway through breakfast with Grams on a Saturday morning, I get a phone call from an animated Robin, who summons me to the O'Leary vacation home but refuses to tell me what's going on. A half hour later, I'm at her doorstep, where she excitedly grabs me by the hand, pulls me in, and leads me toward the kitchen area. I can only hope that her father isn't here.

"Hurry!" she says. "Mom won't tell me a thing until you're here!"

I open my mouth to say something, but she quickly shushes me.

"Go ahead, Mom," Robin says, "she's here!"

Without saying a word, her smiling mom opens a cabinet, pulls out an envelope, and pushes it into Robin's hands. "This is for *both* of you," she says with a smile.

Robin turns to me, and with wide eyes, the two of us open it together—and then freeze. Inside the envelope is a neat clip of hundred-dollar bills.

16

"Wh-what is *this?*" Robin blurts out, looking into her mother's smiling face.

"I know you only have a short time together before school starts," she beams, "so you're going on vacation, just the two of you!"

My brain contorts itself into a pretzel trying to sort out what just happened. This is the woman who, with her husband, was trying to separate me from Robin only weeks ago. Now, she's sending us on vacation together?

"I don't understand," Robin says, looking first at her mother, then me.

"Darling, I can see how happy the two of you are together," her mother says. "And I know once school starts you'll be far apart. You may not realize it, but I'm not so old that I don't know what it means to be young and in love!"

"Seriously?" Robin says. "I-I thought you and Dad—"

"Never mind what you thought. I want you to be you. That's all that's important to me. Your grandfather's condo is available the 3rd through the 9th, which means you'll be leaving tomorrow."

"What about Dad?"

"Don't worry, he's out of town until the evening of the 10th. You'll be coming home on the morning of the 10th, so you'll be just fine. He'll never know." She gives both of us a smile.

We retreat to her room and count out the money. It's one thousand dollars. "Robin, I don't know what to say!"

"Me neither! She's never done *anything* like this!"

It takes me a minute or two to compose myself. "Where exactly *is* this condo?"

She takes my hands and laughs with joy. "Ash, baby, you're gonna *love* it!" she says, smiling ear to ear. "It's in a small town in southern Colorado called Fort Prospect. It's maybe four hours away at the most. There's a lake and lots of mountains! We went there two years ago, and it's so beautiful!"

"Oh my God!" I gasp, shaking my head.

She gives me a quick hug. "Go get packed, then meet me in town. We'll spend the night there and leave first thing in the morning!"

With things moving very quickly, and with Robin's contagious excitement, I find myself in fast motion. I explain it to Grams, and she objects right away.

"Two girls your age don't have any business being out on the road like that by yourselves," she says.

"Grams, we're eighteen."

"I don't like the idea of strangers taking note that the two of you are unaccompanied."

"What? We're accompanied by each other, Grams."

She wrings her hands and sighs. "You're gonna go anyway, aren't you?"

"Yeah, Grams. I am."

After a moment of contemplation, she smiles and rises from the dinette.

"I really need to stop treating you like you're a child. If you're ready to move to Chicago, you're ready for a four-hour drive."

I help her gather up the lunch dishes, give her a kiss, and race upstairs to pack—making sure I don't forget my camera and my two best lenses.

Being in the mountains is excitement enough all in itself, but what really has me revved up is having Robin all to myself for a week, nights included. That in itself is beyond my wildest dream. And for the first time, I feel like we have an adult relationship, where we are totally free to be ourselves.

She comes outside with a big smile on her face as I pull up in the driveway. "Did you get everything?" She peers into the car as I get out. I grab my single suitcase from the back seat and hold it out as we walk back in. It's only slightly larger than a travel bag. "That's it?" she laughs, while ushering me into the master bedroom where her luggage is neatly stacked near the foot of her bed. "My travel bag is a little bigger." And it is. In fact, it's a full-size suitcase that will have to go in the trunk.

"I can already see you're gonna be a travel nightmare," I grin.

We both decide we want to be there in time for lunch, so we're out the door and on the road at 6:00 the next morning. With the sun at our backs, I feel freer than I've ever felt in my life. We jam out for over an hour to her playlist of country songs, then stop at a donut shop in Clayton, New Mexico, to grab a breakfast to go.

It's not long before we can see the rising peaks of the Sangre de Cristo Mountains. "You're gonna be in heaven with that camera of yours," she says through a huge mouthful of cake donut. I'm in hysterics as a few crumbs fly out of her mouth onto the steering wheel, and I reach for my phone to snap an incriminating photo. We've been like this all day. And it's intoxicating. I can't remember being so excited for an adventure.

The sun is still in the morning sky when we arrive. When we get out of the car and take a look around, I see that the condo community itself consists of several large units, all of them alike: four condos per unit—two upstairs and two downstairs, with each pair on opposite sides of the group. Our condo is upstairs, and as soon as we go in, I see a floor made of a highly polished, light-colored wood that gives a stunning open-air effect. The massive living area looks like it's at least thirty feet wide and could accommodate a family reunion. The kitchen is modern, complete with a large island featuring a gas cooktop and a flat grill that reminds me of a hibachi, along with every kind of pot, pan, and utensil needed to cook just about anything, hanging just above. All the appliances, from the oven to microwave, to refrigerator are mirror-like stainless steel.

"You can close your mouth now!" Robin says, beckoning me further. She leads me into a very spacious master bedroom with a king-size four-poster bed in the center of the near wall, a large dresser on the opposite wall, a chest of drawers on the far wall, and a huge, mounted flat-panel TV on the wall above the dresser. All of the furniture is off-white. A French door on the remaining wall leads to a wooden deck patio containing a small table and a couple of lounge chairs, with room left over. Back inside, an adjoining bath radiates a pure white marble floor, a huge circular whirlpool bath to the left, an open shower next to it, and an adjoining closet. There are two sinks with vanity chairs across from the bath and shower area. She points to the bathtub.

"We're gonna have fun with *that!*"

"You said that last time," I smile.

She knows exactly what I mean. "Well, this time we really will!"

I can't help but laugh and put my arms around her waist, lifting her just off the floor, and then spin her around, to which she throws her head back and laughs like a small child. When I set her back down on the floor, she smilingly cups my face with both hands, kisses me, and says, "I'm so happy!"

We spend the next half hour unpacking. Or, I should say *she* does. It takes *me* all of three minutes. In the wardrobe competition, Robin wins by a mile. I can't believe she brought what looks to be easily enough for two, possibly three, wardrobe changes per day. My small wardrobe takes only a dozen hangers and occupies just a small corner of the closet.

She wins the vanity competition as well, with lotions, perfumes, brushes, combs, and makeup taking up all available space around "her" sink area. I love it. In fact, I've come to realize that I'm very attracted to the "girly" side of her personality. When she looks at "my" sink and snickers, it prompts me to walk over and put her in a playful bear hug from behind and kiss her neck behind her ears. This results in the first use of the king bed, and the love-making is incredible. As we lie in each other's arms, I can't help but smile when I look at the near wall.

"What are you smiling about?" she says, looking over her shoulder toward the same wall.

"You don't see it?"

"See what?"

"We didn't even close the bedroom door!"

With that, she throws back her head and laughs.

"We don't have to here!"

"I know!"

She rolls back over toward me to make eye contact. "Ash, you're so fucking hot," she says in a soft voice. She's looking down into my face, perched half-on my chest and stomach, her head resting on her palm with her elbow propped on the other side of me. The mood is enchanting. I want it to last forever.

"You think so?" I whisper.

"Oh yeah!" She leans in and kisses me.

Turning my body and using my arms, I flip our positions to where she's on her back, and I'm straddling her midsection. I return her kiss and then allow my eyes to savor every feature of her exposed body.

"You're pretty hot yourself," I whisper.

"You've got beautiful breasts," she says, reaching up and cupping them. "Mine are way too small." I keep my hands at my sides and allow her unfettered access to everything. She stretches her arms around my body to grab my butt. "But damn, you've got the tiniest butt I've ever seen!" I can't help but laugh as she gives me several playful squeezes, then starts tickling me in the ribs, sending me into spasms. I can't get her off me, so I'm forced to tickle her in self-defense. Laughing hysterically, we finally find ourselves stretched out beside each other again.

"You put a wet spot on my tummy!" she smiles, wiping a spot just below her belly with a finger and holding it up.

"Well, it's *your* spit!" I giggle.

"Yeah, *some* of it!" she giggles in return, giving me a mischievous smile and pulling me close for a long snuggle. We work our way beneath the sheets, entwine our legs, and spend a long time doing nothing more complicated than basking in the simplicity of togetherness.

It's when I open groggy eyes that I realize we've been napping for a couple of hours. I'm a bit hungry, and I turn a little to face her. But right then, as if she's reading my mind, she opens her eyes and says, "What are we going to have for lunch?"

I pull myself off the bed and hold an arm out to help her up. "Let's go look!"

Hand in hand, clad only in our underwear, we find the pantry and size up our booty. With plenty of wine to prod our sense of adventure, we go overboard—ending up with a mid-afternoon smorgasbord of focaccia, three veggie and cheese appetizers, and some kind of layered penne pasta and pesto entree we invented on the spot.

We eat next to each other, standing at the bar and sampling both our own and each other's plates. "This is way too much!" I laugh.

"Let's get dressed," she smiles, wiping her mouth with a napkin. "We're gonna have to walk this off!"

Before we do, we make up another sappy little toast and then drink: "To our red-haired tiny-assed kids!" I say, to which she bursts out in laughter, almost spilling her wine.

We take a very scenic and leisurely late afternoon hike around a foothill lake, and as it starts getting dark, we drive into town to grab a bite and check out the night scene. There's a bar on the main strip with a live band playing country music, so we settle in, eating finger food and drinking beer. We even dance a few songs, including a couple of intimate slow dances. No one gives us any grief, and the acceptance we get is absolutely liberating.

We arrive back at the condo just before midnight. After making love again, I lie in her embrace, noticing that away from the aura of her father, she's completely uninhibited. She's not only playful, but she's also *sexy* playful—and eager to try anything I suggest. I can't find a single downside to this new Robin. Wrapped in contentment, we spoon up and drift toward sleep.

On our first full day, she surprises me with guided horseback riding in the mountains. I get the feeling each day is going to be an adventure, with Robin as my tour guide. We're two in a group of about a dozen, and spend the entire day riding up into the mountains and then back down. Along the way, we make a whole group of new friends.

It's when we're at dinner with the group in a little Mexican restaurant that evening that I notice everyone is in apparent acceptance of us as a couple—and once again, I'm reminded that being open like that in public feels damn good. I vow once again to myself that I'll never again hide who I am from anyone.

The next day is a hiking day—just us—and we push ourselves to the limit. Our reward is a breathtaking vista on the shore of a small mountain lake with snow-capped mountain peaks just above us. I can't recall ever being in the presence of natural beauty such as this. Despite clawing for oxygen in the thin mountain air, I spend the better part of an hour exploring the shores of the lake and snapping photo after photo. Robin patiently follows me around, soaking up my delight and suggesting photo ops, while also showing her mischievous nature.

"Well, *that's* gonna look good on my wall!" I tell her, as she laughingly photobombs a landscape shot with her shirt up and breasts exposed.

By the time we make it back to our condo, we're both too exhausted to cook, so we spread out on the sofa with chips, salsa, and wine, and gorge on *Gossip Girl* reruns. Robin notices my attention to the scenes with Blake Lively. "Guilty as charged," I laugh before she has a chance to rib me about it. Before bed, we enjoy a long bath together, each of us playfully washing the other's hair with some kind of delightfully minty herbal shampoo that Robin brought with her.

Our plans to rent a canoe and spend the next day exploring the local reservoir are thwarted by continuous thunderstorms all day long. Instead, we stay in and play card games, watch old movies, and sit on the covered deck to enjoy the sound and fragrance of the rain. It's a perfect romantic ambiance. As we sit together, I find myself noticing little things, like the way she likes to keep my hand in her clasp. I'm finding comfort and contentment within myself I never knew existed. And I know that our parting in just over a week is going to be as painful as hell.

Midway through the next afternoon, the sun comes out, and with it, we escape to a trailhead in the foothills of the Sangre De Cristo Mountains, where we enjoy a picnic dinner. I'm adjusting my camera settings when I notice she's looking at me with her head slightly leaning to one side—and she has *that* smile on her face. I quickly frame her up and fire off about five or six shots as she silently mouths "I love you."

"You're gonna be all over my wall in Chicago."

"Including my breasts, right?" She lets out with another of her contagious bursts of laughter.

By the time the last evening of the last day comes around, we decide to stay in instead of going out to eat. Around ten, after a home-cooked chow mein dinner, I notice a pale light bathing the patio. Together, we step outside beneath a full moon just now starting its rise in the eastern skies over the mountains.

"Oh my God!" she says, holding her hands outstretched with her palms up, and doing a slow turn. We both break out into large grins and come together in an embrace.

"All we need is a song!" I say.

"I can fix that!" She runs inside and emerges a few seconds later with her phone, and with a tap or two, our song is playing. We come together just as we did what seems like years ago under a distant moon. And as we slowly sway to the beat, hand in hand, heart against heart, my lover sings the song I love so much.

I think I'm just gonna cry myself into a river, but somehow find a way to hold it in long enough to bask in the glow of those beautiful green eyes all the way to the end of the song. As she sings the last few words, she makes sure we're face to face. And as I lose myself in her smile, she sings for me as if I'm the only person in the world.

"I love you so much, baby," she says, pulling me in close until our foreheads are almost touching. "You make me happier than I've ever been in my life!"

"And I'm so glad you're in my life! Seriously, I can't imagine my life without you in it."

"This time, it's forever, baby," she whispers.

"Yes, forever," I respond in a whisper, smiling back my tears.

That night, we're too tired and tipsy to make love. But that's okay. I snuggle up to my beautiful girl, and it isn't long before I can see she's asleep. I softly kiss her forehead and savor the closeness before finding my own slumber.

I wake up the next morning before she does, just as the morning sun is peeking over the mountains. There's just enough light to see. Being careful not wake her, I turn onto my right side toward her. She's on her left side, so we're practically face to face. For a long time, I watch her sleep. Her breathing is slow and deep, and the sound of it is the sweetest of comforts. I slowly caress her with my eyes, all the way from her hairline to her eyes, to her lips and mouth, to her nose, and finally to her neck. That this beautiful creature is mine to love makes me want to never leave the moment. Finally, she sighs and wakes, and when she sees me, she smiles and wipes her eyes.

"Hi, baby," she says in her waking voice, moving closer to bring her hand up and stroke my hair with the tip of her fingernails. I close my eyes and bask in her affection as she snugs herself closer to me. The sun is all the way up before we decide to take our last morning shower together.

It doesn't take us long to pack, and we get on the road just before nine. As we leave, I realize this has been the happiest time of my life. We laugh, reminisce, and sing our songs, but all too soon, we're back in Sagebrush—and our pending separation becomes the elephant in the room. She takes my hand from the center console and slides her fingers between mine.

"Are you happy?" she whispers.

"Are *you* happy?"

"Yes!" she beams, giving my hand a squeeze. "I'm *so* happy!"

I can't help but laugh out loud. "I'm just gonna be honest, baby. Now that I've spent a week with you, I don't want to ever be without you."

She's quiet for a few seconds, then turns to seek out my eyes. "I'm gonna have a hard time when we leave for college, but hearing you say that helps."

"We can do this," I reassure her, pulling her hand in for a kiss. I watch as she blinks back a few tears. We travel the last ten minutes in silence.

"You wanna stay for the afternoon?" she asks as we pull up next to my car in the driveway of her vacation home.

"Thanks, baby, but I think I need to go check on Grams. How about later?"

"Sure! Why don't we just meet up in town? I can stay out until ten or so before I have to be back here."

"Okay, that works for me. Let me check on Grams and then I'll come over. You wanna go out for dinner, or stay in?"

"Let's just cook in, if you don't mind. I'll visit with Mom and then meet you."

When I get home, Grams intercepts me as I walk into the dining room and pulls me in for a long hug. "You girls have a nice time?"

"We sure did, Grams! It was beautiful!"

She turns to the modest cherry wood credenza against the wall and retrieves an envelope. "This came for you."

I take the envelope and notice right away it's from the Winston. Grams watches closely as I open it and take out the letter. It's my dorm assignment.

"I'm in Emily Stephens Hutchins Hall, third floor. Room 383A." I hold the letter up for her to see and she smiles. This makes everything suddenly very real and my mood turns solemn. I slowly fold up the letter and set it down. She notices my downturn.

"Something wrong, sweetie?"

I force myself to smile. "It's nothing." We spend some time visiting, but then I excuse myself to get ready for the evening with Robin. I'm still a little down about the end of summer. It makes me realize how precious time really is. On impulse, I throw a few necessities into an overnight bag and head out. Grams gives me a grin and waves me out the door.

"Keep an eye on the weather," she calls out as I leave. "We're supposed to have storms."

Robin and I both somehow pull into her driveway at the same time. When she gets out of her car, I walk up to her with a smile, holding up my overnight bag for her to see, and pull her into a hug.

"What's that for?"

"I've got an idea, baby," I start. "It's kinda crazy . . . but I'm thinking you and I spend the night here!"

"But my dad is coming back."

I shrug and let out my breath. "But if we're *here*?"

She gets a sad look. "I guess I'm afraid he might come here."

"Can you just do it?" I plead. "I mean, he already knows we're together, and we don't have that much time left."

"I don't know," she says, after a long minute of contemplation.

"He won't really come *here*. Will he?"

Again, there's silence, until she finally says, "I just don't know."

"Whatever." I turn and toss my overnight bag back into the car.

"I feel helpless," she says.

"I guess I'm just having a bit of separation anxiety. I'll be okay."

After a few seconds, she gets an expression of determination. "Okay! I'll do it. And I know *how* we can do it!"

"What do you mean, *how?*"

"He won't be back until after two o'clock in the morning. So, here's what we'll do. I'll call Mom and tell her I'll be out late so she doesn't wait up for me. Then, when I'm sure she's in bed, we'll both drive back out there. I'll quietly leave my car parked there and ride back here with you."

"Why are we doing *that?*"

"Because!" she smiles. "My bedroom door is always closed at night. When Dad gets in, he'll see my car there and assume I'm upstairs asleep. He won't even bother checking. He'll just get in bed and go to sleep. Besides, he'll probably be . . . well, what I mean is he'll sleep late. Tomorrow, you'll drive me back. Doesn't matter if he catches me then!"

"That sounds so crazy!"

"You in?" she asks, giving me a smile.

She already knows I am. And I can't resist that smile. "Yeah, I'm in," I say, to which she literally jumps up on me with her arms around my neck and squeezes tight.

"C'mon, let's go inside!" she says.

I retrieve my overnight bag from the car, and with our arms around each other's waist, we laugh our way up to the door and into the house. We quickly end up in her bedroom, which we now call "our" room, where laughing turns to kissing, and kissing turns to making love.

That evening we cook a really nice meal—and then, for the next few hours, and mellowed out with wine, we spoon on the couch underneath a light blanket. It's my turn to choose the entertainment, so we watch vintage black and white sci-fi movies, laughing ourselves silly at the primitive special effects used back in the day. Right around dark, and true to the plan, Robin calls her mother and informs her she'll be out late.

"She's already headed to bed!" she says, after disconnecting the call. "You're all mine!"

After dropping off Robin's car at her vacation home, we return and do our best to watch a movie that's been on our watch list for a while—until I notice that the day was just too long for her and she's asleep with her arm dangling off the couch. I gently wake her and get her upstairs, where she sleepily peels off her clothes and allows me to situate her in bed. I turn off the lights and climb in beside her.

It's the next morning with the sun behind a cloudy sky when something awakens me. I look over and see that Robin isn't in bed. I'm about to throw off the covers and go find her when she enters the room wearing nothing but her underwear and bra from last night. She's carrying a tray, and the enticing aroma of French toast follows her in.

"Oh wow!" I feel a smile go all the way across my face. In all my eighteen years, I've never once experienced breakfast in bed. I pull myself up into a sitting position and wipe the sleep from my eyes as she carefully sets the tray across my lap. To top it all off, there's a carafe of coffee and a cup as well.

"Aww, this is completely awesome, baby!" I say, giving her a smile. "Hey, wait, where's yours?"

"Hang on!" She goes out into the hallway and immediately returns with another tray. After situating herself beside me, we dig in, both of us stuffing ourselves with French toast and playfully feeding each other. After finishing, I set my tray aside so I can go pee. When I get back, her tray has been placed to the side, and she's seductively reclined on the bed giving me a smile, with *that* look on her face.

"Come here," she says. I approach her, and once I'm near, she laughs, then grabs me by the arm and pulls me on top of her. "It might be a couple of days before we can do this again!" she smiles.

"Damn, for sure you've got *that* move down!" I laugh.

As we're kissing, a loud clap of thunder sounds, followed by the unmistakable sound of a low siren in the distance that gets louder by the second. We both raise our heads at the same time.

"What's that?" she says.

"It's the tornado siren. But that's weird!"

I can tell she's confused. "Why is it weird?"

"Because we don't usually have tornados in August!"

"I've never heard a tornado siren before," she says. We get up and go to the nearest window. There's no wind or rain, but another clap of thunder sounds in the distance. "Should we do something?"

"Let's look outside."

We throw on clothes and go downstairs. It's almost dark outside, telling me that the clouds are thick and low. A flicker of lightning dances across the sky, visible through the top of the living room window. When we walk outside, the siren is much louder. I look up to see a roiling mass of dark clouds. Suddenly, hailstones start pelting the ground around us, little ones at first, but quickly progressing to golf-ball size. We scream and run back inside. Robin is terrified. "I think I should get back home!"

"With the warning siren going off and hail falling?" I pull her in close for comfort. "We can't drive in this hail storm! Forget about it!"

Right then, we hear a strange, low-pitched whining in the distance.

"What is *that?*" she says. I exchange a worried glance with her, and with the hail having suddenly ended, we go outside to take a look. Gusts of wind push at us. The sound is coming from behind the house, so we walk around. What we see is terrifying. Off in the distance, maybe a half-mile away, a funnel cloud hangs low over the landscape, a swirling mass of debris orbiting around it. And it's moving fast—right at us.

"Tornado!" I scream.

"What do we do?" Her voice is filled with terror.

"Do you have a storm cellar?"

"No!" she screams, as the whining of the vortex increases in volume to a roar.

"Quick, follow me!" I take her hand and pull her back into the house and into the living room. "Grab a seat cushion!" With cushions in tow, I lead her to the downstairs bath area, where we hunker down in the bathtub under our cushions. The wind becomes a deafening scream, even inside the house.

"I'm so scared!" she sobs, moving to get as close to me as she can. I'm on the verge of tears myself. I put my arms around her and pull hard, just as the screaming gets so loud I can feel it. Outside, a furious barrage of debris pounds the house, raising a murderous din.

"Hang on to me!" I yell. We cling to each other so tightly I don't think we can breathe. But then, the noise level goes down. And it keeps going down. The sound level of debris hitting the house decreases until it finally stops. Within a minute or two, the only sound from the tornado is a low and distant shrieking.

"Oh my God, we're alive! You okay, baby?"

"Yes," she sobs, still continuing to cling to me for dear life.

"It's over," I say, consoling her and kissing her head. She continues to sob. I realize I'm bawling as well.

When the storm is entirely out of earshot, we come up from beneath our cushions. It's completely dark now, and it takes a minute before I figure out that the electricity is out. After our eyes adjust to the low light, we venture out of the bathroom. Everything seems to be okay except for broken windows in the bedroom, dining room, and living room, where the curtains are billowing inward.

"Damn, baby, I don't think it hit us!"

"Yeah, but what *did* it hit?" she says. We open the front door and take a look outside. Tree limbs and leaves are everywhere on the east side of the property, but my car in the driveway is relatively unscathed, with only small twigs on the top and the hood. Next door, which is about a hundred feet away, the house is still standing. It's only when we exit the house and walk down the driveway that we see torn up homes at the east end of the block. In the distance, we hear sirens from emergency vehicles.

"Oh my God," I whisper. She grasps my hand as if she'll never let go. A sudden thought hits me. "Your parents!" I say. "Which way is their house?"

She looks around to orient herself and then points in the direction from where the tornado came.

"It's that way!" she says in a tearful voice. "I have to call Mom!" We run back into the house and retrieve our phones from the bedroom. She tries to dial, gets a freaked out look on her face, then tries again.

"It won't work!" she sobs.

"Here, try mine!" I say, pushing my phone into her hands. Once again, she tries dialing, then looks around helplessly before wiping her eyes.

"We have to go!" I pull her in close to comfort her, but she pulls away and starts for my car. "Oh, God," she intones through her sobs, as we get out on the highway, "Please let them be okay."

The passage down the highway for the first couple of miles is unobstructed. But from there, the wreckage becomes obvious. About a mile from the turn-off, we see a couple of eighteen-wheelers on their sides. Telephone poles all up and down the highway are either leaning over or broken in two. I look over at Robin, and she has a terrified expression I've never seen.

As we drive the length of Robin's Lake Road, I can't help but notice the landscaping is untouched. Up ahead, we catch our first glimpse of flashing lights. I hear Robin let out a gasp. The road is covered in debris, so I can't go very fast. A half-mile in, we turn through the grove of trees that leads to the house and can now see that the house is still standing.

"Oh, God, it's there! It's still there!" she sobs, wiping her eyes.

"Yeah, but what's with the emergency vehicles?" I ask. We crane our necks forward as I inch the car down the road. When we get close, I can see that the flashing lights are from a county sheriff's car, and next to it there's a white van. As I pull up, a woman emerges from a small crowd and runs toward us. It's Robin's mom.

"Where have you *been?*" she screams. Her face is contorted in distress. Robin comes out crying and rushes into her mom's arms.

"You're okay!" Robin sobs.

"I've been looking everywhere for you!" she yells, holding Robin back away from her. "Where have you *been?*"

"I-I was at home," she manages to say.

At this, her mom breaks down into uncontrollable sobbing. She first tries to pull Robin close, then pushes her back and sinks to her knees.

"Mom!" Robin screams, taking a knee in front of her. "Where's Dad?"

A deputy walks up and leans down to whisper in her mom's ear, after which she wails loudly and crumples to the ground. He then looks at Robin and takes a step forward. "Are you the daughter?"

Sheer, stark, terror crosses Robin's face as she meekly nods.

"I'm sorry to have to tell you, but your father is deceased."

17

The sight of Robin on all fours completely disassembled with grief, alternately sobbing her eyes out and vomiting, is one I never want to see again, nor one I'll ever forget.

I kneel beside her with my arms around her neck, trying my best to give the same comfort she once gave me in a crisis. Across from us, her mom is keeled over in tears. I can see a stretcher being wheeled to the van parked in the distance behind Robin. It's covered in a sheet, but it's obvious Robin's father is under the sheet. Thank God Robin doesn't see this.

When I look up, the scenery is confusing. The house is still standing. In fact, it doesn't seem to be damaged. There are small tree limbs and twigs lying around, but for the life of me, I don't understand how Mr. O'Leary is dead.

Within a few minutes, only a single sheriff's deputy remains on the scene. Gradually, both Robin's and Mrs. O'Leary's wailing and crying ebbs, until finally, with my help, they're able to stand.

"Where *were* you?" Mrs. O'Leary asks of Robin, yet again.

"Mom, I told you!" she chokes out, "I was at the house in town!"

Without turning, Mrs. O'Leary points to Robin's car.

"Then how did your car get here?" She looks first at Robin, then at me.

"I parked it there last night," she says.

"Why?" her mother responds, turning back to Robin.

"Because I was with Ash and didn't want Dad to know!" she says in a timid voice dripping with regret.

Her mom sighs. "Lord, you have no idea."

"I don't understand," Robin replies, looking around. "It doesn't look like the tornado hit our house."

"No, it didn't, but your dad—he was . . ."

"Wh-what are you saying?" Robin replies.

"Your dad—" her mother manages to choke out. "I couldn't stop him. He went outside. I think he died of a heart attack. He just . . . fell down and died. When I got to him, he was already gone!"

"He died thinking I was out here in the storm?" she squeaks.

Holy shit, this is bad. The reality of this tragedy completely shatters me, but my concern is Robin, who must now face up to guilt I wouldn't wish on my worst enemy.

Mrs. O'Leary pulls a sobbing Robin in and clasps her tightly. They stay like this for a long time. I don't know what to do. I want to be the one comforting Robin. The sadness of the entire scene is suffocating. I'm still standing to the side when Mrs. O'Leary leaves Robin by herself and approaches me.

"It's best you go on home," she says. Her eyes are cold and distant.

"What about Robin?" I can feel panic rising. "I can—"

"Just go home."

A familiar uncertainty grips me. "Robin?" I call out as I walk over and take her hand. "Do you need anything?" I need Robin to tell me she needs me. In fact, what I really want to say is, "Do you want me to stay with you," but I don't have it in me to forcefully intrude.

She pulls her hand back and wipes her eyes. "No."

Just *no*. Nothing else. No smile, no thanks, no "see you later," no nothing. Just *no*. Why? I can't think my way past it.

"Please," her mom says.

"Okay," I reply. "If there's anything—"

"I'll let you know."

"Yes, ma'am."

I turn and walk to my car. It feels weird. It feels scary. Nothing about it feels *us;* rather, it feels just like the beginning of a nightmare only recently conquered. I feel nauseous. The drive home seems to take forever, and when I get there, Grams is distraught. Fortunately, our house is on the side of town left untouched by the tornado, and there's no damage visible anywhere.

"Child!" she calls out as she runs toward me before I can even get out of the car.

I get out just in time to take her into my arms. "Grams, I'm okay."

"I was so worried about you," she says, trying her best to maintain composure. "There's people dead. Tom and Lettie Nettles—their home got hit.

And there's more."

I know Grams is upset and needs comfort, but I'm in no condition to provide it when I need it so badly myself. All I want is to figure out a way back to Robin.

"I need to go to my room, Grams."

"Okay, child," she says, releasing me.

I hurry up to my room. Once there, I don't know what to do. I'm a coiled pile of nerves and energy with no place to unwind. I throw myself onto my bed. With cell phone service out, I can't call Robin, and I'm not sure she'd take my call if I could call her. I'm almost in tears. An nightmarish fear is growing within me by the minute. With all my emotional might, I try to push it down.

Later that afternoon, Grams reappears at my door, this time with a soda. "Here, sweetie. You need something to drink or you're gonna dry up." It's all I can do to sit up and take the can. "They think there's only three people dead," she says as I take a sip.

"Well, I know who one of them is," I hear myself respond.

Grams gets a surprised look on her face. "They haven't released any names yet," she says in a puzzled voice. "We know about Tom and Lettie from Reverend Barncastle. Who's the third one?"

"Robin's dad. I saw them take him away."

Grams freezes and a horrified look settles across her face. "Oh, my! How—"

"It wasn't at their house here. They were at their vacation home, and he died of a heart attack."

Grams is momentarily speechless, and she finally clears her throat. "Oh, Robin . . . that poor child!"

"If you don't mind, Grams, I really need some rest." It's a lie. What I really need is what I can't have: to go be with my girl.

I barely get any sleep during the night, and in the morning my stomach is knotted. I'm obsessed with getting to her, but I can't even think my way through that. Then, I start getting the idea she might come over to update me, so that spurs me to get up and get ready for the day.

I'm sitting around in the living room fighting the growing terror in my brain when Orm makes an appearance. Grams lets him in, and he makes an immediate beeline to me and embraces me tightly.

"I just heard. How is Robin?"

"I don't know."

"You mean, you haven't—"

"Not today. I'm waiting, but I haven't heard anything."

"Well, a lot of the phone lines are still down. The cell phone service will be the first to come back online." He eyes me and sees I'm not well. "Do you know how . . . I mean, the tornado supposedly didn't hit any houses out there, and—"

"He died of a heart attack." I wonder if everyone I come across is going to need the same explanation.

"No shit? I hope Robin wasn't the one who found him. How is it you know this? Are y'all—"

"Are the roads clear?"

He gives me a strange look. "Well, yeah, pretty much, except for the neighborhood down the road that got hit real bad."

"Take me to Robin's?" I'm already up and heading to the front door.

"Sure, Ash."

He pulls out of the driveway and after a minute or two, asks, "So, where the hell did you get off to last week?"

"Colorado. Her family has a condo."

"So, I guess y'all are really back together? People were noticing y'all were gone at the same time."

I shake my head and grimace. "Well, before the storm hit, I thought we were."

He gives me a puzzled look. "So y'all broke up again?"

I exhale and look away. "I don't know. It's complicated."

"What does that mean?"

"It means that she could have asked me to stay with her, but she didn't."

"Well, the phone lines are down all over—"

"I was with her, Orm."

"Oh. So . . . she sent you home?"

I let out a long sigh and nod my head.

After a minute or two, he continues. "She's traumatized."

"Yep, she is."

"She needs to pull her self together."

"And that's kind of a team sport. Or at least, that's what I thought."

"You're right," he nods, "it is."

We're silent for a long few minutes. When I look over, he has his eyes on the road, but I know he's listening.

"She was so cold and distant. It was like—" I can't make myself say it.

"Just like when she ditched you?"

Orm giving voice to my worst fear makes me choke up. "Kinda, y-yes."

"Okay, look, maybe she's not ditching you. Maybe she needs you but just can't get in touch with you. Right?"

I let out a single sob, then wipe my eyes. "God, I hope so, Orm."

"I get that she's upset by her dad's death, but those things happen."

"I'm pretty sure she feels his death is her fault."

"Huh? I don't get that part."

"Okay, you might as well hear it from me. Robin snuck out of the house to come into town and spend the night with me at their house here. When the tornado came, her father thought she was outside at the vacation home somewhere, so he ran out trying to find her." I feel a huge lump in my throat. "Then he had a heart attack and died."

"What? Are you sure?"

"Yes. I heard her mom say it."

"Not trying to be disrespectful, but that's bullshit! Wouldn't he think that Robin knows enough to come in out of the rain?"

Whoa. He has a point. "I-I don't know," I finally answer.

"Something's weird about that for sure," he replies, letting out a low whistle. "How's Robin dealing with it?"

"I wish I knew, but I can't call her, and her mom ran me off yesterday."

He gives my shoulder a squeeze, but we're silent for the rest of the trip. As we pull into the O'Leary's driveway, I fight to keep my panic under control.

"Wait here," I tell him as I get out of the car. He nods and kills the ignition. I see that Robin's car is exactly where we left it the night before last. I ring the doorbell. No one answers right away, and as I'm about to ring it again, someone who faintly resembles Robin opens the door and stares at me.

She's colorless, her face is expressionless, and her eyes sunken. It doesn't look like she's even had a shower or bath recently. It's as if she's looking straight through me. I've never seen anyone alive that looks this frightful.

"Baby?" I hold out my hand. "I'm worried about you."

She makes no effort to take my hand. With everything in me, I want to gather her up and take her with me. But she remains frozen in place, almost as if she didn't even hear me. I move closer and reach to touch her hand. Suddenly, the door is opened wide from behind her by her mom.

"She doesn't want to see you," her mom says, stepping in front of Robin.

Before I can say anything, Robin comes to life and asserts herself.

"Will you *please* stop speaking for me?" Her face is contorted in anger as she elbows her mom to the side so she can see me again. Her voice is cracking like she's been weeping for hours. "*God*, I hate that! Dad did it, and now *you're* just picking up right where he left off! It never stops! Just leave me alone!"

Her surprised mom moves a couple of steps back, taking up a position behind Robin and just to the side.

I see my opening. "Do you need anything?"

"No," she says, in a monotone. She continues to stand in the doorway.

"Come with me. Let *me* take care of you." Once more, I hold out my hand for her to take. She eyes my hand but makes no effort to take it. After an awkward half minute, with her mother glaring at me, I drop my hand and shuffle from one foot to the other. Her mom's stern presence makes the conversation awkward.

"I'm fine," she says at last.

"You don't *look* fine."

"Well, I am."

"Just come with me. Let me take care of you, okay?" Her mother looks like she's standing on her tongue.

For another minute or so, Robin gives me nothing but a blank stare. God, I wish her mother would get the hell out of the way.

"I'm fine," she finally mutters.

I study her eyes. "You sure?"

There's another long pause before she answers, "I'm sure."

"Okay, then," I say, taking a deep breath. I almost turn away, but I don't. I'm not going to let that kind of thing get started up again—at least not by something I do or say. I move a bit closer where I can speak in a much lower voice.

"Baby, do you want me to come in and just be with you? I can send Orm away, and he'll come back later and get me. Just, you know, whatever you want me to do."

"You've already done enough," she says, again in a monotone.

"What?"

"You heard her," her mom says.

Robin turns to stare down her mom. I grit my teeth, wanting more than anything to slap her mother. When she turns back toward me, I search her face for any sign of life.

"Baby?" I say, softly. I'm on the verge of getting on my knees and begging her.

"Don't call me that."

I can feel my stomach churning. "What do you mean by *that?*"

She continues with the blank stare, and when I open my mouth to speak again, she finally responds. "Never mind. It's done."

"Hold on, *what's* done?"

"Just forget it, okay?"

"Okay, Robin," I say, bringing up all my courage to speak my mind. "I know you're going through a horrible thing. I'm not going to pretend to know what you're feeling. But I *am* here for you. And I very much want to be with you."

She looks down and lets out a long breath that sounds like an expression of impatience. When she looks up, she has a "why are you still here?" look on her face.

"Okay. So, we're back to *that?*"

She gets a frown. "Whatever, Asher." And with that, she withdraws and closes the door in my face.

I can't believe it. For a long minute, I stay rooted to the spot, hoping against hope that she'll open the door and throw herself into my arms. But, there is no reappearance. Ears ringing, I turn and trudge back to Orm's car.

"Drive."

"Okay." He turns the car around and drives the length of Robin's Lake Road without saying a thing. When we get to the highway, I can feel him take a long, hard stare at me. "I take it that didn't go well."

"We're right back to the first time she rejected me," I say, forcing myself to acknowledge the obvious. "So much for letting her back in. I really feel stupid now."

"So, did she tell you to get lost or something?"

"Pretty much." I'm actually getting pissed.

He thinks about it for a minute, then tries to comfort me.

"Well, she's going through a lot. Maybe you give her a get out of jail free card?"

"I don't know why I'd do that, to be honest. I'm so sick of this!"

We're silent for a long time.

"Are you going to the funeral?"

For the very first time since yesterday's events, I realize that of course, there's going to be a funeral.

"Shit, I don't know."

"I think you go."

"After what she just said, I don't know about that."

Orm breezes past what I just said. "There's a memorial service tomorrow at Our Lady of the Covenant Church. The real funeral will be in Houston."

I say nothing, and instead, fight down the urge to cry.

He reaches over and touches my shoulder.

"I'm here for you, Ash."

"I never told you the half of it." I grab for a tissue and blow my nose. "When she rejected me back in March, it was through the worst kind of cruelty you can imagine. Don't get me wrong . . . I'm old enough to realize that relationships don't always work." I wipe a tear before it runs. "Finally, I got over her. And what did I do? I let her back in." I stifle a sob.

"That's gotta hurt."

"This is a hell of a send-off for college, isn't it?" I say as another tear makes its way south.

When I get home and walk in, Grams is laying out a dress across the bed in her bedroom. It's a navy blue mid-length—one that I've seen her wear to church, but it was several years ago. "It's for the O'Leary service tomorrow," she says, in a tone of voice as if it's assumed I know about it and will be attending.

The rest of the day is nothing but a dull blur of nothingness. There's only a relentless pain, tempered only by a burning desire to have something I can't have. I simply cannot believe I let this happen.

Morning brings a bit better clarity. I know I have to attend. And I know this is going to be a really shitty day for Robin. I wish things were different between us, so I could ease her pain and know what she's thinking. And the more I think about *that*, the more I think my head's about to explode.

I don't even bother with a shower, and instead pick out a dark dress from the back of my closet, pull it on, and fix my hair. Grams and I are silent all the way to the church. My apprehension is rising in a slow crescendo. As we walk into the auditorium I feel I have to be on guard, afraid that Robin will appear out of nowhere to deliver some emotionally devastating remark to me.

It doesn't take long to find her. She's up front, facing forward like a statue, so I can't see exactly what she's wearing, but it's very dark. Her mom, dressed entirely in black with a black veil covering her face, is sitting next to her, doing her part to remain perfectly still. Others are sitting next to and behind them, and one lady reaches forward and lightly touches Robin's shoulder before withdrawing her hand.

The ambiance of the church is devoid of any emotion save despair. Mr. O'Leary's open casket is positioned just in front of the podium and off to the side of the altar. Three people walk up to it and gaze at his face before returning to their seats. The grief factor of it all hits me unexpectedly, and it centers on Robin. That she would have to sit there with her dead father right in front of her really affects me.

I'm completely zoned out during the service. Afterward, the attendees stand and begin to exit. It's when we're outside making our way through the crowd toward our car that I hear a female voice enunciate the word "abomination." I don't know why, but I stop and turn toward it to find a thirty-ish woman who is in a small circle of four other women about ten feet off to the side, and all of them are staring straight at me.

I know Grams heard it too, as she quietly summons me to keep up with her. But something in me won't obey. The women continue to stare at me as if I'm a zoo animal. That's it. I quickly stride right up to them and address the woman whose voice I heard.

"You ladies have something you want to say?" A couple of them inch backward, but the speaker holds her ground, staring down her nose at me. It's as if they regard me as nothing more than an insect. "I heard what you said. Do you want to say it to my face?"

About this time, a man, apparently the woman's husband, walks up and positions himself at her side. He says nothing but gives me a cold stare. I look back at his wife.

"I didn't think so," I say, turning to leave. I've gone maybe five feet when I hear it.

I jerk my head back around in time to see the man wiping his mouth, a large spit stain on the sidewalk in front of him. He stares straight at me and crosses himself, which pisses me off beyond description. I stride right back up to where he is and put my face right in his. While holding eye contact, I turn my head and spit. The women gasp. I then hold up my middle finger only an inch from the end of his nose. The women avert their eyes.

"Goddam whore," the man mutters, turning around to walk away. Grams seizes my upper arm and pulls me away stumbling backward.

"Just ignore him," she says as we cross the parking lot.

As we drive back past the entranceway to the church, I look up and am startled to see Robin and her mom. And Robin is staring straight at me with the same vacant expression she had yesterday. Off to the side, six men are loading the now-closed coffin into the back of a hearse parked near the side entrance. I lock onto her eyes, looking for any little sign: a mouthed word or two, a smile, even a half-smile—anything that will give me hope. But there's nothing. Just cruel indifference. With no warning whatsoever, I feel tears starting to well up. I look out the window to wipe them, so Grams won't see.

The next morning, cell service is restored. After four tortuously long days of not having heard anything from Robin, and with our college departures staring us in the face, I decide to call her, even if she shoots me down. But when I call, it rings for a long time and then goes to voicemail. Later, I call again, and again there's no answer. Knowing that she's purposefully avoiding me kills me all over again. I realize I don't even know her anymore. I wonder if I ever did.

Misery. That's the best word to describe how I feel. And I can't do anything to make it go away. So after a couple of hours in my bed crying my eyes out, I pass a tipping point and decide to just let Robin go. It's all for the best, I tell myself. I salt my resolve with a dose of anger. I know enough to know I can't deal with this kind of on-again, off-again middle school bullshit.

The next morning, I'm lying in my bed trying to summon the willpower just to get up and face the day, when I hear Grams on the stairs, followed by a knock on the bedroom door. I see from my bedside clock that it's just shy of eight o'clock.

Grams opens the door and stands in the doorway. She has a forlorn expression on her face I don't think I've ever seen.

"I've got bad news, child."

"What is it?" I ask, taking a deep swallow.

"Lord have mercy, child," she says, doing her best to hold back tears. "It's Robin. She's at the hospital. They're not sure she's gonna make it."

18

I feel detached from reality.

It's as if I've been transported to another planet and am watching the earthlings through a telescope as they scurry around pretending their lives matter. Grams' voice recedes into the far distance, and I can hear my own heart beating like a drum.

"Wh-what happened to her?" I manage to stammer out.

"I don't know, child. I just got the call from Lorene Bennet down at the sheriff's office. She said they've flown her by helicopter down to Amarillo."

My brain races into overdrive trying to figure out why Robin would be at the hospital in danger of losing her life. Is it an illness? Maybe appendicitis?

Forget letting her go—I've got to get to her. *Now*. I jump up to grab some clothes.

"I'm going down there," I tell Grams, as I quickly pull on a tee shirt and pair of jeans. "Do you know which hospital?"

"I'll go with you," she replies.

I stop tying my tennis shoes and turn toward her. "Not this time, Grams," I say, as gently as I can.

After a few seconds of searching my face, she nods her head in understanding. I grab my phone and find an address for Amarillo Regional Hospital. It's as good a start as any. After giving Grams a kiss goodbye, I'm in my car and on the road within five minutes.

The navigation app tells me it will take two hours to get to Amarillo. My heart is pounding every mile of the distance. I make the trip in only ninety minutes. When the grim facade of the hospital comes into view, my throat tightens, and I break into open sobs. I alternately wipe my eyes and pound on the steering wheel at the unfairness of it all. After parking in a pay lot and grabbing my ticket, I literally race through the front door. The information desk is right up front.

"I'm here to see Robin O'Leary!" I gasp out.

The clerk gives me a once-over before typing on the computer in front of him. He's scrutinizing the screen when my patience runs out.

"Can you hurry, please?"

"I'm sorry, miss, but I have no patient by that name taking visitors."

"Then, can you tell me what happened to her?"

"I'm sorry, miss, I can't say anything else. Federal law doesn't allow us to release any patient information without consent."

"So she's here?"

"Miss, I'm sorry."

"Please!" I beg. "Just nod or something! Don't let her die before I can see her!"

The clerk merely stares into my eyes. Hearing someone else behind me, I stand off to the side. Without warning, tears are streaming down my face. When the last person behind me has been seen, the desk clerk gives me a pitying look and then beckons me over.

"You can go to the ICU waiting area, and maybe they can give you more information," he says under his breath, following with "and you didn't hear that from me."

I'm on the third floor in a matter of seconds, and the signs get me to the ICU. I walk through the entranceway and head for the nurses' station, but suddenly Robin's mom rises from a seat to my left and steps in front of me.

"Where's Robin?" I demand, wiping my tears.

I can see she's been crying as well. It takes her a minute to snap out of her fugue, and she shakily gestures to a seat in the waiting area away from everyone else. After we sit down, she fixes her eyes on mine.

"Robin tried to kill herself last night."

I feel like the breath has been sucked out of me.

"H-how?"

She hesitates and swallows hard. "She drove off into the lake." She tries to continue, but she's on the verge of sobbing. With one hand, she gestures for me to wait until she gets control of herself. It takes a minute or so, but then she continues. "It's her dad. She's been crying ever since her dad passed away." She pauses to blow her nose into a tissue. "Lucky for us, someone saw her and was able to get her out of the car. The EMTs got her breathing again, but she hasn't woken up yet."

I try to speak but only succeed in breaking into sobs that take a minute of fierce determination to bring under control.

"Woken up?" I finally manage. "What does that mean?"

"She's in critical condition and in a coma. They've got her on life support."

"Wh-when is she gonna wake up?"

She looks me square in the eyes. "Asher, she might not *ever* wake up."

"Can I *see* her?"

"No."

"Why *not?*"

"She's in no condition to take visitors."

"When *can* I see her?" I say through tears.

She studies my face, then straightens up and peers down at me. "Never, if it's up to me," she sniffs, in a suddenly icy-cold voice.

I'm dumbfounded. "I'm her *girlfriend!*"

Her eyes narrow. "Not in here, you're not."

"I don't understand! Why are you *doing* this?"

She inhales, as if taking a drag on a cigarette, holds it, then exhales and wipes her eyes once again. "All of this started with the two of you carrying on like heathens," she says. "My husband tried to put a stop to it, and now I see why."

"Heathens? Y-you sent us—"

"It was a mistake. If you two hadn't lied to me, he wouldn't have been out there," she says, turning her head and casting her gaze downward.

"Lied to you? We didn't lie to you!"

"You know what I mean!"

"Are you blaming me and Robin?"

"Stop! Just stop it!"

She takes a second to compose herself, then rises to leave. I'm completely, and in every way possible, emotionally devastated. My thoughts are hijacked by the mental image of Robin in a hospital bed with all manner of tubes and needles sticking into her.

"Please," I mewl, my voice shaking. "I love her! You *know* that!"

She turns back to me. "There's no way I'm letting you anywhere near her!"

"This is *killing* me!" I sob.

"You should have thought about that a week ago, young lady! If you want to help, go to your priest, or preacher, or whatever, and confess."

Fueled by desperation, and from somewhere deep within, I find strength. "I won't leave," I state forcefully, "not until I see her."

She nods, then approaches the information desk and engages the clerk in conversation while gesturing behind herself toward me. Within a couple of minutes, a police officer enters the room and approaches me. I realize I'm out of options. I turn and walk away before he gets to me. Leaving *her*, while she's clinging to life, rips my very soul.

It's on the way back home that the fearsome thought of Robin actually dying seizes my brain and refuses to let go. I imagine Grams telling me that Robin has passed away. My mind goes back to Mr. O'Leary's funeral, only instead of him in the coffin, now I imagine Robin. Thoughts of never seeing her face again, never hearing her laugh or sing, or worse, never seeing that smile of hers, takes me to a hellish place, and by the time I get back to Sage-brush, I'm a mess.

"Oh, God," Orm sighs when he sees me after opening his front door. He grabs my hand and pulls me inside. "What did she do this time?"

"I just got back from Amarillo," I blurt out. "She tried to kill herself last night." I take a deep breath and wipe my tears as Orm's eyes get huge. "She's in the ICU at Amarillo Regional."

"Ho-lee shit," Orm swears. "How?"

"She drove into the lake at their property."

"Fuck! How is she?"

"I didn't see her."

"What?"

"Her mom wouldn't let me. She called the cops on me."

"How can she keep you from seeing her? *Robin's* in charge of who can see her!"

"Except that she's unconscious and on life support."

"Oh, God!" Orm mutters. He leads me to the sofa where he takes a seat and gestures for me to sit beside him.

"We were in Colorado just last week!" I say, dabbing at one eye. "We were so happy. Everything was so *perfect*. Why? Why this?"

Orm pulls me close. "She must have been eaten up with guilt."

"What if I somehow contributed to it? What if it was something I did that pushed her over the edge?"

"You can't go there," Orm replies solemnly.

"I thought she was dumping me again. So, instead of comforting her, I got angry and pulled back."

"Slow down," Orm says. "She pushed you away. I saw it!"

"But I let her," I argue.

"Ash, you went through a lot. You're guilty of nothing more than protecting yourself."

I know Orm means well, but I'm wracked with guilt. Something inside me that's tangled up in fiery passion and promises in the dark tugs at my psyche, telling me that it doesn't matter how much I gave in the relationship, I should have given just a bit more.

After I get home, I'm no good for anything, especially conversation. I hole up in my room go to bed early. I can't sleep at all. I spend the next day half-heartedly going through the motions of planning for my move. But I can't see myself leaving. Not now. When the Dean of Student Affairs at the Winston calls to welcome me to "the Winston family," it's all I can do to speak.

In desperation, and risking the ire of Robin's mother, I call the hospital to ask how Robin's doing. I hope this isn't stalking. The operator rings her room and her mom answers. When she realizes who it is, the tone of her voice ices over.

"Robin is still the same, Asher," she announces. "Is there anything else?"

"Is she asking for me?"

"No, she's not. She's on life support—don't you get that?" And with that, she hangs up.

To counter the urge to drive to Amarillo, I sneak off to spend the afternoon alone at Robin's Lake. I remain parked in the exact spot that she and I occupied that very first time we were here together. I raise my hand to my face and stare at it. The sensation of her fingers entwined in mine comes rushing into my brain, and I instinctively close my hand as if she has just taken it.

Out of desperation, I talk to her aloud, like she's really here and can hear my voice. I tell her how much I need her and love her. I tell her I can't go without her. I beg her to come back to me.

The next day, Grams brings me the worst news yet. It seems that Robin is still in her coma with no sign of improvement, and now the doctors have told her family that they should think about ending life support. My guts literally tie themselves into knots. I'm convinced that I'm the only one fighting for her, and being "nice" or playing by the rules isn't going to cut it. I call the hospital again. This time, I ask to be connected to her room, and her mom answers.

"Mrs. O'Leary, please don't hang up on me!"

"She's still the same," comes a cold response.

"Is it true? That the doctors are saying you have to turn off her life support?"

There's a long silence, and I'm expecting to hear the click of the telephone receiver. But then, she speaks. And surprisingly, her voice doesn't seem to have the sharpness that it did the last time I talked to her.

"It's true," she says. "They reran some tests today, and . . . and her brain activity has not picked up since she's been here."

"Don't do it!" I blurt out. "She's going to come out of this!"

I can hear her let out a long breath. I think she's fighting back the tears.

"We're praying about it."

"Please—you have to tell me you won't do it!"

"I can't tell you that. It's in God's hands now. All of us, including *you*, have to accept that."

"But—"

"This is a *family* matter and really none of your business, Asher." After another few seconds of silence from her mom, during which I can hear a man speaking in the background, the line goes dead.

I've never been in a blind panic before. I let out what must sound to Grams like a primal scream, then rush downstairs and out the door, where I almost bowl over Orm, who is coming up the steps.

"Whoa!" he lets out.

"Stay out of my way!" I sidestep him and head for my car. I'm in the driver's seat when Orm piles into the passenger seat.

"Ash?" I put the keys in the ignition. It's when I go for the gearshift that he grabs my forearm. "Ash! Hang on, will ya?" He closes the door and turns to face me, giving me a long hard stare. "Where are you headed?" It's right then that I realize what he must be thinking.

"I'm not gonna do something stupid, if that's what you're thinking. I've just gotta get out of here!"

"Then take me wherever you're going. I'm not gonna leave you."

Whatever. I put the car in gear, back out, and start driving. I have no idea where I'm headed. Orm displays no concern about that and keeps his gaze on me.

After about ten minutes of silence, he speaks. "You wanna tell me what's got you so upset?"

After another four or five minutes of silence, during which he must think I'm ignoring him, I let it out in a long stream of consciousness filled with expletives and tears. When I finish, I pound my fist on the steering wheel. There's a farm supply store just up ahead with a large parking lot, and I pull in and park just as another crying jag erupts.

Orm appears unfazed. "I'm not gonna say I know what you're going through . . . but I get that it's terrible."

"If they let her die, you might as well just put me in the loony bin."

"Ash," he finally replies, shaking his head slowly from side to side. He reaches over and gives my shoulder a squeeze. "We're too young to have to deal with death. It's not fair you have to do that."

"Yeah." I grip the steering wheel hard and then place my head against it. "Everything moves so goddam fast with her. Do you realize I've known her for barely five months?"

"Mhmm."

"In some ways, it only seems like a few days. And in other ways . . ." I sigh out loud. "Well, it seems like a lifetime."

"It's crazy."

"Hell, just last week we were planning our lives together!"

"Seriously?"

"Yeah! We've even talked about marriage!"

"And she does a one-eighty in a single day?"

I lift my head and turn to Orm. "You know what? I'm going to have to deal with Robin's death right when I'm leaving for college. That's pretty fucked up." I put my head back down. "And the way things are going now, I won't even be allowed to attend her funeral."

"That's a lot to deal with."

I lean back into my seat and stare into the sky. "If I had known all the shit I'd have to go through . . . the pain, all this . . . whatever! I'm just used up. I'm literally used up."

Orm is quiet for a couple of minutes, but then says, "You fell in love. That's worth something!"

"Is it? Is it really worth falling in love if you have to pay a price like this?"

He shrugs and lets out a sigh. "Can't answer that for you, Ash. But for better or worse, you have the memories of an experience that you don't just go out and find every day."

"I think it's for worse. She took me to the highest mountain and then casually threw me off. Twice."

At a little after eight o'clock the next morning, Grams comes knocking on my bedroom door—and a terror seizes me. I know why she's there, and I know what news she bears. I don't want to face it. I just want to be on the other side of the planet, or someplace where bad news can't find me.

With no response from the inside of the room, she opens the door and steps in. She has a dazed expression on her face. I hold my breath and pull my covers up to my eyes as she opens her mouth to speak.

"She woke up. She's gonna live."

19

The phone rings for what seems like forever, and by the time it's answered, I've bitten my lip almost to the point of bleeding.

It's Mrs. O'Leary. I can hear others in the background.

"Mrs. O'Leary!" I shout, "It's Asher! Can I talk to Robin, please?"

"Asher," she begins, and the tone of her voice tells me she's annoyed at my call, "Robin is in no condition to talk on the phone with anyone, least of all you. If you don't mind, we're trying to get her settled in a private room. Goodbye!"

At the moment I hear the phone line go dead, I let out a joyous whoop. The whiplash from terror to joy has my entire body in spasms. Robin, the love of my life, is alive! Knowing I won't have to deal with Robin's death is a relief like no other. I call Orm right away.

"Orm! Did you hear the news? She woke up! She's not going to die!"

"What? Robin woke up?"

"I know, right? It's a miracle, Orm! I'm telling you, it's a straight-up miracle!" I can barely contain myself.

"That's really great, Ash! Are you going to go see her?"

"As soon as I can! Oh my God, you have no idea how good this makes me feel! Can I come over?"

I take what must be the fastest shower in the world, wrap myself in a towel, grab my brush and take two or three good pulls on my hair, leaving a puddle of water on the floor. After throwing on the first random outfit I find, I go downstairs to find something to eat.

"Sweetie, I need to talk to you," Grams says, wiping her hands on a dish towel and motioning for me to take a seat at the dinette. "I just got off the phone with Robin's mother, and according to her, you've made quite a pest of yourself."

"What?!"

"She's asked that you don't try to call Robin, or—"

"Good God, Grams! She's my *girlfriend!* Remember?"

"You might be her friend, sweetie, but—"

"Grams, hold on a minute," I say, raising my palm. "I didn't say I'm her *friend!* I said I'm her *girlfriend.* As in romantic partner. Significant other. Lover. We had this conversation months ago!"

Grams continues as if having been entirely deaf to what I just told her. "Mrs. O'Leary told me that Robin isn't completely out of the woods, and she has some issues—"

"Okay, Grams, stop, please." I wait until she's silent. "I know you're trying to be helpful, but this third-party shit, pardon my French, stops right here. If her mother has something to say, I'm an adult, and she can jolly well say it to me, instead of calling my grandmother."

Back upstairs, I decide to go around her mom and call her cell number, but after ten rings it goes to voicemail, probably because it's off. Once my hair is dry, and I'm dressed, I'm out the front door and headed to Orm's.

"Look at it this way," Orm says, "she knows how to get in touch with you. If she wants to call you, she will." Something about that rubs me the wrong way.

"Are you saying I shouldn't call her??"

He gets a surprised look. "No, I just meant that—"

"What? That she doesn't want to hear from me?"

"Ash, slow down!"

"Why *wouldn't* she want to?"

"She tried to kill herself! You don't just hop back into your life after doing that. There's something wrong, and she's gonna have to deal with it—you know, therapy, or something." He pauses for effect. "What I'm saying is that she's got a lot to deal with that could be more important than calling you."

I tune out big time. I don't want *any* help that involves waiting. I just want to be with her. *Now.* Before it's too late.

"Well?" he asks, after a minute of silence. "What are you thinking?"

"I'm thinking I've only got four days before I leave. I'm thinking I'm going to see her no matter what her mother says!"

"Just make sure you know what you're doing, Ash," he sighs.

It's halfway through the next morning, and she hasn't called. I'm starting to really dislike her mom. I drag myself out of bed and attend to packing.

After a couple of hours of moving in slow motion, nearly all the shelves are empty, and empty drawers are hanging out of the dresser. Most of my clothing is draped across my bed. Is this really what the beginning of my future looks like? What should be a time of joy feels more like an execution date.

I go down for lunch and find that Grams has a meal ready for both of us. I put my arm around her shoulder and pull her in for a long hug. I know my leaving is going to be a massive change for her. We eat lunch in almost total silence. I'm not sure which one of us is saddest.

Shortly after noon, my phone rings. I don't recognize the number.

"Hello?" I say.

There's a loud sigh. Then I hear Mrs. O'Leary's voice, and she almost sounds helpless. "Asher?"

"Yes, ma'am?"

"Robin wants to see you," she mutters, in a tone of exasperation.

"Wh-what? I can come see her?"

"Yes."

There's no time for makeup or wardrobe change. With my heart racing, I literally drop what I'm doing, give Grams a kiss, and sprint to the car. I'm nonstop all the way to Amarillo Regional Hospital. When the desk clerk says, "Room 520," I sprint to the elevator bay, and in a couple of minutes, I'm knocking on the door to her room. Her mom opens the door, contemplates my presence, then steps aside to let me in. She says nothing. I have no idea what to expect. I just know my girl is in there, and she needs me.

Robin's room reeks of a typical stale hospital, with fluorescent lighting emitting a constant low hum. She's in bed, with the back adjusted up far enough to allow her to see around the room without raising her head.

"Mom?" she says, to which Mrs. O'Leary sighs and leaves the room without question. Once she's gone, Robin looks at me in a way I've never seen before, as if she's taken a wrong turn and is looking for a way back.

"How are you doing?" I ask.

She immediately gets a deep frown on her face.

"Well, let's see," she replies, in a slightly raspy, yet sarcastic tone of voice. "Oh, yeah! I tried to kill myself! So, I guess you could say I'm pissed that I couldn't even do *that* right."

I ignore the remark. "I'm so glad to see you!" She looks at me like I just spoke in a foreign language. "I came as quick as I could after your mom called." I walk over and try to take her hand, but she pulls it back and looks away from me.

That catches me by surprise. I thought that maybe after a brush with death, she'd realize she loves me. Looks like I was wrong.

She says nothing for a minute and instead remains mute with her eyes closed and her face aimed away from me. When it's apparent I'm not going to back away, she turns to look up at me.

"Why would you even want to be here with a loser like me?" she says. Her chin has a barely perceptible quiver.

"You asked for me, remember?" I try to address her in my calmest reassuring tone of voice.

"So I did." Her reply is barely a whisper.

"I'm just glad you're going to be okay and—"

"I'm *not* going to just be okay!" she spits back at me. With her left arm, she catches me by surprise and pushes me back.

"I'm not your enemy," I say in a slightly raised voice, moving back up to her. "I'm here because I care about you."

"Care?" she retorts. "I've never heard you say that! What about *love*? I thought you loved me. Guess that's as fake as your smile, huh?"

"Why are you doing this?" I can feel my eyes watering.

"Puhleeze," she says, her voice now raspier than ever. A deep frown contorts her face and she makes no effort at eye contact.

I take a deep breath and, summoning all the tone of confidence I can, try to break through her facade. "Baby, I *do* love you. I love you more than I can describe. You're everything to me. You know that."

Her expression is frozen and she says nothing in reply, yet I can see a tear forming in the corner of her left eye. I lean over her just a little. "Please talk to me," I whisper. "I love you. I want to take care of you."

"Look," she says, her voice now aggressive, "I don't know why I even wanted you to come here. Why don't you just walk out and don't look back?"

I'm getting nowhere with her, and I'm not sure how many more zingers I can take.

"Walk out? You *called* for me! Why do you want me to walk out?"

She gives me a look as if I'm stupid. "Because it's something *I'll* never be able to do," she says as if staring down her nose at an insignificant gnat.

That one goes right over my head.

"Wait, what?"

"She doesn't get it," Robin mutters off to the side as if talking to someone next to her. She fixes her eyes on me. "*I* can't walk out of here because I broke my back."

"Huh?"

"I'm paralyzed from the waist down," she states matter-of-factly, as if it's somehow obvious. "I won't be dancing. I won't be singing. All of it . . . it's gone!"

I'm blindsided. My brain won't let it compute. I feel like all the joy has been sucked from the world.

"Okay, folks," she begins once again, addressing the unseen audience, "move right along. Freak show's over."

"Baby, I didn't know! I'm so sorry—"

"*You're* sorry?" she snarls at me, her face awash in anger. "Like I said—if I could only have finished the job!"

"Will you just *stop* it?"

"Why should I, after all you've done to me? Because of you, I can't even go to college!"

"Robin, for God's sake, *stop!*"

"You stole everything that meant anything to me!" she suddenly sobs, covering her face with her hands.

For a minute, I'm too afraid to move or say anything. But when I see the tears running out from beneath her hands, I hesitate no more. I lean over and slide my arms around her neck and gently pull her into an embrace. At first, she resists by going limp, but after a minute, she slowly puts her arms around me and nestles her head onto my shoulder, after which we both have a good cry.

"Ash, I'm so sorry," she says in a whisper. "I'm so sorry I shut you out. And I'm sorry I tried to kill myself. I'm just so fucked up!"

I shush her and continue to hold her close.

"The only thing that matters is getting well." Her hair is greasy and matted, and she smells like she needs a bath. But I don't care. For the moment, she's my beautiful girl once again, and the world can go to hell. Finally, after what seems a long time, but yet not long enough, she pulls back.

"My shoulders," she says, to which I carefully lean her back onto her pillows and make sure she's comfortable.

I reach to hold her hand, but she pulls back ever so slightly before I can grasp it. "You did steal my scholarship," she says, this time in a calm voice. "I mean, I know you didn't do it to hurt me. But you did."

"Baby," I say, in a soft voice, "that makes no sense. I filled out my application to the Winston way before I ever met you."

"Yeah, but if you hadn't, then I would have been accepted," she counters. I shake my head.

"You gotta stop this. You're gonna kill us." I reach for her hand, but she pulls back.

"I've had nothing but grief since I met you," she says. "I mean, long as we're being honest with each other."

"Okay, *stop* it!" I bark at her. "I've had enough of your hot-cold bullshit!"

"Maybe I've had enough of you trying to ruin my life."

"Oh, geezus!" I shake my head and back away from her. "You said this would never happen again! You said you were sorry you ever did it!"

"Deal with it!"

"Let's just cut to the chase! Do *we* even matter anymore? I mean, I need to know!"

Her face trembles as she replies. "*We* don't exist!"

"Okay, whatever. Fuck it. But you know what? We had a good thing going. We had happiness. We even had plans for a future!" She opens her mouth, but I shush her. "Somewhere in your brain, I know you know that! And for the second time, you've fucked it up! That's what *you're* gonna have to deal with!" I let out a loud sigh and shake my head. "I'm just wondering if you *ever* really loved me."

She screws her face up in anger. "Really? I'll make it easy to understand," she hisses. "I *never* loved you! I *never* needed you! And I sure as hell don't need you *now!*" My head starts spinning out of control as she winds up for the grand finale. "So, why don't you just GET THE HELL OUT OF HERE!" she screams, in a voice so loud both her mother and a nurse come sprinting into the room.

That's all I can take. I brush past both of them on the way out and run for the elevators. It's a long and teary-eyed drive back to Sagebrush. Somehow, I manage to call Orm and ask him to meet me at Dave's. And like a rock, he's there when I pull in. I'm still a mess. He takes one look at me as I climb in, then pulls me over for a hug.

"Robin's paralyzed," I manage, after a minute or two of sniffling and dabbing at my eyes.

He pulls me away from his body and stares into my eyes. "Ash, I'm so sorry!"

"She's paralyzed from the waist down, but she's so fucking full of fire." I give him the entire sordid episode.

"She's mental. She's completely mental."

"What do I do?"

He sucks in a deep breath with wide eyes and shakes his head. "Hell if I know! What do *you* think you should do?"

"That's what's so confusing! I want to run *away* from her, but then I want to run *to* her."

"You're really conflicted, Ash."

"Yeah, I am," I sigh as I slump down. "I mean, I get it that not all relationships work out, but is it too much to ask for a soft landing? Or a warning sign? Something?"

"I guess that would be nice." He gives me a nod of sympathy.

"This is the second time we've been cruising down the highway at eighty, only to smack right into a brick wall. I tell you, Orm, I'm broken. And in a couple of days, I'm expected to be a thousand miles away in Chicago."

"Yeah. I know."

"Should I go?"

Orm is strangely silent. I can see he's deep in thought, and he stays that way for a long moment. "You still love her?"

I hang my head. "Honestly? Yeah."

"Even after everything she's done to hurt you? Why?"

"What if I don't know?"

"How can you *not* know?"

"Because she's just so . . . complicated! Sometimes I wonder if she's from another planet. She can love you like there's no tomorrow! And when *she* loves you, believe me, you *know* it!"

"I believe you."

"It's not an exaggeration! You *feel* it. You're *alive*, just like you said. And if she commands you to fly, you *can* fly. She gives you the kind of love that sets your soul on fire. But then, on a whim, she dishes out the worst kind of cruelty—and laughs when you cry." I take in a breath. "You wanna know the scariest part?"

"What's that?"

"She can talk you into doing it all over again the very next day!"

For a long time, he stares, as if trying to bore his way into my head. "She's a big project," he finally says. "She could ruin you."

"Probably." He's right. I really need to remember that.

"I have to ask . . . exactly *what* is it you hope to get from her?"

"Hell, I don't know! All I can say is I love her. It's scary, but I love her. Beyond that, I just don't know."

He gives me a reproving look.

"She doesn't have anything you need, and has a lot of what you should run from."

I can't disagree. All I can do is shrug.

"Ash, what *does* it take to crush your love for her?" His tone is dripping with bewilderment. "I mean, what does it take for you to say 'I give up'?"

"I just don't know. I mean, I thought I already did it, but now I know I didn't really. I guess I'm just pathetic."

"Well, you better grow a pair, or you're gonna be in the same rut right here in Sagebrush ten years from now, without a college degree, waiting tables at Big Sam's, and wishing you had gone to Chicago."

I stare at the floorboard. I can't think of what to say in response, but thankfully he doesn't push his point. Deep inside, I suspect he's right. I don't want him to be right—but I think he is.

"Thanks, Orm. Guess I better finish packing." I open the car door and stand.

"Will I see you before you leave? I mean *if* you leave?"

He rolls down my window as I close the door. "I promise."

A small tumbleweed hurries itself across the parking lot and scoots between me and Orm's car as he pulls out. I watch as he drives away.

Grams already has dinner on the table as I come trudging in, and motions for me to take a seat. At first, we eat in silence.

"I went to see Robin today," I finally confess.

She gives me a wistful look. "Lord, child," she says, in a voice just above a whisper, "I wish I could take the heaviness off your heart."

"I-I'm having a tough time, Grams," I choke out. "I don't know what to do." I can feel my throat tightening.

She gives me a pat on my hand. "You know I don't understand this *gay* thing," she says, trying hard not to struggle in her choice of words. "But I don't doubt for a minute that you love her. So leaving her to go to Chicago is hard to do. Is that close?"

I close my eyes and nod. "I've cried every tear I have, Grams."

She sighs and wipes her mouth with a napkin before putting it back beside her plate. "I wish I could tell you the right thing to do, but I think you're meant to find out for yourself."

"You think so?" I so want to just crawl up, sit in her lap, and put my arms around her neck like I used to.

"There's someone you should talk to."

I open my eyes and allow them to focus on hers. "Who?"

"Her mother."

"You think I should ask for advice from her *mother?*"

Grams gives me a nod, then pats my hand again. "Make your peace with her. You need her on your side. She needs you, as well. And you never know, she might have some good advice for you."

I spend the rest of the evening in tortuous solitude, staring at my worldly possessions sorted out in my room. And I contemplate life without Robin. Have I really lost her again? Did I ever have her? Amid all the "what ifs" and "could've beens" that float through my brain, I think about what Grams told me. It takes me a while to see the wisdom in her advice, but eventually, and little by little, I do.

A big part of me is afraid to talk to Robin's mother. I mean, what do I say? It's close to ten p.m. when I say "to hell with it" and reach for my phone. After three rings, she answers.

"Mrs. O'Leary?" I hear the faint sound of breathing on the other end. "Mrs. O'Leary, it's me, Asher," I say into the silence.

"Yes, Asher," she says, "what do you want?"

"Um . . ." My throat is suddenly thick. "I guess I'm having a hard time dealing with . . ." I clear my throat. Why can't I talk all of a sudden? Now I'm annoyed with myself. I grit my teeth and force it out. "I'd like your advice on something." There's a long silence, and I wonder if she's already ended the call. "Are you there?"

"Yes," she says. Her voice is barely a whisper.

"Mrs. O'Leary," I start again, determined to spit out the problem before she hangs up on me or I have a change of heart, "I-I don't know what to do about leaving for college. I've got less than two days now, and I don't think I can leave Robin." Again, silence. "I guess I was hoping . . . well, maybe you'd have some advice or something."

The silence lasts another painfully long minute, and I'm on the verge of giving up when she finally takes a breath and speaks. "*Why* would you stay when you have a scholarship to the Winston Institute?" she asks.

"Because," I sigh, seeking the courage and strength to say the truth, even though I know she might slap me down, "I'm in love with Robin."

"She doesn't love you."

That hurts. "So you think I should leave?"

I hear her breathing heavily. "I shouldn't have said that. Maybe a better way is to say she's not capable of loving someone right now. She's not all together if you get what I mean."

"She's not? I-I don't understand."

"She's struggling with misplaced blame."

"That much I get. She blames *me* for losing the Winston scholarship. She blames me for *everything.*"

"That's because she doesn't really know," comes a terse response.

"What is it she doesn't know?"

"She didn't lose the Winston because of *you.*"

"I know, and I tried to tell her. She just wouldn't hear me."

"She didn't lose the Winston because of *you,*" she says again. "She lost the Winston because her father withdrew her application when he found out you had applied as well."

"Wh-what?" A sudden dull throb pierces my brain.

"He withdrew her application."

"Why?"

"He was determined to keep her away from you," she says. I hear her inhale deeply. "That's why he did it. He didn't want the two of you to end up at the Winston together. So, he withdrew her application."

My head is spinning.

"I don't get it. How could *he* withdraw *her* application? I assumed all along she was in charge of her own application!"

"Asher, there's so much you never knew. He managed a lot more than her college application. He controlled—or tried to control—nearly every waking moment of her life. And that included who she dated."

"Oh my God!"

"When she found out you got a scholarship, and she didn't, she was crushed. He told her they skipped over *her* because *you* got in *and* that they would never accept two from the same high school. He told her it was your fault because you were trying to follow her there."

"And you *let* him get away with that?"

I hear a sigh, but she says nothing.

"I'm not believing this!" I fume. "You're just as guilty as him! Do you realize what you *did?* That was her biggest dream! It may have been her *only* dream!" I hear her start to say something, but I cut her off. "You're insane! The two of you, you're fucking insane!" Once again, tears spill down my cheek. "You robbed her of *everything!* How could you *do* that to her?"

"He thought he was saving her. He blamed *you* for her . . . *condition.*"

"*Condition?*"

"That's him, not me."

"He thought I made Robin gay?"

"Like I said, that was him."

"It was you, too! I remember what you told me at the hospital!"

I can hear another sigh. "Asher, I didn't think you *made* her gay."

"But you thought there was something wrong with her being gay. And you didn't stand up for her."

"It might have been in the beginning. But I've learned a lot since. I know now there was never anything *wrong* with her. I wanted to openly acknowledge her. I wanted to free her. She desperately needed it. But Brendan . . . oh my God! *Damn* his Irish stubbornness! He put his foot down on the matter. No child of his was going to be . . . be . . ."

"Gay?"

"Yes," she whispers. "God *damn* him and his thick head! And now look where we are."

I'm having a hard time catching my breath. "It wasn't just him. *You* let her think I robbed her of a Winston scholarship when you knew it was him. *You* let her carry that anger and sorrow around for months! Why?"

All I can hear is a long, heavy sigh—the kind borne of regret.

"You could have at least told her the truth *after* her father passed," I say.

"I didn't want to make her *hate* him."

"Well, it's pretty plain she hates *herself,* especially with her father's death! But, hey, what's a little more hate when you've got plenty to go around?" I have to stand on my tongue to keep from making an accusation that even I would regret.

I hear a sigh. "Asher, she's not to blame for her father's death."

"Maybe you should have told her that before she—"

"You're not hearing me. Her father died due to his own drunken stupidity."

"Wait, he was drunk?"

"He was drunk most of the time." I feel my head spin. "It's why he was outside in the first place, stumbling around like an idiot. Once he realized she wasn't in the house, he was furious. He knew exactly where she was and who she was with, and he was going there to confront you both. I tried to stop him but couldn't. He staggered out the door in a rage, but fell before he even got to the car. He was dead before the storm ever got to us."

"So, Robin had absolutely *nothing* to do with her father's death?"

"Yes. You're right."

"God damn *both* of you!" I scream into the phone. I'm surprised she doesn't hang up on me. "I heard what you told her that day! You said he was looking for her because of the storm! You made her think it was *her* fault that he died. *Why?* Why did you say that? Why did you put that on her?"

She's silent in response, but then her voice cracks. "Don't you think I've been asking myself the same thing?"

"Tell her! Tell her what you did. She deserves to know. You can at least take that much off her mind!"

"I did. I told her, but she still feels she's to blame."

"Why?"

"I'm pretty sure she believes he drank to excess *because* of her . . ." Once again, her voice fades.

"Because she's *gay?*"

"Yes," she replies, almost like a little girl afraid in the dark.

"Oh my God! You knew that, and you could have shielded her. You knew she was drowning in guilt. And in her moment of need, you didn't rescue her . . . you pushed her under."

"God forgive me," she whispers.

For what seems a long time, I'm so mired in a toxic brew of anger, sorrow, and disgust that I can't speak a word. But then, what can I possibly say? What can I say in the face of that kind of dysfunction? That kind of sickness? That kind of domination?

"What's going to happen with her?" I finally ask.

"She's got a lot of issues," her mother sighs. "Guilt about her father, physical rehab, accepting life as a paraplegic—and she's got some serious internal injuries as well. She'll need a lot of surgery. As soon as she can be transported, we'll be going back to Houston where she'll be close to the medical facilities she needs."

"She won't be living in Sagebrush?"

"No. We still have our home in Houston. We're going back home."

It suddenly occurs to me that Robin and her family are being erased from Sagebrush—almost like she was never here—like her father is finally getting his way from beyond the grave.

But she *was* here. And we were lovers. And she changed me. I'm trying my best to make sense of it all when Mrs. O'Leary seems to finally realize we're at the moment of truth.

"Don't lose *your* dreams, Asher," she says. Her voice is emotionless but soft and genuine. "Let there be at least *one* dream held by the two of you to come true."

"But what if she still loves me?"

"She's no good for you. She'll destroy you. She has to learn to love herself again before she can love another. Leave, Asher. Leave, and live your dream while you still can. In time . . . maybe."

Maybe. Seems like that's the best description of Robin I ever had. *Maybe* she loves me. *Maybe* we can be together. *Maybe* she can please her father. *Maybe* she doesn't mean it when she says she never loved me. Robin seems to be little more than a riddle wrapped up in *maybe*.

For a long time after my phone call with Robin's mother, I lie on my bed and stare at the ceiling of my room. Just ten days ago, I was deliriously happy in Colorado—just me and my girl. Just ten days ago, Robin's father was alive. Just ten days ago, Robin could walk, and we had a bright future. But, ten days ago now seems like a faraway remnant of a past life on the other side of the universe to which I can never return.

It's after midnight before I finally start feeling sleepy. As I lie in bed gazing at the boxes stacked neatly off to the side that contain all my worldly possessions, I'm tortured with painful indecision. Do I listen to my head or my heart? I still love her. But, do I still love *us*? Was my love for her ever met in equal share? Or was I carelessly over-invested the entire time?

I don't know.

But it's time to climb out of the abyss. Is it time to grow a pair, as Orm put it? Or, is it time to sacrifice all in the name of love? Better yet, is there anything left to sacrifice? I decide to punt. This dilemma can only be solved by seeing her one more time—and then making a choice that will be the most profound decision in all my eighteen years.

20

It's just past seven a.m. as I get started toward Amarillo.

I check my back pocket for a certain folded sheet of stationery. Yep, it's there. Orm waves as I pull away from The Okie Diner on the outskirts of Sagebrush. Taking me for breakfast is his show of support for the tough decision I'm going to make, even though *I* don't yet know my decision.

The sky is uncharacteristically gray for this time of year. An endless prairie is tall with corn, and I shave off mile after mile of farm crop until finally, I see the skyline of Amarillo in the distance. The mere sight of my destination puts me on edge. I have to admit I'm afraid I'll make the wrong decision.

As I get closer, thoughts of Robin drown out all others in my brain. There's a part of me that's still in mourning over the failure of our second time around, but perhaps a more significant part that remains angry about how quickly it happened. It reminds me of just how fleeting the present can be, and that it can be rearranged with even the merest breeze of whimsy.

Getting started on the right foot with Robin this morning is important, and I decide the best way to begin on a cheery note is to bring flowers. I stop at a flower shop just a block from Amarillo Regional Hospital where I almost choose a dozen roses but instead take a summer floral collection of daisies, pink tulips, green poms, purple monte casino, and, by my own request, a few wisteria sprigs.

Just as I approach the door to Robin's hospital room, I meet her mom coming out. She gestures for me to step to the side so we can talk. I follow her to an adjacent hallway that is out of Robin's earshot.

"Those are pretty," she says, lightly touching one of the tulip petals. "Robin will like them."

"I'm hoping she does."

She searches out my eyes. "I spoke with her neurosurgeon this morning.

While she's making good progress recovering from the near drowning, it's her spine that's the real problem. It's broken in two places, and that's why she's paralyzed."

The blunt medical assessment frightens me.

"It *will* heal, though, won't it?"

"While the fractured vertebrae will heal, there's no guarantee that she won't be paralyzed."

"Will she be permanently paralyzed?"

"That's the issue," she says, raising a finger. "Her spinal cord isn't severed. He thinks that with some surgery to relieve the pressure on her nerves, she might be able to regain some use of her lower body. But it could take several surgeries, and years of rehab."

"That's good news! She could walk again!"

"Asher, that type of surgery carries serious risk."

I'm struggling with a response, and in seeing that, she reaches out and touches my shoulder. "That's enough for now," she says. "Anyway, I'm leaving everything up to Robin. You go on in now."

After waiting for her mom to disappear around the corner, I step up to Robin's hospital room door. I hold the bouquet close, and taking a deep breath, I give out with a cheery "Hello!" as I push the door open and enter the room.

When I first catch sight of Robin, she's craning her neck forward to see the doorway. With a backward push of my arm, I close the door as I walk toward her.

"I brought you something to brighten up the room!" I place the vase onto the windowsill right in front of her. When I turn, I notice she no longer has her IV, although she's still hooked up to a device that appears to be displaying her blood pressure and pulse.

"It's nice," she says. "Thanks."

"You're welcome." I give her a smile, worrying whether the pain behind my smile is visible. I pull up the bedside chair so that I'm close. "It's terrific to see you."

"You're a liar!" She raises an eyebrow and then looks away.

I take an emotional step back and have to force myself to breathe. That's the power her words have on me. I'll never know when she's gonna put the next knife in me. My trust in her is completely destroyed.

Like a tsunami that wipes the beach clean of all objects of distraction, her demeanor lets me finally see our bare naked truth with no obstacles. Nothing in front of me to confuse me. No shades of gray to give me wiggle room. It's inescapable. It's at this exact moment that I finally understand: our story is at an end.

"Well, I couldn't leave without seeing you," I reply in a whisper after gathering my wits.

Her expression sags. And for an awkward minute, neither of us says a thing. She looks down at her hands and I can see her fingers moving ever so slightly, almost as if she's lost in thought. Finally she looks up at me. Her face is a gloomy portrait of resignation.

"When do you leave?"

I bite my lip. This is hard. Really hard.

"Tomorrow." I try my best to be gentle.

She speaks, but the words come out haltingly. "There was a time when I thought it would be *me* leaving Sagebrush for Chicago."

"Yeah," I sigh, "and I once thought . . ."

I pause, but she picks up on my unfinished sentence. "You thought it would be both of us?"

I feel my chin quivering, and we lock eyes.

"It's what I hoped for."

For what seems a long time, she's silent, as if recognizing that hope has all but left her. Finally, she speaks.

"It's all my fault," she says in a voice that's so hoarse it cracks. "I've been thinking about it a lot . . . I have so many regrets. It really sucks that I basically fucked up the best thing I ever had."

"Isn't that what you said to get me back?"

She grimaces, but then only shrugs.

"What was going on with that, Robin?" I ask, trying hard not to sound resentful. "Why was it so easy to hurt *me*? I never even once hurt *you.*"

She surprises me with her quick reply. "It's true, you didn't." She gathers the shoulder of her hospital gown and wipes her eyes. "When I let myself think about it, it scares me. There's a dark side of me, Ash—a side I can't control. I hate myself when it comes out. And when it does, it has a life of its own. It scorches everything in sight. It . . . it makes me wish I was dead."

I don't think I've ever been in front of someone who's fallen as far as Robin. There was a time when I envied her—when I thought she had everything: talent, popularity, beauty, and confidence. I see now she had hardly anything of what she needed most, with peace of mind being at the top of that list. And I see now that she *never* had what I had—the luxury of just being at ease with *herself.* Or with *us.*

He wouldn't allow it.

There was always that dark cloud for her.

There was always *him.*

"You don't have anything to say?" she asks, jerking me back to the present.

"About what?"

"Maybe about why I was so destructive? Why I hurt you? Why I hated myself most of the time?"

I give her a slow nod. "I think you were at war with yourself."

"Meaning?"

"Meaning, you never accepted yourself for being who you are. I get that, because early on, I almost went down the same path."

A frown emerges onto her forehead. "Ash, I really, really *hate* being who I am," she says. Her fists are balled up.

"And *that,*" I say, raising my forefinger, "is what opens the door for all the guilt and self-doubt. Don't get me wrong. I *know* what he did to you. I know how he treated you. And I really hate that he put all that on you. But you're gonna have to learn there's never a happy ending when you can't accept yourself, and especially if it's something you can't change. If you don't love yourself, you'll never truly be able to love someone else."

"You think?" she replies sardonically.

"Yeah. At least I've learned *that* much."

"Good for you, Ash. You love yourself. Nice. I guess your big mistake was getting mixed up with *me.*"

"For God's sake, Robin, we could have had it all! We were in *love!*"

"Love?" She stares straight through me. "I'm glad *you* say so. Dad said it *wasn't* love, that it was just lust and the sins of the flesh."

"What the hell did *he* know about whether or not you were in love?! Why couldn't you just trust *yourself?*"

"I don't know," she says, in a helpless tone of voice that is the perfect silhouette of the mess she is. She looks toward the flower arrangement in the window as her eyes brim with tears once again. "When I started dating Dill, my father started talking to me again. But when he found out I was with you, he disowned me. Again. I couldn't even go to Mom because she told

Dad everything I said. I literally had no one."

"You had *me,* goddammit! Geez, Robin!"

She uses a tissue to dab at her eyes, then gives me a teary, mournful look.

"I'm losing you, aren't I?" she says. It takes a few seconds of concentration to summon the courage to answer her.

"I think so, yeah."

The thought that my response is causing her pain is itself painful. I wonder how deeply I'm wounding her. I search deep within her eyes—still green and beautiful, even though missing their usual sparkle—and find only sorrow. Her response is weak, and reeks of desperation.

"I wish it didn't have to be this way."

"Hey." She looks up. "There *were* good times. There were some very good times."

"You promise?" she squeaks, dabbing at tears that are slowly tracking down her face. When I reach over to wipe them away, she gently clasps my hand before I can withdraw it. Slowly, very slowly, she slides her fingers between mine while holding her gaze on my face.

"Yes, I promise," I tell her in a gentle voice. "You took me higher than the sky. You gave me the best moments I've ever had. I fell in love for the first time in my life. In so many ways, you're the best thing that ever happened to me."

"I feel the same, Ash. I really do!"

"I'm not lying when I say you'll always have a piece of my heart."

I see her hesitate and then swallow. "That's scary. It sounds like goodbye."

"It's just time for me to get out of this town and start over."

She sniffs and wipes her eyes with her free hand. "With all my heart, I wish *we* could start all over again and be long-distance girlfriends while you're in Chicago." There is only sad resignation written across her face as she searches my eyes for a long time. Finally realizing I have no response, she swallows hard. "I'm really messed up."

I force a teary-eyed smile. Seeing her wallow in her own self-pity and tragic circumstance is almost too much to bear.

"I don't know what I'm gonna do without you," she mewls. She sounds so defeated that it's hard to restrain myself from gathering her into my arms and telling her that I didn't mean any of it and that I'm never going to leave her. But I don't. I can feel my own inner strength kicking in.

"Get yourself healthy, baby," I tell her. "It'll be hard work, but you'll be ready for love again someday, and when you are . . . wow! That next girl is gonna be one lucky girl!"

"She is?" She gives me a weak smile, and I know she senses the conversation is almost at an end. She reaches for a tissue, and I get it for her.

"Yeah, she will be!"

She wipes her tears then looks straight into my eyes. "I *never* loved anyone like you, Ash. I know I didn't always show it, but I never loved anyone like you!"

"And I never loved anyone like *you,* baby," I whisper. I can see she's terrified, and I wish I could take away that fear. I know all too well how crushing it is.

"Can I ask a question?" she squeaks while wiping her tears.

"Sure."

She looks up at me and starts to speak but is overcome with a soft kind of sob that tears at the fabric of my soul. I don't think I've ever seen such a piteous expression of helplessness than the one I see right now. After soaking several tissues, she takes a breath and speaks.

"Can I have a goodbye kiss before you leave," she chokes out. "Please?"

Wow. That's playing with dynamite. I know enough to know I shouldn't do it. It would completely disarm me. I open my mouth to tell her "no," but the word won't come out. Despite all the effort I summon to push it out, my mouth refuses to obey. As tears spill down my own cheek, I finally break.

"Yes, baby, you can," I manage to choke out as I bend over her.

She receives me with two open arms, placing one hand on my back with the other one cupping my face. Our lips meet, tentatively at first, but in a few seconds, the kiss is torrid. All of the familiar and emotionally laden tastes and sensations are there, as if the story of our romance is flashing through my mind like a movie in fast motion. With my eyes closed and my body powerless against her, my surrender is complete. I allow her to hungrily devour my mouth for a long minute or two. I'm not sure I want it to end. But finally, she slows, and then she hesitantly withdraws.

I look into her eyes, maybe for the last time in a long time, and once again gently wipe the tears from her cheeks and mouth. She softly kisses my finger as it passes near her mouth and the sight of her doing it gets to me again. She might be paralyzed, but her ability to kiss me stupid is as potent as ever.

We stay in this position, looking into each other's eyes, for what seems forever. I hope she sees in my eyes how much I love her. Because I do. I really do, and it sucks things have to turn out like this. I really wish things could have been different.

Then, I slowly pull myself straight up. Our hands are still locked together, and as I try to withdraw mine, she squeezes ever so slightly, but then allows my hand to come free. Our fingertips linger on each other's before finally separating.

"Goodbye, my love," I whisper.

She's doing the best she can to accept our finality, but I can tell she's on the verge of losing all control. I'm not much better. I almost take out the folded sheet of stationery and hand it to her, but something tells me at the last second to keep it until I know the time is right.

"Goodbye, my sweet Ash," she whispers back. The expression on her face is one I'll never forget.

Stifling my own sobs, I turn my back to her and walk from the room. Just getting to the door seems to take forever, like my legs weigh a ton. Once outside, I hear uncontrolled sobbing. I slowly close the door behind me, pulling until I feel the latch catch. I lean forward and keep my forehead and hands on the door for a long time, lost in hesitation and despair as my own tears drop to the floor. It seems a long time before I'm finally able to suck in a deep breath and exhale without shaking. Knowing that the girl I love is just inside that door, I turn and walk away. It's the hardest thing I've ever done in my life.

Outside, a dark sky cries down on me as I find my way back to Sagebrush. It takes me twice as long to get home as it did to get here. As I pull into my driveway, I see that Orm is there. I knew he would be. I exit my car and run to him, where I find safety in his open arms.

"Well, I did it," I manage to croak, after unloading a gallon of tears into his shirt.

He nods his support, then pulls me in even closer. It's all I can do to keep from crying all over again. Once I pull myself back together, I look him in the face.

"It was so hard," I manage, in a cracked voice. I can tell he knows my pain. He always knows.

"It's hard to say goodbye to someone you love," he says softly, releasing me so I can wipe the rivulets of moisture from my brow and eyes. The rain is just a light sprinkle now.

I let out a long *whew*. "The sooner I'm outta here, the better."

"I know."

We take a seat in his car, and he puts on some music, just like old times. We listen to a couple of them in silence. But they sound different somehow, as if they have different meanings. Something tells me they'll never again mean what they did when I was in high school.

"I was just thinking," I say. "Do you reckon you'll ever get back with Charlene?"

He gives me a wide grin. "You're a hopeless romantic, Ash! But, yeah! I hope so!" He pauses for a moment or two before continuing. "But I also know that life is a train that's always in motion. You choose a general direction, but as you go along, you're in charge of where you end up. You have to keep an eye out for the right track—the one that's gonna take you where you want to be. And sometimes you don't end up where you thought you would."

"What does that mean?"

"It means I hope we cross paths, Charlene and me, but also that if I *don't* find her again, I hope she finds happiness with someone else."

His casual acceptance of tragic romance knocks me a little off center. But then I start to see his point. Life does go on. There *will* be someone for me. That's Orm for you. Always keeping me grounded.

For a long time, we listen to music while saying hardly anything. With my visit to Robin behind me, I feel like I'm starting a brand-new chapter in my life's story. This time tomorrow, Sagebrush will be in my rear-view mirror. That sounds a little scary, but I'm ready to be brave. As for me and Orm? He's been my rock steady go-to for so long I can't imagine surviving somewhere he isn't. Yet that's precisely what I'm going to have to do now.

"You won't forget where I am, will you?" I say, breaking the silence.

He gives me a reassuring smile. "Hell no!" he laughs. "Don't forget, I'll be at K State. That's not so far from Chicago that I can't keep my eye on you!"

I have to choke down a lump in my throat as he takes my hand and squeezes. We spend another hour together like this, cozied up in our own little world while listening to music, before I say my goodbye to him.

Early the next morning, with the sun painting a scarlet horizon, I take a last look through my loaded-to-the-hilt car before I bring Grams outside for our goodbye. She holds me tight, and I can feel her holding back sobs.

"You'll come home for the holidays?" she asks.

"I have a better idea, Grams. You come see *me* anytime you want!"

With one last hug, I'm on the road. About ten minutes outside of town, I turn off the main highway and head down a small country road. After one more turn and a couple of minutes or so, I'm beside a small lake, and I pull over. Just one last goodbye to give.

After rolling down the window, I take a deep breath, gathering in a familiar fragrance as the sun's first light kisses the water from the tops of the trees on the far shoreline. I lean back in my seat and allow my eyes to close. All that is and ever was my love of Robin O'Leary plays out in my mind: innocence, self-discovery, first love, risk, intimacy, and yes, heartbreak. It seems the most important story of my life began right here, down Robin's Lake Road. And now, as I leave Sagebrush for college, it looks like that story is going to end right here as well.

Knowing my time on this stage is up, I take my exit. In only a few minutes I'm at the stop sign at the highway. I swallow, then take my foot off the brake and gently accelerate onto the roadway—not toward home, but instead in a direction toward distant, new horizons.

There's no other traffic in sight. "I'm really doing it," I tell myself. For what seems a long time, I keep watch through the rearview mirror as the many miles of my past fall away behind me. There's a feeling of sadness at the closing of this chapter of my life, yet there's also a feeling of change, like the opening of something brand new and mysterious.

After a melancholy few hours, I feel my spirits begin to lift just as I make my way into Springfield. By the time I'm able to see the statuesque skyscrapers of downtown Chicago, I feel a rising excitement. Just then, my cell phone rings, and when I glance down I see it's Amsra—and I realize I haven't spoken to her in over a month. I raise the phone to my ear and answer.

"Hey, girl!"

The sound of her voice is sweet, and it makes a smile spreads across my face. She asks how I am.

"Great," I say in reply, "in fact, best day ever!"

Epilogue

Five years, almost to the day, have passed since I last drove on this road in Sagebrush.

It's a hot August afternoon, the sun is mercilessly torturing the landscape, and dust devils dot the prairie. I'm sure the temperature is over a hundred degrees. As I pass the city limits sign, it doesn't take more than a second to realize the cityscape looks exactly the same. Change comes slowly to the small outposts in life like Sagebrush.

I had actually hoped Orm would be in town so we could explore the old town together. I've kept in pretty good touch with him over the last five years. He graduated from Kansas State with his degree in engineering and now works for a telecom company in Dallas. I remember last year how thrilled I was when he attended my graduation ceremony at the Winston. But Orm found a wife while he was in college, and with him being married now, I have to share him, and he's not always able to run off to see me.

I drive through the business district out toward Grams' house, and as I turn the corner onto my old street, my eyes instantly lock onto a residence halfway down the block. I half expect to see Grams' car parked in the driveway. But, of course, I don't, as Grams passed away two years ago. That's what finally got Mom to come back to town, as she was in charge of selling the house. The funeral was held in Olathe, Kansas, where Gramps is buried. Orm met me there for the service. At least Grams had three visits to me at the Winston before her stroke. And that's three more times than Mom ever visited me.

The exterior of the house looks just like it did that day I hugged Grams' neck in the driveway before leaving. I park next to the curb and stare out the window for a few minutes, craning my neck to see the second-floor window that was my world.

I'm lost in my thoughts when a couple of young children, a boy and girl, emerge from the house with a dog, and begin playing in the front yard just below my old bedroom window. I chuckle to myself. The old house now has another family's story to tell. Life goes on. There's no one from my past left in Sagebrush. Except Robin.

I stay maybe another two or three minutes, and then put my car in gear and drive away.

My next stop is the high school. This one's kinda tough. I pull into the old familiar parking lot and park my car. I almost expect to see Orm in the seat next to me. I can practically hear all the old sounds of the morning rush as students hurried into the school building before the doors were closed. To the left and in the distance, I see the football field, and my eyes lock onto the place where years ago, on a carefree spring day, a geeky high school senior once fell in love for the first time in her life.

My eyes wander to the right and settle on the entrance to C wing. The most important things that ever happened in my life are all tied to that one building. All that I am, or ever will be, was discovered, experienced, celebrated, and yes, mourned, right there.

I'm in my own dream world when I take a look at my watch and realize I've been here for over two hours. It's time to go, yet I find it a bit of an effort to drive away. I know where I'm supposed to end up today, and what I'll be doing there, so maybe that's what delays me. I slowly drive out the same way I came in.

I decide to drop in on Big Sam's. Nothing's changed. The aroma around me is the same, and it triggers powerful memories of what was important to me during high school. I can remember as plain as day the first time I ever talked to Orm about Robin. It was right here in this very seat. I wonder if that was the first time he ever suspected I might be gay. Honestly, I don't know if I could have navigated life without Orm.

When I glance at my watch and see it's already after seven, I remind myself that today really belongs to Robin, and I don't want to shortchange my visit. There's still time, though. I mean, she's not going anywhere. I sit in quiet meditation for another half-hour before standing. It's time.

I have to mentally psych myself up to start the car in my intended direction of travel. But, I knew a month ago, as I planned out my trip, that this would be difficult. The drive has barely begun before I notice the first wave of nostalgia and, yes, grief. As I take the highway, it's almost as if I was back in high school on one of the many days a laughing Robin and I would sneak out here to be alone with each other.

I come to Robin's Lake Road, take the turn, and proceed at a snail's pace down the lane until I come to the lake where it's closest to the road. It's at this spot that I notice there's a new sign that reads "Robin's Lake." Up ahead, and in the distance, the familiar outline of a residence sits at the end of the road. I won't be going up to the house. Besides, I don't know who's living there now. No, *this* spot—this *exact* spot—is right where I want to be. I put the car in park and turn off the engine.

It seems that everything that was important to me five years ago begins and ends in this place. Like a memory from just last week, I recall the first time I was ever here with her. I can't help but let out with a soft chuckle. We were so clumsy and innocent. I hold up my hand in front of my eyes, and I swear I can feel the sensation of the first time she ever put her hand in mine. The softness, the smoothness, the sensuality—all of it's here, right now. But then, ever so slowly, the memory of that last tragic trip together down this road emerges and occupies center stage.

Do I wish for a do-over? I don't know. Maybe. But then again, no. It's not like I'm incomplete without Robin. After all, I'm happy at my station in life. I have a fantastic girlfriend, Melody, whom I plan on making my wife. We met at church. Yeah. I'm back in church. Only this church is welcoming to all. I actually look forward to Sunday services.

I have a degree from the Winston Institute, and a gallery and studio in downtown Naperville, just outside of Chicago. And I have plenty of business and a growing reputation in the Chicago area. I've even been interviewed in three periodicals. I have over ten thousand followers on Twitter, and my thousands of followers on Instagram wait with bated breath for each new work of art that I post.

Yet this shadow—this incomplete chapter of my life—is always on my mind. And that is the reason I'm at this spot.

After I left five years ago, Robin's mother sold their property in Sagebrush and moved the two of them back to Houston. Robin and I kept in touch for that first year with phone calls, then dropping back to text messages, and finally to sporadic text messages.

Robin never was one to talk about her medical progress, so I had to get that from her mom, who would call from time to time to tell me about the results of the latest surgery. She always expressed a curious kind of optimism—one that seemed to believe that *just one more* surgery would completely restore Robin. I can still hear in my mind how confident she was before Robin's last surgery. I'll never, ever forget the sorrow in her voice when she called me a full two weeks afterward to break the sad news. The resulting month-long fugue I endured tested my endurance for grief.

Making peace with Robin is actually Melody's idea, although deep inside, I knew it had to eventually happen. Melody is the fourth girlfriend I've had since Robin, and we've been going strong for two and a half years now. I'm delighted, very much in love, and now know how the game of relationships is played. Still, I've struggled to push Robin out of my mind. She's always there. But that never bothered Melody. It was Melody who suggested that maybe Robin's not meant to be pushed out of my mind and that instead, I just need closure on the "Robin" chapter in my life. It took a while, but then I realized she was right.

You see, there was a time, and there was *this* place I'm in right now when I thought I had the most profound love possible. That means something. That's not something you causally toss aside.

I roll down the window and listen to the gentle lapping of the waves on the lake. Then, I open the car door and get out. I'm immediately immersed in the familiar bouquet of wisteria, just as I was the first time I was here. A hummingbird or two flits in and out of the blooms in the shrubbery, and in the distance, trees still hug the far shoreline. A gentle, aimless breeze washes over me, and as it finds its way over Robin's Lake, it sings out the wind song that is her name—and I smile. I know I'm in the right place, at the right time, doing the right thing.

As I rest against the side of the car and look out over Robin's Lake, the memories of *that* moonlit evening find their way back into my mind. I lean my head back and close my eyes. Even after all these years, I can still hear the chirping of the frogs, feel the warm caress of her lips on my neck, and smell the vanilla fragrance of her perfume. Of all the sensuous moments I've ever enjoyed in my life, Melody included, those few moments I shared with Robin, dancing in the moonlight with our bodies entwined, were the most intense and erotic I've ever experienced. With great effort, I force myself back into the present.

Strangely, I feel like a smiling Robin is watching my every move, probably from behind a nearby tree. I turn to look all around. But, she's not here— although if she were, she'd probably give my neck just enough of a gentle kiss to make me touch the spot and call out her name.

It's time. I reach into my hip pocket and take out a folded sheet of old stationery. It's pale yellow now, and Robin's lipstick imprint is only barely visible. The sheet contains my own handwriting, but the words are not mine. They are the lyrics to a song—a song sung twice to an audience of one. I can feel my throat tighten as I hesitantly read the words aloud.

Since we met on Monday, no day is complete without you,
No joy is worth remembering without you,
No life has meaning without you,
So, with you I'll stay, living a passion every day,
Singing every joy, down this path I've chosen,
Hand in hand, my darling, my one and only love.

There's a small clearing just in front of me, where the aquatic vegetation that hugs the shoreline most of the way around the lake has parted. I know what I have to do. I slip off my shoes and wade in until the water is at midcalf. Her presence overwhelms me. A single tear forms and slowly descends my cheek until it drops into the water. I take one last look at the sheet of paper, then slowly stoop and place it face-up on the surface of Robin's Lake.

The water almost immediately soaks through, but the sheet remains floating on the surface. I kiss my forefinger and lightly touch the paper as it slowly begins drifting out toward the middle of the lake. And as the waves on the lake that bears her name gently pull it away, I say my final goodbye to Robin.

"Rest in peace, my darling. Rest in peace."

ABOUT THE AUTHOR

C. L. Avery makes his home in Texas. Before giving in to his inner passion for creativity, he was a college professor. In addition to writing about anything he wants to, he enjoys spending time with his much loved and eclectic group of friends, while also enjoying photography, nature, hiking, and travel. *Robin's Lake Road* is his third novel, after *Mary Full of Grace* and *On the Edge of Darkness.*

CPSIA information can be obtained
at www.ICGtesting.com
Printed in the USA
LVHW052101040720
659749LV00001B/65

9 780960 033522